My mother is trying to kill me.
Sitting here, on a 2-pound puddle-jumping
plane rattling harder than Denis Leary's
lungs, it's suddenly become so clear.
She wants me dead. ~~This~~ This is why
she insisted I move to Fort Nowhere.
Why she made me leave my entire
wardrobe at home, including my
brand-new, just-got-out-of-rehab
Marc Jacobs floral silk sundress.

I can't believe I got sober for _this._

Oh god, I think we're about to land.

Also by Lola Douglas

More Confessions of a Hollywood Starlet

True Confessions

OF A

HOLLYWOOD STARLET

A NOVEL BY

LOLA DOUGLAS

razOr bill

True Confessions of a Hollywood Starlet

RAZORBILL

Published by the Penguin Group
Penguin Young Readers Group
345 Hudson Street, New York, New York 10014, U.S.A.
Penguin Group (USA) Inc., 375 Hudson Street, New York, New York 10014, U.S.A.
Penguin Group (Canada), 90 Eglinton Avenue East, Suite 700, Toronto, Ontario,
Canada M4P 2Y3 (a division of Pearson Penguin Canada Inc.)
Penguin Books Ltd, 80 Strand, London WC2R 0RL, England
Penguin Ireland, 25 St Stephen's Green, Dublin 2, Ireland
(a division of Penguin Books Ltd)
Penguin Group (Australia), 250 Camberwell Road, Camberwell,
Victoria 3124, Australia (a division of Pearson Australia Group Pty Ltd)
Penguin Books India Pvt Ltd, 11 Community Centre, Panchsheel Park,
New Delhi - 110 017, India
Penguin Group (NZ), Cnr Airborne and Rosedale Roads, Albany,
Auckland 1310, New Zealand (a division of Pearson New Zealand Ltd)
Penguin Books (South Africa) (Pty) Ltd, 24 Sturdee Avenue, Rosebank, Johannesburg 2196,
South Africa

Penguin Books Ltd, Registered Offices: 80 Strand, London WC2R 0RL, England

10 9 8 7 6 5 4 3 2

Interior design by Christopher Grassi

THE LIBRARY OF CONGRESS HAS CATALOGED THE HARDCOVER EDITION AS FOLLOWS:

Douglas, Lola.
  True confessions of a Hollywood starlet / Lola Douglas.
    p. cm.
  Summary: Teen movie star Morgan Carter retreats to a small midwestern town to
recuperate anonymously after an overdose and rehabilitation, recording her thoughts
in a diary.
  ISBN 1-59514-035-2
  [1. Actors and actresses—Fiction. 2. Rehabilitation—Fiction. 3.Diaries—Fiction.]
I. Title.
  PZ7.D74737Tru 2005
  [Fic]—dc22

                                                          2005008150

Razorbill paperback ISBN: 1-59514-093-X

Printed in the United States of America

*If you're going to go through hell . . .
I suggest you come back learning something.*
— Drew Barrymore

True Confessions

OF A

HOLLYWOOD
STARLET

8/16

My mother is trying to kill me.

Sitting here, on a two-pound puddle-jumping plane rattling harder than Denis Leary's lungs, it's suddenly become so clear. She wants me dead. This is why she insisted I move to Fort Nowhere. Why she flew me all the way from LAX to Chicago in *coach*, replacing my usual luggage with one small carry-on, a hideous nylon thing she bought from a street vendor ("Normal teenagers don't have Louis Vuitton, Morgan"). Why she made me leave my entire wardrobe at home, including my brand-new, I-just-got-out-of-rehab Marc Jacobs floral silk sundress.

I can't believe I got sober for *this*.

Oh God, I think we're about to land.

8/16—*Later*

So I am now officially a Fort Wayner. Waynean? Whatever. The puddle jumper hurtled onto the tarmac at the Fort Wayne International Airport a little after 8 p.m. "Aunt" Trudy (as I'm supposed to call her) was waiting for me in the terminal. She's thin—painfully thin, Mary-Kate-before-rehab thin—and when she hugged me, I could feel her ribs poking into my side. I've never liked hugging people I don't really know, even though I've been forced to do it my whole life. Strange how I still haven't gotten used to how awkward and uncomfortable it is.

Trudy isn't entirely a stranger; she's my mom's best friend from childhood, a recent divorcée-slash–Fort Wayne transplant (much like me). Mom says I've met her before, when I was still wearing Pampers. Needless to say, I don't remember.

Since I didn't have any other bags to claim, we went out to the parking lot and loaded into Trudy's pickle green Saturn Ion. It's surprisingly comfortable for an economy car. She asked me if I was hungry, and I was, so she took us to this little Italian place called Casa D'Angelo. The restaurant was mostly cute, and they braise their calamari in a light tomato sauce instead of breadifrying the hell out it like I figured all Midwesterners would. I was glad to have something to put into my mouth, because ever since Crapplewood, my ability to make small talk has been severely diminished.

There everything was about "being real" and "stripping away the layers." Apparently, I was *all* layers, and when I got done stripping them away, I realized there wasn't much left.

Trudy chattered on about my new high school, Snider, and how tomorrow we could go shopping for clothes and school supplies. I said, "Can I get a SpongeBob lunch box, too?" but she missed the sarcasm. Then I felt like a total wank, since it's not Trudy's fault I'm here. She's the one who was nice enough to agree to let me hang at her place during this year of enforced normalcy.

Speaking of, Trudy's house is . . . I can't even find the

words. There are four bedrooms and two and a half baths, but it was built in the seventies and you can totally tell. The kitchen's done up in avocado and orange—how very Brady!—and the floors are all this gross laminate trying to masquerade as wood. Worse, the room that's been designated as mine has crazy yellow wallpaper and a *full-size bed*. I haven't slept in anything less than a king since . . . I don't know, since I was in a crib?

This house definitely needs some love.

8/17

Trudy's in the bathroom, so I only have a few minutes, but we just finished breakfast at Cindy's Diner, which is this totally old-school kind of establishment. It looked familiar for some reason, and then Trudy mentioned that this was the diner they used in Neil LaBute's *In the Company of Men*. Apparently he's from the Fort (as Trudy likes to call it) and still shoots movies here whenever he can.

I know it's stupid, but suddenly I feel like I've found a little piece of home.

8/17—*Later*

My mother must be on crack. She seriously expects me to buy an entirely new wardrobe for under $500. I mean, really. I have *sandals* that cost more than that!

Me + Glenbrook Square Mall = total disaster. I blew through the entire $500 in about an hour flat, and that was mostly on jeans (Gap), shoes (Marshall Field's), and underthings (Victoria's Secret). I realized I was out of money when I tried to be cool and pick up the tab for Trudy's and my lunch at Red Robin. So embarrassing. I ran into the women's bathroom and dialed Mom on my cell.

ME: I need more money.
MOM: What? What happened to the five?
ME: I spent it.
MOM: You *spent* it? *All* of it?
ME: Be real. You spend like double that every time you walk into a salon.
MOM: That's not the point, Morgan. You've been in Fort Wayne for thirty-six hours!
ME: Right. And thanks for calling, by the way.
MOM: I figured you'd call me.
ME: Which I just did. To tell you I need more money.
MOM: No.
ME: *No?*
MOM: No.
ME: What am I supposed to do, then?
MOM: Figure it out.
(*click*)

I immediately burst into tears. How can she do this to me? My own mother. And it's not like it's even *her* money. I'm the one who earned it. I didn't see her busting ass in fourteen films over the past nine years.

After a good cry, I cleaned myself up and went back to the table. I mumbled something to Trudy about being out of cash and she reached across and patted my hand. Then she said that she'd pick up the check and that I shouldn't worry, but maybe I should rethink my new $200 Stuart Weitzman mules?

"I have a thing for shoes," I confessed.

She nodded. "The thing is, you're trying to shop like

Morgan Carter, Hollywood starlet. But remember, when you're here, you're Claudia Miller, average American high school student. Would Claudia Miller wear Stuart Weitzman mules to Snider High?"

"I guess not."

"So what do you want to do?"

We ended up returning everything I'd bought. *Everything*.

Then we drove to CVS, where I picked up some no. 2 pencils, a pack of Uniball pens, half a dozen college-ruled notebooks, and an At-a-Glance school planner. How responsible of me. The planner had a solid navy blue cover, which seemed like the kind of thing "Claudia" would want to buy.

Oddest moment of the day? Realizing that even in the largest mall in all of Fort Wank, not a single person recognized me.

Not *one*.

So I guess the disguise is working. Either that or I've become instantly irrelevant, like Tina Yothers or Justin Guarini.

Trudy's got her divorced women's support group tonight, so I'm on my own. Plans include eating an entire pint of Häagen-Dazs pistachio ice cream, giving myself a pedicure, and watching obscene amounts of trash TV. If I have any room left in my rapidly expanding stomach, I may just go ahead and order in Chinese. Although I'm a little scared about what those wholesome Hoosiers will do to my down-'n'-dirty kung pao beef.

Tomorrow, I have got to get my ass (also rapidly expanding) to an honest-to-goodness gym. I'd prefer a tight-abbed personal trainer who came to my house four times a week, but that doesn't seem to be part of the new regime.

What have I gotten myself *into*?

Dear Sam,

I just tried to call your cell but got voice mail, so I figured I'd write a letter instead.

Well, I'm here, in Fort Wayne. I have to admit this place is a bit of a culture shock. It's like Extreme Suburbia—strip malls as far as the eye can see! But I guess it's not *that* bad. I mean, remember that two-week shoot I did in Thailand—the one where there wasn't any indoor plumbing? *That* was bad. Still, one of the worst things about hiding out here is not being able to see the ocean every day. I don't think I've ever lived in a landlocked state before. It makes me feel sort of . . . trapped.

That's kind of why I'm writing, actually. Sam, you've been my manager since I was six months old, and you have guided me through every stage of my career. More than that, you've been like a dad to me, and you never stopped believing in me, even after that night at the Viper Room. You were the first person I saw when I woke up in the hospital, and I know it was you, and not Mama Bianca, who arranged for me to have that private suite at Applewood.

Rehab I understood. You were right—I needed to get clean. And if it hadn't been for you . . . I know you feel guilty because you didn't tell Mom about my "habits," but you shouldn't. If my time at Applewood taught me anything, it was that *I* was the one steering the ship. You were the one trying to throw me a life preserver (literally).

This is why I'm trying really hard to understand why you sent me here. I know you think that if I drop out for a year, make myself over as anonymous Midwestern high school student Claudia Miller, and ultimately resurface with a tell-all autobiography, it will save my career. But Sam, I have to tell you, it sounds like the plot to a really bad movie. Do you really think I can last a whole year without a single person recognizing me? I mean, I know I've put on some weight, and after that doctor who fixed the hole in my septum took it upon himself to make some slight artistic adjustments, I *do* look kind of different. But still, it seems really unlikely that I can fly under everyone's radar for that long.

I trust you, Sam, more than anyone, so I'm trying to make this work. And I'm doing what you asked—writing as much as possible down in this journal. I'm staying clean, too, and on Thursday I'll go to my first Narcotics Anonymous meeting here. I'm trying, Sam—trying hard to be the girl you've taken such good care of all these years. I promise I'll make you proud of me again.

All my love,
Morgan

8/18

Emerged from my kung pao coma around noon. Too much MSG, not enough H_2O. I feel . . . what's the word? *Thick.* I used to scarf a plate of scrambled eggs peppered with Tabasco and four ibuprofen to cure my hangovers, but I have no idea how to make myself feel less puke-tastic today.

God, I'm depressed. Last night on *E!* they were showing clips from this PETA benefit that in my former life I so totally would've been invited to. Instead, I was here, in my Nick & Nora pj's, eating full-fat ice cream. If that's not sad enough, I finally see my best friend, Marissa Dahl, for the first time in more than seven months and it's on *television*. Joan Rivers was interviewing her and her latest co-star-slash-*boyfriend* Evan

7

Walsh—impossible, of course, since everyone knows Evan is gay. I can't even describe how hard it was not to snatch my cell and call up Marissa, because if she's "dating" Evan, it means she's really hooking up with someone who has a very public girlfriend (or even wife) and using Evan as her cover. *I want to know who Marissa is seeing!*

I hate hate HATE not being on the inside. And I miss Marissa so much. She's probably the only true friend I've ever had. We met six years ago when we both did guest appearances on one of the *Law & Order*s. A "ripped from the headlines" episode in which Marissa and I played classmates traumatized by a school shooting. Fun stuff for eleven-year-olds, no? Anyway, we terrorized the set—stealing double chocolate brownies from craft services and hiding under the table so we could eat them without our mothers flipping out on us.

(NOTE TO SELF: Buy brownies *ASAP*.)

I wonder if Marissa is worried about me. Is it possible that she hasn't even realized I'm gone? She didn't visit me once during the six very long months I spent at Crapplewood, although she *was* sweet enough to send me a whole case of La Perla lingerie when, in my last month of rehab, I had my 38 DDs shrunk to more manageable 36 Cs. Still, we haven't talked in ages—haven't even e-mailed since the day after my release, because she was shooting in Toronto and I was practically chained to Mama Bianca's side in L.A. Actually, that's one really good thing about being here. Not having my mother scrutinize every facial tic, convinced that if I see anyone I used to know, I'll immediately want to break sobriety and therefore jeopardize years upon years of potential income she's expecting me to make so the two of us can live in the lifestyle to which she's become accustomed.

Trudy just came in and asked me if I wanted to try clothes shopping again. I politely declined. She (equally as politely) reminded me that school starts in five days. I politely told her I didn't give a flying—

Christ, I should go apologize.

8/18—*Later*

Trudy is gone (?) and didn't leave a note. Not very Trudy-like. I must've really pissed her off.

8/18—*Much later*

Okay, so I didn't piss Trudy off. This is because Trudy is a saint-type lady who has empathy for everyone and everything around her. Seriously, you should hear her talk to her plants. She names them all—for example, the Chinese evergreen is Albee, for reasons I have yet to uncover—and she will gingerly touch "his" soil and say things like, "Well, hello there, Albee—you're feeling a little dry today, aren't you? Here, let me give you a little drink." (I should note that I'm not making fun of Trudy for doing this—it's actually kind of cute.)

So where *did* Trudy go? To the store. She came back with Betty Crocker brownie mix (how did she know? HOW?) and a stack of magazines—*Seventeen, CosmoGirl! Teen Vogue.* For research, she said.

We plan to spend the rest of the day combing the mags and making a list of what I need to transform myself into

Claudia Miller, quintessential Midwestern high school student. And oh! Tonight the Style Channel is running a marathon of *The Look for Less*. Marissa once did a segment on that show—putting together a complete outfit for under $100. Maybe I can get some ideas from there as well.

THE LOOK FOR LESS—Claudia Miller Edition

Clothes

- Jeans, 2 pairs
- Nice pants, black, 1 pair
- Cargo pants, khaki or olive, 1 pair
- Knee-length denim pencil skirt, 1
- Flouncy miniskirts, 2
- T-shirts, solid colors—black, white, gray, 1 each
- T-shirts, funky, 2
- Button-down oxford, white, 1
- Classic cardigan, black or navy, 1
- Hoodie, 1
- Fitted blazer, corduroy, 1
- Denim jacket, 1
- Peacoat, 1

Shoes

- Good boots, black, 1 pair
- Sneakers (Skechers?), 1 pair
- Mary Janes, black, 1 pair

Accessories

- Belt, black, 1
- Monogrammed purse, 1
- Pearl earrings, 1 pair

- Small silver hoops, 1 pair
- Trendy necklaces/bracelets
- Tights, black, 2 pairs
- Socks, asst. colors, 12 pairs
- Scarf/mittens/wool knit cap, 1 each

Misc.

- Bras/underwear, 12 each
- Pj's
- Bonne Bell lip gloss (preferably with sparkles)
- Umbrella

8/19

I finally understand why Oprah loves Target.

It was incredible. Such prices! Such fun things! And why didn't anyone tell me Isaac Mizrahi had his own line there? I got two of his long-sleeved T-shirts for $20 and a black-and-gray angora sweater for the same price, and these adorable piqué polo shirts in black and red with cutie white collars for $14.99 each. I also got a seriously cute clutch purse with the initial *C* on it (although I'd originally picked up *M* before Trudy reminded me I was shopping as Claudia now, not Morgan. Oops).

After we'd ransacked Tar-jay, Trudy and I went over to Old Navy, where I picked up two pairs of jeans for $14.99 each and this beautiful striped sweater for all of $9.99. Then we hit Wal-Mart (bras and underwear), Payless (more shoes, messenger-style book bag), and CVS again (makeup and hair stuff).

Total spent: $479.81.

Who rocks the house? *I rock the house.*

Unfortunately, I have to stop rocking the house long enough to work the steps. Tonight is my first meeting in Fort Wayne. I'm not sure what to expect—the few meetings I went to during my brief hiatus between Crapplewood and here really were more like industry events. I even sat next to Robert Downey Jr. at the last one I attended and he gave me a big hug and said, "You can beat this thing, kid." It was the nicest thing any non-Crapplewood-affiliated person had said to me in months.

More soon.

8/20

Last night was a total disaster.

I don't even know where to begin. Maybe with the panic attack I had while Trudy was driving me to my meeting? See, back home, practically everyone's in treatment for something, and even before I got sober, I knew which A-list celebrities attended this meeting or that meeting. But here, it's different. Here, I wouldn't be another face in the crowd—someone might actually recognize me. And I don't believe for one second that a roomful of recovering addicts would honor the "anonymous" part of NA if they had an opportunity to sell out a former child star (i.e., me).

So, yeah. We're pulling up in front of the church and I can barely breathe, I'm so freaked out. Trudy's going, "What's the matter? Do you have asthma? Where's your inhaler?" And I can't stop hyperventilating long enough to explain that no, I don't have asthma, but I sincerely wish I could pop a Xanax right about now.

Eventually I calmed down enough to tell Trudy what was really wrong, and she gave me a sideways car hug and told me that I didn't have to go in—that she'd take me home and we could try again another night. But no. I had to go in. The whole Witless Protection Program was built upon two things: (1) assimilating into Fort Waynean high school society and (2) staying sober. Besides, I promised Sam I would, and Lord knows I've already disappointed the man enough for eight of my nine lives.

So I went in. It was a typical church meeting room, albeit in a slightly shabbier church than I'm used to. A long table lined one wall, boasting an impressive, industrial-sized coffee machine with all the fixings and six trays of doughnuts (for the recovering heroin addicts, I presume—for some reason those guys can eat their weight in sugar). A large, misshapen circle of folding chairs took up most of the rest of the space. And the smoke! It was so thick, I felt like my eyes were coated in cheese-cloth. At Crapplewood, there were specific lounges for the smokers, which was a good thing, because I'm not one of those people who traded narcotics for nicotine. I have a very sensitive nose—not surprising, considering how much junk I snorted up it once upon a time—and the smell alone made me want to puke. Which is sort of funny, if you think about it.

Anyway, I sat down and no one seemed to recognize me, which made my breathing slightly easier (or it would have, had I not been choking on the cigarette smog). This is proba-bly because I was the youngest person at the meeting by a good twenty years. Gaby, the woman who facilitates the Thursday night group, came up to me before she started the meeting because she thought I was looking for the Alateen meeting down the hall. I assured her I was in the right place.

Gaby started the meeting by welcoming the newcomers and asking us to make a brief introduction. "Us" turned out to be just me and Valerie, a horsey-looking woman with very small, Chiclet-shaped teeth who'd been battling a ten-year-old amphet-amine addiction she'd developed while trying to lose weight. She had a big ass and cottage cheese thighs, though, so obviously all Val had gotten from the drugs were those many stints in rehab.

And then I had to make my introduction, and I was so nervous I said, "Hi, I'm Morgan," and everyone said, "Hi, Morgan" in unison, and I could literally feel all the blood drain out of my face. I had one line—one!—"Hi, I'm Claudia"—and I blew it. I BLEW IT. My heart started beating all crazy, and I said, "Actually, I'd prefer it if you call me Claudia, because that's my real name, the one that's on my birth certificate and every-thing." My voice came out all squeaky and the words were too rushed, and for half a minute I was certain someone would realize who I was. But if anyone made the connection, their faces didn't show it. Maybe I was never big in the Midwest? Whatever the reason, I was so super-grateful, because after the name snafu all I could do was mumble that I'd been sober for twenty-eight weeks. The number got a modest round of applause, which I have to admit felt sort of good.

But I was so nervous about being found out that I could barely listen to a word anyone was saying. I just kept scan-ning the room, my eyes combing over each person to make sure they were oblivious as to my identity. I must've looked like I was jonesing for a fix, because I seriously couldn't sit still. The minute we finished the closing serenity prayer, I hopped up and practically ran back to the parking lot, where Trudy was waiting for me.

Trudy thinks that to truly become Claudia Miller, I need more of a costume. So tomorrow we're buying me a pair of glasses and dyeing my hair dark brown. It seems a shame, especially since my mom splurged on $600 honeyed highlights not two weeks before I left L.A., but Trudy's right—if I'm going to think like Claudia Miller, I really do need to look the part.

8/21

Me + 1 bottle of Nice 'n Easy 120 + 1 pair squared-off tortoiseshell glasses – all traces of makeup = girl who now looks as invisible as she feels.

Only thirty-six hours of freedom between me and a public high school education.

I can hardly contain my excitement (not).

8/22

Trudy is so cute. She packed me a lunch for tomorrow—a PB&J sandwich, an apple, a Baggie of pretzel nuggets, two chocolate chip cookies, and one of those squeezie boxes of Juicy Juice. She also stuck a couple of dollar bills in there in case I wanted to buy something hot from the cafeteria. The money was pinned to a napkin with a note on it: *Good luck today, CLAUDIA! See you tonight. Love, Tru.*

She's such a mom. I don't know why she never bothered to have kids of her own, but seriously? She's so much more a mom than my mom ever was, is, or ever will be.

But that's another entry entirely.

I should try to get some sleep. My alarm is set for 5:30 a.m., which is truly obscene.

8/23—aka "The First Day of School"

TOP FIVE MYTHS ABOUT THE AVERAGE
AMERICAN PUBLIC HIGH SCHOOL,
AS PORTRAYED BY THE TEEN MOVIE UNIVERSE

MYTH #1: In the movies, girls get dressed up for the first day of school—sexy tank tops, miniskirts, kitten heels, designer backpacks with their initials embroidered on the front flap. This is not the case in lovely Fort Wayne, Indiana—at least not at scenic Snider High. Here, the first-day uniform consists of baby T-shirts emblazoned with the logo from some nearby college, low-rise short shorts, broken-in Saucony sneakers, and J. Lo–size silver hoop earrings.

This means that girls who show up in, say, a white button-down, lightweight black vest and knee-length plaid skirt don't exactly *blend*. And it's not the kind of non-blending where you show up at the Oscars wearing a vintage Chanel in the perfect ballerina pink that makes girls like Scarlett Johansson weep with envy. No, you stick out like you're auditioning for the role of stereotypical prepster nerd and figure you might as well have written *NEW GIRL* on your forehead with a black Sharpie, because *everybody knows*.

MYTH #2: In the movies, when the new girl arrives at school, she stops in at the front office to get a copy of her schedule and meet the student guide that's been assigned to her—usually a hot jock boy who just happens to be in all of her classes.

This is a total fallacy. In the real world, the new girl has to register for her classes the week before school starts (or, in my case, has to have her manager register for her, using a fake birth certificate and falsified transcripts). She's mailed a printout of her new schedule ahead of time and therefore has no need to check in at the front office. Instead, she stumbles through the hallways, feeling the weight of evil, unfamiliar eyes judging her every move, praying she finds her homeroom before the first bell rings. She is relieved to know that there are actually bells and that they do actually ring.

MYTH #3: In the movies, the mean-but-beautiful school princess will approach the new girl in one of her morning classes, saying something like, "Hey, you're the new girl, right?" She will be flanked by her two best friends–slash–cronies and she will introduce herself with a semi-smug smile and a mischievous glint in her big blue eyes. Ominous music plays in the background, and you know this will not be the new girl's last run-in with the princess—odds are, she's about to steal the princess's boyfriend/best friend/homecoming queen title.

At Snider, everyone will look at the new girl but not a

single soul will bother with anything beyond a customary head nod of acknowledgement. She will manage to make it through all of her morning classes saying three words: *here*, *present*, and *here* again.

MYTH #4: In the movies, lunch is a sociological study of high school hierarchy. Tables are divided into groups like brains, stoners, and band geeks. The new girl will take a deep breath as she exits the lunch line, holding her mold-green tray and looking for the right place to sit—either by the hot jock boy guide, by the princess and her cronies, or by the princess's boyfriend, which makes the princess glare at her and start hatching diabolical plans of retribution.

In the real world, the dividing lines are not crystal clear, and no one—and I mean, *no one*—invites the new girl to dine with them. In fact—

You know what? It was so horrible I can't even write about it in a witty way. I just stood there, looking around the room, searching for a safe place to sit. I ended up on the fringes of this one group, just trying to look like I was actually with them instead of the add-on I truly was, until one of the girls turned to me and said, "Are you, like, a freshman or something?" To which I replied, "I'm new." I might as well have said, "I have herpes," because she turned away from me so fast she could've gotten whiplash. I wanted to die, I was so completely embarrassed.

And then I went to wipe my mouth with my napkin, and I saw Trudy's note, and I swear to God, I almost started to cry. Right there, in the middle of lunch.

Tomorrow I'm going to eat in the library. Or the girls' bathroom. Or anywhere but the hell that is that cafeteria.

MYTH #5: In the movies, the new girl gets a ride home from school with the hot jock boy, who's already asked her out for Friday night. She's become so instantly popular that she's got a handful of gal pals vying to be her best friend, an invitation to try out for the cheerleading squad, and a very cute, very young male English teacher who winks at her and makes her feel like she's really super-special.

This new girl, on the other hand, took the bus back to Trudy's house, devoured yet another half pint of ice cream, and cried herself senseless as Oprah unveiled her latest book club selection.

That Oprah pick looks good, though. Maybe I should buy it—take up pleasure reading for a hobby. Pleasure reading could be my new "thing." I could be like Rory Gilmore and take a book with me wherever I go. Big, smart books, too, like *Madame Bovary*. And I'll take this journal with me wherever I go and I'll order lattes at a cool, non-Starbucks coffeehouse and take notes about everyone and everything I see. That way, when I publish my memoirs, I can be like, "I'm so over acting. What I really want to do is *write*."

8/26

Tomorrow is Friday, which means this weeklong exercise in humiliation is almost over. Only thirty-five more until I'm officially a senior. The minute I turn in my final exam, I am so totally out of here.

At least, I think I am. That was the plan, right? Sam swears that this is a surefire way to make a comeback. Much more effective than me doing five hundred hours of community service, becoming the new spokesperson for the hottest anti-drug organization, and talking about how I found God in rehab. That's all been done. *This* will be different.

I will be different.

The thing that normal people don't realize is that when an actor or actress gets publicly busted for drugs (or, in my case, almost ODs on a mixture of E and OxyContin), they become virtually uninsurable and therefore a major risk to the studios. So, like, even though Spielberg was all about casting me in his modernized remake of *Gypsy*—a part I was born to play, by the way—the other top dogs at DreamWorks nixed the idea because (a) the premiums for insuring me would blow out the already huge budget, (b) no one can predict whether or not rehab actually "took," and (c) I haven't actually made a quality film in like a year and a half anyway, so why would anyone risk their project on a washed-up has-been like me?

On that depressing note, I think I'll go to bed.

8/27

It's been discovered that Trudy has the box set of *My So-Called Life* DVDs, so tonight we're ordering pizza and hunkering down for a mini-marathon of our favorite episodes. But first—

MY WEEK, IN REVIEW

♦I neglected to mention before that I got stuck in a

second-period gym class. Also that my gym teacher, Ms. Vineyard, is a former Olympic hopeful in volleyball and is dead serious about the sport—so much so that she's making us take a test on its history and rules next Tuesday. (NOTE TO SELF: Study for volleyball test!) Anyway, second-period gym class means you're gross and sweaty by 10 a.m. And even though the girls' locker room does have showers, apparently they're just for show. Ms. Vineyard leaves us exactly three minutes to get changed before the bell rings for third period, so we all spray ourselves down with deodorant, perfume, or a combination of the two. Mostly you just *feel* disgusting for the rest of the day, but sometimes I actually look pretty disgusting too—sweaty, stringy hair, pungent post-workout scent. Not that anyone seems to notice!

♦Mr. Pinzer, my chemistry teacher, assigned us lab partners on Wednesday. I got paired up with An-Yi, this very tall, very striking foreign-exchange student from Hong Kong. I mistakenly thought that since she's new too we might become friends—or at the very least, comrades—but no. She spent the entire period snatching beakers out of my hands and saying things like, "Give it here, stupid, and let me do it right." In impeccable English, too, which was a little unexpected. Turns out that An-Yi isn't your typical foreign-exchange student: even though she was raised in Hong Kong, she was born in Connecticut and has been educated at English-speaking schools all of her life. Her father is the one who insisted she spend a year in Indiana getting a "true American experience" before she graduates. It occurs to me that the two of us are on similar missions, which I'd love to explain to the girl if she'd stop looking down on me for thirty seconds.

♦Today I accidentally left my lunch at home, which meant that if I wanted to eat, I had to buy food in the Cafeteria of Doom. But this turned out to be a good thing. Emily Whitmarsh, this sort of quiet girl in my English class, was behind me in line and she tapped me on my shoulder and asked me if I'd understood what Mr. Garrett, our teacher, had said about *Siddhartha* being a secret treatise on consumerism. (For the record, I hadn't.) We were still talking when the cashier rang me up, so Emily said, "Wait for me, okay?" I did, and the next thing I know, I'm eating cold, rubbery mac 'n' cheese with Emily; her twin brother, Eli; and a handful of their friends. Score!

The pizza is finally here, and I'm stoked to watch some MSCL and rediscover "why Jordan can't read," so I guess I'm signing off for now.

8/28

It's Saturday. In a former life I'd be shopping for something hot to wear clubbing with Marissa. In this life, I'm getting ready to attend my second Narcotics Anonymous meeting in Fort Wayne. I skipped my Thursday meeting because I was feeling so blah—which, actually, is the exact reason why I should've gone. But whatever. I'm going today, and then Trudy and I are going to check out the YMCA. Last night we polished off a large pizza, an extra-large bag of white-cheddar popcorn, yet another pint of Häagen-Dazs, *and* half a jar of peanut butter (don't ask).

In the middle of our lonely-girl binge, Trudy told me that after her divorce, she pretty much stopped eating for six months and dropped something like thirty pounds (hence the Mary-Kate thinness). I told her she must've FedEx-ed those pounds to my ass and thighs, because I've gained so much weight I'm too chicken to step on a scale. The last time I did was right after I left Crapplewood, which is when I found out I'd put on twenty solid pounds during my six months of rehab.

Good news: Mom sent Tru a check for two thousand dollars, which she said "should cover Morgan's room and board for September." Hello, does she think she's boarding a *horse*? Trudy was going to send it back when I suggested we use part of it for gym memberships and the rest on a salon day—Euro facials, mani-pedi combos, hot stone massages. She said, "How can I spend your mother's money like that?" but I reminded her that technically it was *my* money and that my mother was only babysitting it until I turned eighteen. Eventually she said, "We'll see," but we *are* going to the Y today, and I'm going to do a little Googling later to see what Fort Wayne has to offer in the way of high-end spas.

8/29

Feeling thoroughly depressed. At yesterday's meeting, this very overweight woman told the story of getting off smack only to become addicted to snacks. She said she's put on more than 250 pounds since getting sober, and now she feels just as worthless as she did when she was an addict. She broke down sobbing and it was just so heartbreaking. Granted, I never got near heroin—oddly enough, it was the one drug that freaked me out—but supposedly detoxing from Oxy is almost as bad and, let me tell you, not a pretty sight.

Carlie, the Saturday meeting facilitator, talked about how we're all addicts for a reason—that there's something in our personality that makes us prone to addictive behaviors—and how that's why so many of us end up smokers, even if we never touched a cigarette before rehab. Then she started talking about food and how easy it was to find ourselves abusing it because it's just another form of self-medication. Through all of it, the four-hundred-pound woman kept blubbering, and all I could think about was how much ice cream I'd ingested since moving to Fort Wayne and how maybe I was becoming her—becoming addicted to food—and oh yeah, I had to work really hard not to bolt from the room.

At the end, Carlie gave us information about an Overeaters Anonymous meeting that takes place on Tuesday nights, which made this one guy start ranting about recovering addicts who become addicted to twelve-step groups. And then the four-hundred-pound woman shrieked at him, "You don't understand, you'll never understand!" At that point I *did* bolt, because I seriously couldn't take any more chaos and carnage.

Speaking of, I'm supposed to be working on my first review for film class. I don't think I've written about Mr. Sappey (pronounced Sap-PAY), my film teacher, but let me just say, I've never met a bigger wanker in my life. He speaks in this very affected accent, sort of like Madonna's after she decided she wanted to be British, and wears corduroy blazers with leather elbow patches even in eighty-degree heat. Anyway, this weekend our homework was to watch a "lowbrow" comedy and write about the elements that make it lowbrow. When I asked him for an example of what he considered lowbrow, he said dismissively, "You know, like anything by the Farrelly brothers."

So I said, "Well, obviously they're the kings of gross-out humor, but haven't they made an art of it?"

He rolled his eyes at me and then replied, "I would hardly call jokes about semen 'art.'" He didn't actually say this last part to me, mind you. He said it looking around the room, like my fellow classmates were going to validate his feeling that I am a total idiot.

I couldn't let it drop. I cut in, "Wasn't there was a time when Shakespeare would've been considered lowbrow? Look how he's regarded today."

"That," Mr. Sappey snapped, "is *theater*." He said it with such disdain, too, which is beyond ridiculous. Anyone who's actually done theater knows it's like fifty thousand times harder than film.

I raised my hand again, but Mr. Sappey told me he'd heard enough from me and would I mind giving the rest of the class a chance to speak? Which was total BS, because no one ever participates in that class. I think this is because we all know how much Sappey likes the sound of his own voice.

Anyway, I decided I was going to write an essay comparing the musical narration of *There's Something About Mary* (via the most excellent Jonathan Richman) to the use of minstrels in Jane Fonda's 1965 comedic Western *Cat Ballou*, which Marissa made me watch a couple of years ago when she was going through her whole cowboy boot fetish. According to IMDb, *Cat Ballou* received five Academy Award nominations, including a Best Actor nod for Lee Marvin, who actually *won*.

So there, Mr. Sappey!

8/30

Dear Marissa,

It's 3:30 a.m. and I can't sleep. I keep thinking about that time you and I crashed Paris Hilton's birthday party, and you made out with her Backstreet Boyfriend, and I ended up playing Texas hold 'em with Ben Affleck's crew and winning twenty-five grand of their money. And how the next day we put on our sluttiest clothes and went shopping on Rodeo, pretending we were Julia Roberts in *Pretty Woman* and spending crazy amounts of cash on red leather cowboy boots and those silly Rebecca Taylor ballerina skirts. Those were some good times, weren't they?

But then I remembered what happened *after* our shopping spree—how I snorted all those lines in the bathroom at the Teen Choice Awards and then, coked out of my mind, almost got into a fistfight with Hilary Duff.

I guess that's the sort of thing that landed me here.

Where is "here"? I'm not supposed to tell you. I can, however, tell you that I'm okay and that I'm still sober—two things I'm really grateful for, even when I'm dead bored and totally lonely. Oh, and I'm in high school. Real high school, with a cafeteria and everything. It was Mama Bianca's idea—well, hers and Sam's—and they swear that dropping out for a year is the only way I'll ever make a comeback. I hope they're right, because I keep having these deep fears that my "comeback" will consist of me being added to the next cast of *The Surreal Life*, alongside people like Joey Lawrence and that blond chick from *Sabrina, the Teenage Witch*.

Oh! Oh! I read in this week's *Entertainment Weekly* that you beat out Sarah Michelle Gellar for the new Wonder Woman movie—nicely done, M.! I know you'll be a kick-ass super-friend. Take that, Buffy!

I miss you. Is that a given? You don't know how many times I've picked up my cell to call you, but that's against the rules of the Witless Protection Program. There's so much I want to tell you about—and even more I want to ask you about. Like, what's up with you and Evan Walsh? How was that shoot in Vancouver? And have you seen the fall line from Stella McCartney? I'm *drooling*.

In exactly four hours, I will be in geometry class. They had to put me in with the sophomores because my math skills are so "severely lacking." I feel like such a cliché.

Just for fun, I've printed the rest of today's schedule below.

I'm going to mail this letter to Bianca and ask her to forward it to you. Hopefully, she will.

As Paris would say, "Love you, bitch!"

—M.

SCHEDULE:

7:45 a.m. to 7:55 a.m.—homeroom w/ Mr. Pickles (his real name—swear to God!)

8:00 a.m. to 8:55 a.m.—geometry w/ Mrs. Chappelle (way too sexy to be a math teacher)

9:00 a.m. to 9:55 a.m.—phys ed w/ Ms. Vineyard (mean ex-Olympic volleyballer, should've been a shot caller)

10:00 a.m. to 10:55 a.m.—U.S. history w/ Ms. Kwan (awesome feminist)

11:00 a.m. to 11:55 a.m.—English w/ Mr. Garrett (stuck in the sixties, thinks Big Brother is out to get us all)

12:00 p.m. to 12:25 p.m.—lunch (second-most-torturous 25 minutes in my day, next to running laps for Ms. Vineyard at 9 a.m.)

12:30 p.m. to 1:25 p.m.—chemistry w/ Mr. Pinzer (remind me to tell you about my lab partner, the exchange student from hell)

1:30 p.m. to 2:25 p.m.—Spanish III w/ Senorita Ferguson (thinks muumuus are an acceptable form of fashion)

2:30 p.m. to 3:25 p.m.—film w/ Mr. Sap-PAY (total moron, bane of my HS existence)

Dear Mom,

   I'm enclosing a letter to Marissa. It doesn't say anything about where I am, so please just make sure she gets it, okay?

Thanks,

Morgan

8/30—Later

I wasn't sure if Emily Whitmarsh's invitation to lunch on Friday had been a fluke or not, but seeing as Margaret, the school librarian, has a no-food policy and seeing as how the few days I choked down my lunch in the bathroom were really, really gross, I decided to chance it. After English, I walked with Emily down to the cafeteria, making light conversation about Mr. Garrett's latest harangue on *Siddhartha*. When we reached the table, I paused, not sure if I was still welcome. But the minute I hesitated, Emily said, "If you need to go buy something, I can save you a seat."

"Thanks," I said, sliding into the one across from her. "I actually remembered to bring my lunch today."

The table quickly filled with the rest of Emily's crew, causing me to revert to silence. It was good, though, because it gave me more time to observe my fellow dining companions. They include:

• Emily—quiet, sort of serious, but clearly a leader in this group. Everyone looks at her immediately after they say something, almost like they're seeking her approval.

• Eli—Emily's twin brother, also quiet, also sort of serious. Is way more focused on what he's eating than he is the conversation going on around him. Can't tell if this is because he isn't a talker or if he's just really bored by the kind of talking the others engage in.

• Debbie Ackerman—Emily's best friend(?), slightly plump and super-chatty, but not in a perky kind of way. More like an if-I-never-stop-talking, you-have-to-acknowledge-my-existence kind of way. Has barely acknowledged my existence.

• Bethany Parker—Says grace before every meal. Seemed interested in knowing more about me until she asked which church I belonged to and I admitted I'm not completely down with God in terms of organized religion. Immediately ceased speaking to me. Is most likely praying for my soul.

• Joey Harkus—The male Bethany. Must have fairly severe asthma, as I've seen him use an inhaler three times over two lunches. Could be cute if he let his military-issue buzz cut grow out some.

• Kevin Roach—Eli's best friend(?)—calls him "E.," which clearly denotes some sort of increased intimacy. Plays soccer, judging from his well-muscled legs. Would probably be in a different social group altogether if his acne weren't so severe. Seriously, his face is completely red and pitted. Would love to recommend dermabrasion, but if his knock-off Nike sneakers are any indication, he most certainly could *not* afford advanced skin care.

So there you have it. My brand-new circle of best friends. Not exactly the kind of people I would've hung out with back home. "Claudia's" place on the food chain should depress the hell out of me, but I have to keep in mind that if it weren't for these people, I'd still be scarfing my PB&Js in stall number four of the second-floor girls' bathroom.

Gag.

8/31

This is only my second week of high school, and I already landed myself in the principal's office. Why, you ask? Well, yesterday I was supposed to meet with the guidance counselor, but since our little tête-à-tête was scheduled during my fourth-period history class—the only class I actually like—I skipped it. You'd think my dedication to education would be seen as a good thing, but no. I got in T-R-O-U-B-L-E.

That's not the worst of it. Turns out that the reason I

was supposed to see Ms. "Please, call me Janet" Moore in the first place was because my mother thought weekly sessions with her would be an ample substitute for the $400-an-hour shrink I used to see back home. Trudy told me this last night, after I confessed to skipping.

Bianca's response? "Normal kids can't afford $400-an-hour therapy sessions."

Well, *duh*.

I asked her how she thought I'd get counseling when I was supposed to be Claudia 24/7, and she told me to "improvise."

"Improvise?" I asked. "Improvise what?"

She sighed impatiently. "Talk about whatever you'd talk about with your regular therapist, Morgan. Just . . . you know. Be Claudia."

Yeah, Mom. That makes so much sense. Thanks for clarifying.

The official party line, according to Ms. Moore, is that I was kicked out of my last school for falling in with a bad crowd, and I require weekly meetings with her to make sure I stay focused. Focused on what, though? Pretending to be someone else?

Ms. Moore—er, *Janet*—is really young and really enthusiastic. She's maybe five feet tall and looks like she stole her wardrobe from the Gap's showroom, right down to the trendy striped scarf knotted on the right side of her neck. She picked me up from the principal's office and showed me to her own, where she immediately offered me peanut M&Ms from a chunky crystal dish. I declined at first until I saw her dogging down a handful. I reached in and grabbed a few for myself.

She said, "So, Claudia, why don't we talk about why you skipped out on me yesterday?" I told her I didn't want to miss history, and she said, "Yes, Ms. Kwan's pretty great, isn't she?" Then she said, "What can I do to make this easier for you? Some incentive for you to come in one day each week."

"Let me come in during my gym class."

"Done," she said with a smile, and offered me some more M&M's.

So now, once a week, I have an official pass to skip Ms. Vineyard's torture sessions. And if she's giving a test during my meeting, I get to make it up later, like after school. My standing appointment with la guidance counselor takes precedence over anything Ms. Vineyard throws my way.

(NOTE TO SELF: Bring Ms. Moore—*Janet*—a big bag of peanut M&M's.)

To be honest, I'm not sure what to make of Ms. Janet Moore. She seems fairly innocuous—like today, all she wanted to do is talk about my class schedule and ask me how I felt about making the transition to Snider—but then again, who knows what kind of nefarious plan she's got cooking under her perfectly coiffed hair?

I guess I'll find out next week.

9/1

I realize I haven't written much about the Whitmarsh twins, which is odd considering that they've become my closest—er, *only*—friends at Snider.

I'll start with Emily: She's a little bit shorter than me, maybe five-foot four, and has shoulder-length, light brown

35

hair in serious need of some highlights. Heart-shaped face, clear skin, and nice, hazel green eyes that would really sparkle if she actually wore a little makeup. Her usual uniform consists of a baggy T-shirt tucked into tapered-leg jeans that make her hips look bigger than they need to, a plain brown leather belt she could've stolen from her grandpa, and white sneakers that always look a bit too clean.

Eli looks exactly like his sister, minus the breasts. He's a photographer for the yearbook, so he runs around with this digital camera around his neck, taking random snapshots of everything—kind of like Brian Krakow from *My So-Called Life*. He sort of dresses like Brian too, even though he'd be way cuter if he ditched the prepster look for some Adam Brody–inspired geek chic. But I get the feeling that fashion isn't a top priority for the Whitmarsh twins.

That's how people refer to them, too: the Whitmarsh twins. I wouldn't exactly call them popular—I'm guessing they could be, with the right clothes and attitude—but everybody seems to know who they are and they're generally well liked and respected. In addition to working for the yearbook, Eli is a member of SWAT (Students Working Against Tobacco) and a volunteer tutor through Study Connection. Emily, on the other hand, is the president of VIP, which stands for Very Involved Panthers (a shout-out to our school mascot). It's a service organization that does stuff like organize blood drives and collect gifts for poor kids at Christmas. She also heads up this big haunted house every year, the proceeds of which go to the local children's hospital.

Their parents must cream themselves regularly for having such wholesome, well-rounded children.

Here's some fun news: I'm actually going to meet Mr.

and Mrs. Whitmarsh this weekend. The twins have an extra ticket to Saturday's Fort Wayne Wizards baseball game—originally intended for Debbie Ackerman, but since she has to babysit or something, Em asked me if I wanted to go instead. At first I was like, "No way," but when I told her I thought I was busy, her little face fell. Seriously, she looked like a sad puppy who'd been denied a juicy treat.

Then I remembered that I've never actually been to a live sporting event and how that might make for a good scene—you know, when I sell the film rights to my autobiography. The fallen ingénue, experiencing her first baseball game with the all-American family—realizing that if she had grown up in their world, maybe she would never have fallen to begin with. (That kind of crap always wins the audience over.)

So eventually I said yes, and Emily grinned so big I thought her lips would crack. And all because of a baseball game!

This should be interesting.

Gotta run—tonight Trudy and I have our fitness orientation at the YMCA. Time for me to shave off some of my rehab gut!

9/1—Later

Can't move a muscle. Everything hurts. I swear to God, I'll never let myself get this out of shape again. I hurt so bad that even writing these few words is making me wince in pain. Tru's sore too. Since neither of us is strong enough to cook dinner, we ordered in a pizza, which should be arriving any minute. And yes—I see the irony. At least we skipped the pepperoni and opted for veggies.

Today it occurred to me that I've been having lunch with "the crew" for almost a full week, and the only one who's bothered to ask me anything about myself is Emily. And even then it was basic questions like, "Where are you from?" and, "Why did you move to Fort Wayne?" Claudia, it turns out, is from Pennsylvania and moved here to "make a fresh start." I figured that last bit just begged for more questioning—something I was actually looking forward to, as I had been playing with Claudia's backstory since the flight from L.A. and was eager to try it out—but no. Instead, Debbie asked Eli if he was shooting the soccer matches after school, which got Kevin talking about this year's team, which left me with absolutely nothing to say and, even if I'd *had* something to say, no one to say it to.

On a completely unrelated note, I got my film paper back from Mr. Sappey this afternoon. It had an enormous *D* scrawled across the top. Underneath he'd written, *Nice try, Ms. Miller, but comparing two pieces of drivel doesn't support your argument that lowbrow comedy can be high art. Try using source-based material to back up your points next time.* Then I found out that LaTanya, the girl who sits behind me in class, wrote her paper on how the success of the *American Pie* trilogy epitomizes everything that's wrong with today's moviegoing audiences. Sappey gave *her* an A-plus.

LaTanya said, "Girl, where have you been? It's not about how smart you are. It's about how well you can figure out what the teacher wants. Parrot back to them what they spoon-feed to you, and you'll end up with a perfect GPA."

That can't possibly be true, can it? The only formal education I've had has been from on-set tutors, which are kind of a joke. They put in the bare minimum amount of time on school stuff—just enough to comply with state laws. Even so, not one of my tutors ever punished me for disagreeing with them. In fact, alternate viewpoints were always encouraged.

So, I ask you: who's really getting the joke-worthy education here?

9/3

I've been feeling dark and stormy since yesterday, and I guess it showed up on my face because in English today Emily asked me what was wrong. I said, "Nothing," which is what you're supposed to say when someone asks you that question, but she wouldn't leave it alone. Finally, at lunch, I told her about Sappey's D and what LaTanya said. Once I got going, it turned into this really heated rant. Like, the kind where if I'd been a cartoon character, steam would've been shooting from my ears. Eli kept staring at me and shaking his head and smiling like I amused him in some way.

"What is it?" I snapped.

"Nothing," he said. "I've just never seen you like this."

Emily read through the paper and Sappey's comments, thoughtfully chewing on her tuna sandwich. "The thing is, Claudia, he's got a point. You didn't use any supporting sources."

"It was supposed to be a review!" I seethed.

"But you didn't write it like a review—you wrote it like an analytical essay."

I could feel myself giving her evil death glances. "It doesn't matter," I said, snatching the paper back from her.

"It's clear that he gave me the grade based on the fact that I disagreed with him."

"Maybe," Emily conceded. "Next time, though, you should follow the assignment exactly. Then if he still gives you a bad grade, at least you'll know it's personal."

At home I filled Trudy in on the situation, including what Emily said, and wouldn't you know it? She agreed with Em too.

I've decided I need to burn off some of this aggression, so Trudy and I are going to a 7 p.m. kickboxing class at the Y. Oh, the glamorous life I lead!

9/4

I just spent the last four hours doing homework, and I feel stupider than ever. (Stupider? More stupid? Whatever.) I've failed the past two geometry quizzes, I'm behind on my *Siddhartha* paper for Mr. Garrett, and yesterday An-Yi asked Mr. Pinzer—out loud, in front of the whole class—if she could have a new lab partner because I was "holding her back." The only class I'm doing well in is history (which I love). That and Spanish III, but that's just because I did a six-month shoot in Mexico when I was twelve and Senorita Ferguson is still teaching us how to conjugate simple verbs.

I so do *not* want to go to the Wizards game with the Stepford twins and their perfect parents. I already feel bad enough about myself as it is. But Trudy says it would be rude of me to cancel now, especially since they're picking me up in two hours. So, as Mama Bianca would say, I've got to "suck up and deal."

Speaking of Bianca, I've left her two messages this week

and still haven't gotten a return phone call. This means my mother is either (a) dating someone new, (b) out of the country, (c) avoiding me on general principle, or (d) all of the above.

It wouldn't bother me so much if I'd heard from Sam at all, but he's MIA too. So mostly I walk around feeling irrelevant, which is *grrr*eat for someone working on sobriety, let me tell you.

Sometimes I really hate my life.

9/4—*Later*

Baseball is maybe the most boring sport in the world. This surprised me, because there are a ton of baseball movies that have made me cry, like *Field of Dreams* and *The Rookie*. But real baseball can be a total snooze fest.

Even so, I had an okay time.

This also surprised me, because the day got off to a rocky start. I'd had Trudy drop me off at the Whitmarshes' house so I wouldn't have to worry about them finding some Morgan-identifying items at our homestead. Turns out that they live in this really ritzy neighborhood with well-manicured lawns and mile-long driveways. I didn't know Fort Wayne knew such luxury, but there it was.

Anyway, you know how you get an image of a person stuck in your head, and then you meet them and they look completely different? I think I was expecting Mr. and Mrs. Whitmarsh to be Ned and Maude Flanders, but instead, they looked more like Kurt Russell and Goldie Hawn. No joke! And they were totally charming, too, all genuine smiles and firm handshakes.

The problem was, they liked to ask questions. *Lots* of questions. Things like, "So, Claudia, how does Snider stack up to your old high school?" and, "Is it hard being away from your family?" These were not topics I'd considered when building my backstory. Luckily, I inherited Bianca's talent for thinking on my feet and responded (in complete seriousness), "The kids here are so much more positive, and I adore my history teacher," and, "Sometimes I miss my mom, but mostly I'm just focused on my studies." (Now that I see it written out, I realize it's all pretty much true, but at the time I felt like the world's biggest liar.)

I used an old trick of Marissa's and turned the questions back onto the Whitmarshes, thereby diverting attention from myself and making them think I was an excellent con-versationalist to boot. (Quoth Marissa: "People are only really interested in talking about themselves. Ask them a ton of questions and they think you're kind, sensitive, *and* bril-liant.") I found out that Mr. Whitmarsh is actually a city councilman and Mrs. Whitmarsh is the founder of Fort Wayne's largest accounting firm (the aptly named Whitmarsh and Associates). Oh, and Mrs. W. also volunteers at the Washington House Treatment Center, which is—you guessed it!—a drug and alcohol rehab facility.

My blood turned into insta-ice. Of course the mother of my new best friends would work closely with recovering addicts—and therefore have the tools to identify me as one, if she looked hard enough.

Fortunately, Emily emerged from the kitchen just as I was certain I was going to pass out. She wore the exact same uniform she wore to school every single day, only this time her drab hair had been pulled into a ponytail and threaded through the opening in the back of her Wizards baseball cap. Dorkness to the extreme, until Eli came pounding down the steps *wearing the exact same hat*. If that weren't enough, he lifted the camera he always wears around his neck and took a very candid snapshot of me and Em. Instinctively, I raised my arms across my face, like a vampire shielding herself from sunlight.

"What's wrong?" Eli asked, concerned.

"Nothing," I said, because the lie was easier than explaining to him why I didn't want any part of me photographed by anybody anywhere, including him. "I'm just camera shy," I offered. More of an afterthought than anything, but Eli ate it up with a spoon.

"Sorry," he said. "I shoot before I think."

"I'll have to have you arrested then," I joked, but he didn't get it. I tried again: "Assault with a digital weapon?" Eli just stood there frowning at me in confusion. "Your camera is *digital*," I explained patiently "You *shoot* pictures with it. Like, *bang bang!*"

"Oh," he said.

After a few more minutes of awkward small talk, we all loaded into the Whitmarshes' pristine white Ford Explorer and headed for Memorial Stadium. Mr. Whitmarsh had barely turned on the ignition when he started in with even more questions: "I hear you and Emily are in the same English class. Tell me—is Mr. Garrett *really* as bad as Em makes him out to be?" I was about to respond when Emily jumped in and said, "Dad, please stop cross-examining Claudia." Then she turned to me. "I'm sorry. My father used to work in the DA's office. Sometimes he forgets that it's impolite to give my friends the third degree."

"Fair enough," Mr. Whitmarsh quipped. He turned on the radio and started singing along with this old Jay and the Techniques song. I, on the other hand, momentarily lost the ability to breathe. What are the odds that my only two sort-of friends in Fort Wayne are the progeny of a treatment center volunteer and a former district attorney? No way are they going to buy my cover story for long. I'm going to be outed before I finish fitting in—and then there's the fact that two weeks in hiding isn't nearly long enough to warrant a career-resuscitating memoir.

Then I reminded myself that I still hold the record as the youngest Oscar nominee for Best Actress (I beat out that *Whale Rider* chick by a whole six months!) and that Sam wouldn't have sent me here if he didn't think I could pull off the role of a lifetime. So I took some slow, deep breaths, chanting a silent mantra: I am Claudia Miller. I AM CLAUDIA MILLER.

Slipping into full-on Claudia mode isn't that hard, actually. It's all about speech patterns and facial expressions. Claudia Miller is mostly cheerful, and there's a smile hidden in every sentence she speaks. She grins a lot too, hoping that the curve of her mouth will distract people from looking at her face as a whole.

To cover my discomfort, I started chattering on about how much I like Fort Wayne and how different this place is from my hometown of Lancaster, Pennsylvania. I've never actually been there, but I'd watched enough episodes of *Amish in the City* to fake it.

Then I made the mistake of saying something about being excited because I'd never been to a baseball game—or any other game, for that matter. I say "mistake" because suddenly the Whitmarshes were all about making this the

44

quintessential baseball experience. The minute we arrived at the stadium, Mrs. Whitmarsh insisted on buying me my own Wizards T-shirt and cap, and then she shooed me into the bathroom to change into my new ensemble.

Meet Claudia Miller, walking billboard.

But it's just a costume, right? At least, that's what I tried to tell myself. When I came out, Mr. Whitmarsh and Eli were in line buying snackage and Emily and her mom were deep in private conversation. I say "private" because their heads were bowed close together and I heard Mrs. Whitmarsh whisper something about Claudia—er, *me*—being even prettier than she'd expected. When Emily realized I was standing there, she looked horrified and elbowed her mother in the waist.

It was a weird moment, but I didn't dwell on it long. I mean, I was a baby model when I was just six months old, so people have always been commenting on my looks (or, in those awkward pre-teen years, my lack thereof). But later, after we'd gone to our seats and I polished off one of the best-tasting hot dogs I'd ever known, I told the twins about my homework disaster earlier in the day. Mr. Whitmarsh said, "If you're interested, Eli would be happy to tutor you, wouldn't you, Eli?" I was just about to take him up on the offer when I saw Eli turning redder than the hot dog he still held in his hand. He forced a laugh and said, "Come on, Dad. You know Emily's way better at geometry than I am. Chemistry too."

For a second I thought, *Does Eli Whitmarsh have a crush on me*? But then I figured if he was so eager to pass me off to Emily, he probably didn't have a crush on me after all.

It was weird, though, because the idea of someone

crushing on me felt completely foreign. For one thing, at Crapplewood they drill it into you that you shouldn't become romantically involved with anyone during the first year of recovery. You're not even supposed to make out with anyone, even if you don't think of the guy as boyfriend material.

But the other thing is that even though I've had several so-called boyfriends, they were mostly other actors I met on-set, and those relationships tended to implode the minute a shoot wrapped. When I was using, I was always hooking up with random losers—but that's something I try not to think about too often because let's face it: not my finest hour(s). My point is, it wasn't like anyone ever asked me to the prom or anything. So if Eli actually *did* have a crush on me, I wouldn't even know how to respond.

Good thing I don't have to worry about that.

Back to the game: the Wizards lost 11 to 3, but I was barely paying attention. Sometime during the third inning I asked Emily when we'd get to do "the wave," and she looked at me like I'd lost my mind. So I said, "Fine, I'll make a one-woman wave," and then proceeded to swoop up and down until I was dizzy and the twins were laughing themselves silly.

There were some pathetic fireworks after the seventh-inning stretch, and they were blasting all of this cheesy classic rock out of bad, tinny speakers to accompany it. Mr. Whitmarsh pulled his wife up into the aisle and they were doing some middle-aged dancing—you know, the kind where they hold hands and swing their hips and think they have rhythm.

I whispered to Emily, "Your parents are hot."

"Ew," she said, making a lemon-pucker face.

"No, really. They must do it, like, *all the time*."

I don't know why I started baiting her like that, but it was sort of fun, seeing unflappable Emily get flapped. I mean, Marissa and I used to mess with each other's heads all the time. It was *entertainment*.

I kept digging at Emily until she literally put her hands over her ears and yelled, "Shut up, Claudia!" Which made Mrs. W. give her a look and say, "That wasn't very nice of you, Em." She muttered an apology, but I could tell she was pissed.

And then I felt bad, because even though she and Eli can be sort of lame, having lame friends is better than having no friends at all. Not to mention the fact that I really did need a tutor. So when we were leaving the game, I told her I was sorry—told her I was being bitchy because I was PMS-ing hard-core. I also thanked her for inviting me and thanked Mr. and Mrs. Whitmarsh for buying me all the Wizard-pride gear, and Mr. W. tapped the bill of my cap and said, "Anytime, Claudia. Anytime."

Back at Trudy's, Emily walked me to the door. I asked her if she was still mad at me and she said, "Don't be silly! Everyone gets moody once in a while, right?" Then she hugged me. She actually hugged me! It was like a scene from *7th Heaven* or something. She also said that she'd call me tomorrow about setting up some tutoring sessions and that she'd had a really fun time and hoped we could hang out again sometime soon.

To quote the great Cher Horowitz: *As if!*

It is now 1 a.m. and I've been scribbling so long I've lost all circulation in my fingers. Tomorrow morning Trudy and

I are taking a yoga class at the Y and then we are having our big spa day. I AM SO FREAKING EXCITED! Midwestern air doesn't agree with my pores. Either that, or it's all the junk food I've been eating . . .

9/5

As I write this, there is a very large, very Slavic woman named Ludmilla rubbing heated essential oils into my lower back muscles. Can you say "heaven"?

Oops—gotta go. She wants to do my hands now.

9/5—Later

Trudy has left the building.

We were having a perfectly good day—facials! pedicures! eyebrow waxes!—and then afterward we went to Sakura, because I've been dying for some sushi. And then, in the middle of dipping part of her crunchy yellowtail into a dish of soy sauce, Trudy started crying. Like, *sobbing*. I asked her what was wrong, but she ran into the ladies' room and locked herself in the handicapped stall and refuses to come out.

What the hell just happened? Is she having a reaction to the wasabi? Posttraumatic stress from her divorce?

How am I supposed to write a three-page critical summary of *Siddhartha* when my de facto guardian is having a nervous breakdown in the john of Fort Wayne's swankiest Japanese restaurant?

9/6

Dear Marissa,

Me again. Having yet another night of insomnia, but writing these 3 a.m. letters seems to help me get to sleep quicker. Of course, a Xanax would be much more efficient, but as a recovering addict, I no longer have the luxury of taking prescription drugs. (NOTE TO SELF: Look into valerian root as potential sleep aid.)

I had sushi for dinner tonight, and it reminded me of that time we were in New York and ended up at Masa with Lindsay Lohan. (Oh God—just thinking about that white truffle tempura is making my mouth water. But anyway . . .) We kept pounding back the sake and got so wasted we ended up ordering a round of . . . what was it called? The blowfish, the one that can kill you if it's not made right? Fugu, I think. And then Lindsay wanted to go dancing, so we took a cab to the PM Lounge and you and I had a contest to see who could do the most shots of tequila without puking (I won). I'm pretty sure that was the night that you and I got up on the bar and traded bras while everyone watched. Too bad we didn't see the Page Six photographer snapping candids of our naughtiness. The press had a field day with those, remember?

Is it me, or were so many of our good times good because we were smashed? Or high? I know you weren't really into the drugs, and you were always trying to get me to lay off them, but Marissa—I remember us sneaking into the Dresden Rooms when we were *twelve*, stealing everyone's drink remnants and flirting with the older pervy boys just so they'd buy us pink champagne.

How did that *happen*?

Life is really different where I am now. Here, rush hour traffic means a five-minute delay in your commute. Here, the only music on the radio is country, christian, or classic rock. Here, pale blue nail polish is still very "in."

I don't really fit here, but I'm starting to think I wouldn't fit back home, either. I'm like . . . *displaced* or something.

I belong nowhere, with no one.

Depressingly yours,

Morgan

9/6—Later

I woke up this morning with Tori Amos's cover of "I Don't Like Mondays" running through my head. Totally felt like death on a stick until I remembered—

I don't have to go to gym class today.

boogie

Over breakfast—Special K, skim milk, and half an orange (part of our new health kick)—Trudy and I finally talked about her bathroom breakdown yesterday. She said the massage freaked her out because it was the first time in nearly a year that anyone's touched her naked skin. I've heard things about how deep tissue manipulation can unlock repressed emotions, but I'd never seen it in action before. Powerful stuff.

Anyway, then she told me she's decided to quit her divorced women's group because she leaves every meeting bitter and depressed and that's not what the group was supposed to be about. I said, "Does that mean I can quit my meeting too?" She looked horrified until I told her I was joking (mostly).

Geometry whizzed by; normally I'm taking frantic notes, but today I didn't bother, because Emily and I have our first tutoring session tomorrow night. Then it was off to Ms. Janet Moore's office. She was psyched to get the one-pound bag of M&M's I bought as a thank-you gift for rescuing me from Monday-morning gym class. And I would've been totally happy to sit there and shoot the shit with her for fifty minutes but—get this—she wanted to head-shrink me.

The school guidance counselor. Head-shrink *me*. I've had psychiatrists who charge more per hour than Ms. Janet Moore's yearly M&M budget, but she thinks it's perfectly okay to delve into my psyche and start poking around.

No goddamned *way*.

She goes, "You look angry, Claudia." When I didn't respond, she said, "It's okay. You're allowed to be angry, you know."

I started to laugh. "I hate to break it to you, but we're not exactly starring in the sequel to *Good Will Hunting* here, okay?"

Her face lit up. "You relate to movies, don't you?" she asked.

Insert deafening silence, during which my blood turned to ice water yet again.

Ms. Janet Moore poked around some papers on her desk. She held one up and said, "I see from your schedule that you're taking film class with Mr. Sappey. How's that going for you?"

Relief! I told her that film is my least-favorite class. When she asked why, I said, "Because he's a moron, that's why." She looked like she was blushing, which threw me off.

Until, that is, I spotted a small, heart-shaped picture frame in the middle of her desk.

Guess whose picture was glued inside?

"Are you actually dating that asshole?" I asked.

She flipped the frame photo-side down and said, "I'd rather not discuss that, Claudia."

"Yeah?" I said. "Well, I'd rather not discuss my anger. Or whether or not I relate to movies. Or anything of any kind of substance—at least not with *you*."

She cocked her head to one side like a puppy. "Why is that, Claudia?"

I wanted to say, "Well, for one thing, my name's not Claudia, and if you ever found out who I really am and what I'm doing here, you could make ten times your yearly salary by selling the information to the tabloids."

But what I really said was, "No reason."

Then we stared at each other for the rest of the period. So in the end it sort of was like a scene from *Good Will Hunting: The Chick Version*.

I spent the rest of the day in a supremely crabby mood, which culminated in Sappey giving us another writing assignment. This time I'm supposed to explain the difference between movies and films. The answer is, movies make money, films win awards. Or rather, movies *hope* to make money, and films *try* to win awards.

Now, how am I supposed to get 1,500 words out of *that*?

Trudy's calling me—we're celebrating her decision to quit her divorced women's group by taking an all-eighties spinning class at the Y.

9/6—Even later

Thighs still burning, ass still vibrating, pits still dripping sweat. Trudy called dibs on first shower or I'd be soaking my broken body right this second. Since I'm on dinner duty, I think I'll call for Chinese.

9/7

I had my first tutoring session today. After school Emily, Eli, and I went to the main branch of the Allen County Public Library. We were going to go to the Whitmarsh house, but at the last minute, Mrs. Whitmarsh's friend Sheila called and asked Eli if he'd mind working with an eighth grader struggling with English and reading comprehension. Since Sheila works at the library, and since she wanted to facilitate the introduction, we ended up there instead.

The minute we sat down, Emily was all business. That girl is *smart*. We started with geometry, since I'm struggling with that even more than chemistry. Em looked at my last two quizzes (the ones I failed) and then copied the problems I got wrong onto separate sheets of notepaper. Then we went over each individual one, her coaching me until I got the right answers. When she was satisfied with my progress, she pulled similar questions from the practice tests in the back of my book and had me do them too.

Surprisingly, I got six out of ten correct on the first try.

"Impressive," I said.

"Yeah," she agreed. "You're doing much better."

"No—I mean *you*."

She shrugged. "All I did was show you how to work the problems."

I told her that she was being too modest. She shook her head and asked me to take out my chemistry text and show her where I was having trouble.

Two hours later, we were finished, and I felt 33 percent less dumb.

Emily said she was hungry and asked if I wanted to grab a bite before going home, so I took my cell outside to call Trudy and let her know. On the way back in I passed the kids' reading room. Sitting at a tiny plastic table, his knees up to his chin, was Eli. Aurora, the eight-year-old he was tutoring, was sitting next to him, a huge smile plastered to her face. It was the kind of smile that said, "I've got an enormous crush on you." *So* cute. Eli must've been explaining something to her because his hands were flying everywhere and his eyes were so wide, he could've been an anime character. Aurora started to giggle; not long after, Eli joined her. He has a nice laugh.

I was so intent on watching the two of them that I didn't hear Emily sneak up behind me.

"You think someone might have a crush?" she asked, smiling.

Assuming she meant Aurora, I said, "Maybe."

Then Emily got a big goofy grin on *her* face and said, "Really?" It was the wrong kind of look, and it confused me. But then I remembered the other night, at the game, and what Mrs. Whitmarsh had said.

Was Em asking if I thought Eli had a crush on me? Or was she asking me if I had a crush on Eli?

Neither option was appealing.

I wanted to clarify my position to Emily, so I said, "I think Aurora's the one with that crush." But I said it so fast, I'm not sure she heard me. Sheila the librarian heard me say something, though, if the deep frown and the pointer finger to her mouth shushing me were any indication.

Eli wrapped up with Aurora, who gave him a hug before wandering off starry-eyed. Then we all loaded into the twins' car—a late-nineties Toyota Camry; how very *practical*—and drove to Munchies, this cute little restaurant over on Dupont. I had started to look at the menu when Eli said, "No need—we always get the same thing."

"Maybe Claudia wants something different," Emily said.

I said I'd have what they were having plus a diet soda. The twins burst out laughing at the same time.

"What?" I asked. "What's so funny?"

Eli said, "You can't order a soda. Not unless you want a *club* soda."

"I don't get it," I said.

"Around here it's called 'pop,'" Emily explained. "You want a diet pop."

"I want," I said tightly, "a Diet Coke. Please."

The twins exchanged a worried glance, which made me feel like even more of an idiot. Why did I have to get so pissed off about it? Pop, soda, Coke—it's all the same damned thing. And by responding so hotly, I'd now given the twins reason to think that Claudia is a stuck-up priss who can't stand to be corrected.

Just like her alter ego, Morgan.

I hate it when I screw up.

Anyway, Eli asked for a double order of something called Scooby Snacks with extra Munchie dip. I was afraid, until our sort-of-hot waiter delivered two heaping baskets of potato wedges seasoned with Old Bay and three saucers filled with the most exquisite mixture of sour cream and cucumbers.

Needless to say, I dug right in.

Eli was staring at me again, and it was beginning to get annoying. I said, "What, do I have dip on my face?"

He shook his head and said, "No. It's just—"

"What?"

"Besides Em, you're the only girl I've ever seen eat Scooby Snacks like . . . well, like a *guy*."

The potato wedge I was holding up to my mouth dropped to the mini-plate in front of me. How many times could I feel deeply embarrassed in a twenty-minute span? I must've made a face, because Emily cut in. "He didn't mean it as an insult. Eli has this pet peeve about girls who starve themselves. Tell her, Eli."

He shrugged. "I just think it's stupid. That girl I was tutoring—Aurora? She's only eight and she's already on a diet. Did you see how skinny she was? The girls at school are like that too. At lunch they eat a Baggie of baby carrots and half an apple and talk about how stuffed they are, but then they sit there eyeing your chili like rabid dogs. Totally annoying."

I laughed, but truth be told—I used to *be* one of those girls. The standard industry lunch for a hot young thing in Hollywood consists of a chicken Caesar (hold the croutons, light dressing on the side) and either a Diet Coke or water with a lemon wedge. And it's considered really decadent to leave less than half the serving on your plate. Before rehab, the only person I ever felt comfortable eating around was Marissa, and even then we did our "real" eating in private.

When the press started talking about my weight—at fourteen, I committed the unpardonable sin of putting on ten extra pounds—my manager's secretary suggested I try bulimia on for size (so to speak). I told Sam, and he fired her the next day, but the seeds had already been planted. But yakking up meals daily wasn't nearly as efficient as large amounts of speed and coke were. The drugs took those extra pounds right off. They also took most of the lining in my nose, but hey—at least I was thin, right?

Right.

It occurs to me as I write this that sometime in the next year I'm going to have to shift firmly back into the never-ending-diet mentality. (Albeit this time, I'll have to do it the right way—without any of my "special supplements.") The thing is, it's fine for me to be wearing size seven jeans in Fort Nowhere, but back home, in my real life? They'd be packing me off to a fat farm by now.

Back to Munchies: Emily started yelling at Eli for making me feel self-conscious, but I told her I was fine. To prove my point, I crammed two Scooby Snacks into my mouth at the same time (yes, I really did that. Oh God, I'm never going to work in Hollywood again). Then Eli grabbed four and shoved them into his mouth. Emily, not wanting to be left out, took a whole handful. The next thing I knew, we were laughing so hard we were sneezing potato.

Eli held the door for me when we left Munchies, and he opened my car door first too. It's polite, and Eli is a very polite kind of guy, so I still can't figure out whether he does or doesn't have a crush on me.

I have to ask myself: whichever it is, do I even care?

9/8

Who's going to an *actual pajama party* Saturday night?

You guessed it—*yours truly*.

The soiree is being held at Debbie Ackerman's house. Debbie is a very old friend of the Whitmarsh twins—their moms took prenatal classes together—and she's one of those rabbit-food eaters that Eli was complaining about yesterday. Even so, she's like thirty pounds overweight (not that I have any room to talk). She'd be cute if she got some contact lenses—maybe blue ones—and stopped trying to blow out her naturally curly hair. Mostly she looks like she's wearing a frizz-mop wig on top of her Moon Pie–shaped face.

Something else about Debbie: she's totally in love with Eli. She looks at him with these adoring eyes and turns red every time he says her name. I'd like to see them hook up, because I think they'd be really cute together. A slightly nerdy version of an "it" couple.

Anyway, we're all sitting around the lunch table—"all" being me, the twins, Debbie, Bethany, Joey, and Kevin—and Debbie starts talking about this party she's having at her house. And Joey and Kevin are like, "Hey, how come we're not invited?" and Debbie goes, "Duh—no boys allowed." So then I'm thinking, *Hey, how come I'm not invited?* Not that I really wanted to go or anything. I mean, I can easily think of two dozen better ways to spend my Saturday night. (Unfortunately, most of them aren't exactly sanctioned by the twelve steps.)

But then Emily says, "You should come, Claudia. We do this every couple of months and it's always a lot of fun."

Now, I can't imagine what Emily's idea of "fun" is, but I'm guessing it's fairly different from mine. I was going to politely decline, but then I saw Debbie's eyes flash in Em's direction. Like she was pissed that Emily would invite me to her stupid party. Enter Morgan, who, unlike Claudia, cannot stand the thought of some chubby loser girl thinking she's better than her. Better than *me*. So with Morgan-me firmly in the driver's seat, I decided to play ball. "Wow—I can't wait! Should I bring anything, Debbie?" I offered up a saccharine-sweet smile and savored the way Debbie squirmed when she said, "Just you is more than enough."

That pretty much killed conversation for the rest of the lunch period.

How is it possible that by Fort Wayne standards, *I* am a social pariah? Look at the company I'm keeping! It's not like they're the crème de la crème of Snider High society.

I used to party with princesses—actual *princesses*—and now I'm reduced to accepting a pity invite to Debbie Ackerman's pajamarama?

God, I am sad.

Sappey's film-versus-movie essay is due Friday, and I haven't even started it. I know what I *should* write (the LaTanya-style regurgitated class lecture). But what I want to write (an in-depth look at the films of Steven Soderbergh) is pretty much guaranteed to get me another D—or worse. Hello, paralysis!

The thing is, Sappey's *wrong*. Blockbusters aren't always bad movies, and art-house fare isn't always of good quality. You'd think a guy who teaches a film class would know that, right?

The worst part is, I don't even know why I care. I mean, Sappey can give me straight Fs, but when it comes right down to it, which one of us has worked with Steven Spielberg, Ang Lee, *and* both of the Coppolas? I have the kind of education you can't get from a textbook or watching too many episodes of *Ebert & Roeper*. What's Sappey got? Failed dreams of being a world-class filmmaker is my guess.

In unrelated news, it's now been over a week since I last spoke with my mother. Not like we're best friends or any-thing, but Jesus—you'd think she'd *want* to know how I was doing, marooned in the Midwest. What's worse is that I can't get ahold of Sam, either. I've left him half a dozen mes-sages and *nothing*. No response whatsoever. It's very unlike Sam, and that makes me nervous. Maybe he's angrier with me than I thought? I wonder if it was that letter I sent him right after I got here. All that talk about him giving me one more chance—maybe he's just decided that when it comes to me, the costs far outweigh the benefits.

Sometimes I wonder if they sent me here just so they wouldn't have to deal with me there.

Or maybe I'm just being a drama queen.

9/8—*Later*

Emily just called to "say hi," and since I didn't really feel like talking, I told her I was in the middle of working on my film paper. I said it in this really bitchy way, too, but either Emily didn't register the tone or she pretended not to. She started to talk about Debbie's party and how she and her friends began hosting these girls'-night-in get-togethers last year, and at first it was just her and Deb and Bethany, but now there are about a dozen girls who routinely show.

The whole time she's talking, all I can think is, *Why are you being so nice to me? What do you want? What do you need? What do you* know? In my experience, it's always one of the above. Everyone's got some ulterior motive, even if it takes you a while to figure out what it is.

I must've zoned out because the next thing I know, Emily's saying, "Hello? Claudia, are you still there?" I said yeah and she sighed, sort of softly, but I heard it anyway.

"What's wrong?" I asked.

"Nothing," she said. "It's just—"

"Just what?"

"Sometimes I get the feeling that you don't really want to be my friend."

She said it exactly like that, too. So blunt that it completely knocked me off guard.

"That's not true," I said, after a longish pause that most likely indicated the opposite. "Look, I have a hard time being close to people. It's just not my style." Which isn't a lie, if you think about it, because outside of Bianca, Sam, Marissa, and now Trudy, I don't let anyone get to know the real me.

"I had a feeling," Emily said. "Is it because of your old friends? The ones your mom wanted you to get away from?"

"Sort of." Again, not a *total* lie.

"Well," she said, "I just wanted you to know that I'm here, you know, if you need to talk or something. About anything. I can be a really good listener."

And okay—maybe I was being paranoid, but the way she said that last part? All I could think was that I am Emily Whitmarsh's new charity project. Me! Morgan freaking Carter! It all adds up, though: the fake invite to Debbie Ackerman's, the tutoring sessions, the ticket to the corny baseball game. Like part of some covert operation, "Pity the New Girl" or some crap like that.

Needless to say, I don't like the idea of being anyone's charity case. Especially not when the "benefactor" is so clueless she hasn't figured out that tapered-leg jeans haven't been in style since the late eighties and that they make her hips look twice as wide as they actually are.

Whatever. I'm going to bed.

9/9

I wanted today to be Friday, but instead, it's Thursday.

Off to another fun-filled NA meeting!

9/9—*Later*

Dear God,

It's me, Morgan.

You know that pretty blond-haired woman who was staring at me from down the hall as I exited my Thursday night meeting? Please don't let her be Mrs. Whitmarsh.

That would be really, really bad.

Love,
Me

9/10

It's the end of my third week of high school, and I am beyond ready to drop out. How does anyone survive this hell for four whole years?

Here are some highlights from my day:

• I overslept the alarm because I was up until 4 a.m. working on my paper for Sappey's class.

• My extraordinary lateness meant sacrificing my morning shower, so when I got to school, I looked tired *and* greasy—not a great combination, even for my ultra-bland alter ego Claudia Miller.

• Despite Tuesday's tutoring session with Emily, I proceeded to fail yet another geometry quiz. What is wrong with me? Did the drugs kill that many brain cells?

• In gym class some Amazon bitch spiked the volleyball square between my eyes, thereby smashing the cheap frames of my fake glasses. Only no one knows they're fake glasses or that my laser-corrected vision needs no assistance, so I had to spend the rest of the day squinting and pretending to be half blind. The result? A dull, nagging headache.

• All through lunch Debbie Ackerman gave me a furtive death stare, but due to my faux blindness I wasn't supposed to notice and therefore couldn't call her out on it. Can't wait for that party!

• Last, Sappey's lecture today was about—who else?—Steven Soderbergh. Fifty minutes of Sappey ranting about *Erin Brockovich* and *Ocean's Eleven* (and *Twelve*) and how talented indie filmmakers sell out to The Man just so they can buy extra-large hot tubs for their Hollywood Hills homes. Of course this would come on top of me screaming Soderbergh's praises in my stupid paper. Hello, F!

If this were a movie, and not my actual life, we'd rapidly be approaching the scene where the hot senior guy rolls up in his sleek silver convertible and says, "Hop in." And we'd drive off to the lake, where we'd sit on a soft patch of green grass and he'd confess that he'd been interested in me for a while. "Who *are* you?" he'd say, a glimmer in his eye. I'd shoot back, "Wouldn't you like to know?" only seconds before he'd lean in for a music-swells-up kind of kiss.

Instead, I got on a school bus that reeked of someone's forgotten lunch—tuna fish, no less—and came home to a dark, lonely house where I proceeded to eat an entire bag of mint Milanos.

Trudy should be home from work in an hour, and then we're going to check out the Irish step-dancing class at the Y. Too bad we can't cap it off with a thick pint of Guinness. I'm not even joking when I say I could *really* use a drink.

9/10—*Later*

Change in plans. Trudy walked in and found me in the fetal position on the couch, crying. When I told her the part about wanting the Guinness, she said, "I think you should go to a meeting." So that's where I am now, waiting for the festivities to begin.

Right before she dropped me off, Trudy asked me if I had a sponsor—you know, the person you're supposed to call whenever you need support so that you don't fall off the wagon and morph back into the obnoxious alcoholic-slash-addict you once were. I told her I hadn't been in L.A. long enough to get one and it hadn't even occurred to me to find one here. She (gently) suggested I ask tonight's leader for some suggestions.

So the writing's on the wall. Trudy's getting sick of my shit too, and when that happens, where will I go? When you're young and beautiful and making $3 million a picture, everybody loves you. But when you're a sixteen-year-old unemployable has-been, they pass you off like you're poison.

Ugh! I have *got* to stop feeling so goddamned sorry for myself.

9/10—*Much later*

The meeting helped. Gaby, my Thursday night group leader, was there. I asked her about finding a sponsor, and she offered to be mine herself. Which is cool because I kind of like Gaby, even if she does wear the same ugly pair of shit-kicker boots to every single meeting.

Trudy's dishing up slices of bacon-and-scallop pizza from Bertucci's. I know I shouldn't be eating things like pizza (especially not with bacon as a topping), but I'm too worn out to care. Besides, Tru found out the Aquatonics water aerobics class meets Saturday mornings at 9 a.m., so I can work off the extra calories then. I'd better start doing that, too, or I'll look so hideous in my bathing suit that I won't even want to go to Aquatonics in the first place.

A tragic catch-22.

9/11

What the hell are you supposed to pack for a slumber party? Besides pajamas and a toothbrush, I mean. Do I bring a sleeping bag? A pillow? A tube of cookie dough?

(NOTE TO SELF: Pick up replacement pair of non-prescription glasses so night won't be spent fake squinting and helping premature wrinkles to form.)

Part of me wants to call Emily and tell her I'm sick—anything to get out of this party. But doing that would mean making Emily feel more insecure about our "friendship" and I've realized I can't risk losing my safety net. Also, I don't want to give Debbie Ackerman the satisfaction that my absence would bring.

Okay—maybe I'm a little curious, too. I've never actually been to one of these things. It seems like just another rite of passage I missed out on by being a child star.

I wonder if Haley Joel Osment ever stops to think, "Gee, what would it have been like to play on a Little League team?" Probably not—I've only met him once, but he seems like a really old man trapped inside a teenager's body.

Must go finish packing!

9/11—*Later*

I just realized that it's September 11.

Maybe I'm being melodramatic, but there's a part of me that feels really wrong about "honoring" the anniversary of the attacks by going to a slumber party.

9/11—*Much later*

This evening has been completely surreal.

When Emily and I arrived at Debbie Ackerman's house, she and ten of her closest friends were already seated around an enormous dining room table, waiting for Mrs. Ackerman to dish up her traditional spaghetti dinner. There weren't two open seats next to each other, so Em went to sit between Debbie and Kelly Capo, whereas I got sandwiched between Bethany and Lauren Johnson. For some reason I had a minor-league panic attack—like I'd had my safety blanket (Emily) snatched away from me.

Being separated from her, though, gave me plenty of time to observe my fellow partygoers—truly a cross-sectional representation of what Snider High society has to offer. At the risk of sounding like a broken record, it's not like it is in the movies. There aren't well-defined cliques, and there isn't any one queen bee that every girl aspires to be like (or that the boys aspire to be liked by). Like at this party: Kelly Capo is the goalie on the girls' soccer team, and I guess by some standards she's a jockette, but she's also student council secretary. Bethany, my Jesus-loving lunch buddy, not only heads up a church youth group but doubles as captain of the dance squad—which can't be confused with the cheerleading squad, of which Delia Lambert is a member. Delia also does math league, as does our welcoming hostess, Debbie Ackerman, but Debbie's main extracurricular activity is serving as managing editor of the yearbook, where she can keep close tabs on her star photographer, Eli Whitmarsh.

My point: it's a diverse group. Except for the fact that we're all white and upper middle class (besides me, that is). Race is the one truly dividing line at Snider. There aren't a lot of black kids who go there, and those who do tend to stick together. Like LaTanya—I'd like to get to know her better, but even though we share the same lunch period, she barely acknowledges my existence when we're in the caf. The postmodern segregation is just . . . accepted. No one questions it or tries to change the way things are—not really.

Actually, when I stop to think about it, it's not unlike the industry I grew up in.

Back to the party. After scarfing the last meatball, Delia announced that she'd brought a bunch of "classic" DVDs. Everybody was like, "Ooh, ooh—what did you bring?" She pulled them from her *Go Panthers!* duffel and spread them out across the carpet. There, among select volumes from the *Dawson's Creek* collection, *Bring It On*, and *Legally Blonde*, was *Girls on Top*. With *my* thirteen-year-old face taking up 33 percent of the cover. (Yes, exactly thirty-three percent. It was in my contract.)

Girls on Top—despite its unfortunate name—was originally conceived as a teenage homage to feminism. The story in original form followed three strong, smart young girls in different stages of sexual development. The one thing they all have in common is that in terms of sex, they are the ones calling the shots—not the boys. During the course of the film my character, Natalie, discovers the joys of self-love, and there was one particularly funny scene—written in an early draft of the script—in which Natalie conducts an impromptu masturbation "class" for her two best friends.

The screenplay was written by a twenty-year-old NYU dropout by the name of Holly Swenson. She sold her script to Ova, a production company that focused on female-friendly indie films. She was slated to direct and in fact was the one to green-light the cast (myself included). Then, only days before shooting was set to begin, Ova went under, and Miramax swooped in to pick up the pieces. The studio loved everything about the project—except Holly. The next thing we knew, she was gone and a thirty-something former pop-video director who went by the name of Datsun was at the helm.

Datsun's vision of the movie was way different from Holly's. The masturbation scene, for example, ended up being this weird, pseudo-lesbian romp involving coconut suntan lotion and a bunch of bananas. Oh God—it's embarrassing just thinking about it. At any rate, he chucked the girl-power right out the window and camped it up so much our parts could've been played by boys in drag.

I didn't want to do it—the movie, I mean—but Bianca thought that Datsun was charming and that I was crazy to want to quit what was sure to be another Oscar contender (ha!). Translation: she wanted the money. I thought Sam could help me out, but despite his doubts, he was way more concerned about my image. How bad it would look for me to pull out at such a late date. "Committing studio suicide," he'd said. "Unless, that is, the movie tanks—and then they'll call you brilliant instead of just a pain in the ass."

Anyway, that's the story of how I ended up co-starring in one of the most offensive teen films ever made.

Here's the kicker: despite the fact that *Girls on Top* was universally panned by the critics (*tanking* is too kind a term), a small-but-loyal audience fell head over heels in love with the film. It was a cult phenomenon, like *Donnie Darko*. Within a year, there were thousands upon thousands of Web pages devoted to the film (and everyone in it—me included). If I actually *had* died that night outside the Viper Room, *this* would probably have been the movie I'd be most remembered for, as pathetic as that seems.

I'd only seen the movie once—at the premiere—and I vowed never to watch it again. The idea was particularly unappealing when you factored in a room full of Midwestern high school girls I didn't know. Not to mention that watching it could totally blow my cover—and I couldn't let that happen.

So here's me: "Ohmigod, like, I haven't seen *Bring It On* in forever!"

Here's them: "Let's watch *Girls on Top*!"

ME: "But *Bring It On* is so much better!"

THEM: *"Girls on Top! Girls on Top!"*

ME (turning to Delia, desperate): "You're a cheerleader. Wouldn't you rather watch a movie about cheerleaders?"

DELIA: "Not especially."

I pouted, folding myself into an oversized easy chair in the corner while the rest of the girls gathered around the Ackermans' TV and cackled cattily at the sheer magnitude of the movie's cheesiness.

Wait—it gets better.

Twenty minutes into the film, Kelly Capo pointed to "Natalie" on the screen—i.e., *me*—and goes, "Isn't that the girl that OD'd last year? Megan Carter?"

"Morgan Carter," Delia corrected. "And yeah, that's her."

"I hate her!" shrieked Lauren Johnson, who up until this point had said maybe two words all evening. "She used to go out with Harlan Darly—you know, after they made *Perfectly Imperfect*? But then she cheated on him with that dude from Hanson—the little one—and she totally broke his heart!"

Oh. My. God. Besides the fact that I have never met a single Hanson brother (let alone hooked up with any of them), hearing Harlan Darly's name made me want to puke. It's a long story—one I've never told anyone, not even Marissa—but suffice it to say that he is evil. Pure evil. And he was never—NEVER—my boyfriend. Not ever.

While I was still reeling from Lauren's verbal explosion,

Bethany—sweet, churchgoing Bethany!—chimed in. "That girl is such a slut. I mean, who gets implants at thirteen?"

To which Lauren replied, "She's mental! You'd have to be mental to cheat on Harlan Darly!"

"But that guy is such a flaming asshole!" I cried, causing eleven heads to swivel in my direction. Then in a more controlled tone I said, "At least, that's what I've heard."

"That's a lie," Lauren said coldly. "He raises money for kids with cancer. And he has *four* dogs."

Then Emily jumped in and said, "Come on, guys—are we watching the movie or what?"

Debbie hit the rewind button and everyone fell silent for maybe six minutes before the insults started up again.

LAUREN: "She can't even act. *I'm* a better actress than she is."

KELLY: "I heard she signed a contract with *Playboy* promising to pose nude the day she turns eighteen."

BETHANY: "Look at her boobs. You can't tell me those are real. Am I right? Am I?"

Finally, my new best friend Delia Lambert shouts, "Shut up, you guys! Morgan Carter is like really, really talented. So lay off!"

"If she's so great," Lauren sneered, "then how'd she end up hooked on heroin? She used to prostitute herself for the drugs, you know."

This was all news to me. Not just because I'd always avoided H like the plague, but also because I'd only had sex with one person, *once*, and it wasn't an experience I wanted to repeat anytime soon.

It was almost more than I could stand, hearing them argue about exactly how horrible a person I was and why. All based on unfounded gossip, no less.

I stared at all of them, my mouth hanging open. This, of course, was when Debbie Ackerman said, "Claudia kind of looks like her, don't you think?"

Delia, my *ex*-new best friend, rolled her eyes. "I don't think so. Morgan's a blonde."

"So?" Debbie shrugged.

"*So?* Are we even looking at the same person?" Delia said. "Morgan's got a completely different face. Not to mention twice the bra size. She's also, like, way skinnier—no offense, Claudia."

Through gritted teeth I said, "None taken."

"Enough!" Emily shrilled. "I can't listen to any more of this! None of you know anything about Morgan Carter."

This elicited several rounds of, "Chill out, Em," and, "Yeah, what's your deal? We're just *talking*." Thankfully, during the melee, Delia popped out her DVD, put it back in its case, and deposited it in her duffel. When everyone started to protest, she said, "It's *my* movie, and I don't like watching it with you guys. Let's do something else."

For about thirty seconds, I thought the universe was giving me a break. Instead, Debbie goes, "Let's play truth or dare!"

I wished I were daring enough to walk the hell home. But I didn't.

Sadly, the rest of that story will have to wait until tomorrow, as it is now 3 a.m. and I'm beyond exhausted.

9/12

Well, I survived the slumber party of doom.

But just barely.

I knew from the start that truth or dare was a colossally bad idea. What I didn't know was that the only reason Debbie wanted to do it was so that she and her friends could play "grill the new girl."

It started off pretty tame—like with Lauren asking Kelly how far she and her boyfriend, Ben, had gone (third base, but only once) and Kelly daring Bethany to go onto the Ackermans' front lawn and flash the neighborhood (she did). Then Bethany asked Debbie if she had a crush on Joey Harkus (are you kidding me?), and this is when all hell broke loose.

DEBBIE (to me): Is it true you got kicked out of your old school for doing your boyfriend in the cafeteria?

EMILY: Debbie!

ME: Uh, no. Who told you that?

DEBBIE (ignoring me): So why *did* you get kicked out?

ME: I thought you could only ask one question per turn.

Emily mouthed an apology to me, like it was her fault that Debbie had such bad manners. What, had they been talking about me behind my back? Speculating how a bad girl like Claudia could end up in a nice school like theirs?

I was *pissed*.

ME (to Emily): Is it true you're only friends with Debbie because your mom forces you to be nice to her?

DEBBIE: What? Emily—did you actually say that?

EMILY: No! Of course not! Claudia, why would you even ask me that?

ME (giving Debbie an evil grin): No reason.

The game proceeded in a less bitchy fashion for a while until Lauren kicked it back to Debbie, asking which of her body parts she hated most (thighs). Debbie wasted no time whipping around and practically growling at me, "Truth or dare?" This time I chose dare.

DEBBIE: I dare you to tell everyone who you have a crush on at school.
ME (smugly): I don't have a crush on anyone at school.
DEBBIE (menacingly): Really? *No* one?
ME: I said no, didn't I?
DEBBIE (under her breath): Liar.

My instinct was to pounce on Bethany and ask her something like, "Which girl in this room has the fattest ass?" knowing very well that it was Deb. But I'm coming in a close second these days, so I didn't want to risk it. Instead, I dared Kelly to eat a chocolate cupcake off the coffee table with her hands behind her back (lame).

As soon as she'd licked the last splotch of frosting off the corner of her mouth, Kelly turned back to me and went, "Truth or dare?"

"But I just went!" I said.

She repeated, "Truth. Or. Dare."

I chose truth.

KELLY: Isn't it true that you have a massive crush on Eli Whitmarsh?
ME: Didn't we already cover this? I don't have a crush on anyone.
KELLY: Seriously?
ME: Yes, seriously.
DEBBIE (jumping up): She's so totally lying! Emily told me herself!
ME (to Emily): What? Why would you say that?

EMILY: I thought you said you liked him. At the library that day.

ME: I was talking about the eight-year-old he was tutoring!

DEBBIE: You have a crush on an eight-year-old?

ME: No! I said I thought the eight-year-old *girl* had a crush on Eli!

EMILY: Oh.

DEBBIE: Oh.

ME: *Yeah.* So thanks a lot for spreading rumors about me.

I'm not sure what possessed me to say this next thing, but I kind of blurted out, "Besides, I already have a boyfriend."

Eleven girls, practically in unison, asked, "You do?" And then:

DEBBIE: Does he go to Snider?

LAUREN: Is he from your old school?

BETHANY: Is he the guy you had sex with in the cafeteria?

I replied, "No," "Sort of," and, "You live in a Lifetime TV movie, don't you, Bethany? No, I've never had sex in a cafeteria and no, he's not why I left."

"So what's his name?" Emily asked, in a quiet voice. I said the first thing that came to mind:

"Evan Walsh."

Why? Why did I say that? Why couldn't I have said Jim Smith? Or Dan Jones?

No, I had to name the hot actor boy my best friend is supposedly seeing, even though he's a closet homosexual.

Lauren shrieked, "Evan Walsh! Like the actor?"

"No!" I said. "I mean, yeah. They have the same name. But, uh, they're not the same person or anything."

"I didn't think so," Lauren said. "I mean, you? Dating Evan Walsh the actor? That's funny."

If only she knew *how* funny . . .

The pretense of the game was dropped; everyone starting shooting questions at me, rapid-fire. Where was I from? Why did I move to Fort Wayne? Did I miss my boyfriend? Did we have sex, and if so, what's it like? (That one was Bethany's. I swear, that girl is sex-obsessed!

Just when I thought I couldn't take any more, Debbie Ackerman herself came to my rescue. "All right, all right. Let's leave Claudia alone now. This is supposed to be fun, not the Spanish Inquisition!"

She smiled at me, a nice, friendly smile.

What's up with that? I wondered. A second ago she was giving me the third degree and accusing me of lying; now we were suddenly best buds?

Then a lightbulb popped up over my head. The only reason Debbie Ackerman had "hated" me was because she thought I was after Eli Whitmarsh! Now that I had a "boyfriend," I was no longer a threat to her.

I went into the kitchen with Deb to help her put together a tray of desserts. As she removed a pan of brownies warming in the oven, I said, "So why haven't you asked Eli Whitmarsh on a date?"

Debbie flushed a hot red. "Who says I like Eli? We're just friends."

"Come on," I said. "I see how you look at him over lunch. You're totally sweating him."

"Even if I did like Eli—and I'm not saying I do, but if I did—it wouldn't matter. He's not into dating. He's too busy photographing the world."

"That's true," I conceded. "But it doesn't have to *stay* true."

"Meaning?"

"Meaning we just have to get Eli to stop looking at you like a yearbook editor and start looking at you like a girl."

She blushed again. "How do you propose we do that?"

"We'll go shopping, of course." I grinned. "A hot outfit, a little makeup, some cute earrings. You'd be surprised how those tiny changes can make a huge impact."

Debbie's smile faded. "Why are you being nice to me? Until now I've been a total bitch to you."

I shrugged. "You thought I was after your dude. I would've been bitchy too."

She surprised the hell out of me by throwing her arms around my neck and giving me a tight hug. "Thanks, Claudia," she said. "You're a lot cooler than I gave you credit for."

That's when the music should've swelled, signifying a turning point in my character's story arc—the point where she becomes accepted and beloved and lives happily ever after.

Instead, the second Debbie and I took the tray out to the girls, Emily said, "Claudia, can I talk to you for a minute?" and dragged me back into the kitchen.

"What's your problem?" Emily demanded, crossing her arms over her chest like a disapproving parent.

"What do you mean?" I asked.

"Well, for one thing, you tried to tell Debbie that I hang out with her against my will," she replied, raising her voice slightly.

"I was just playing the game," I fired back. "You heard what they were asking me. Why are all your 'friends' gossiping about me to begin with?"

"Claudia," Emily said sighing, "Debbie just has a crush on my brother. That's all."

"Yes, and why exactly does Debbie think that has anything to do with me?"

Emily paused, looking at me hard. "My brother is kind of into you," she said. "Like, he talks about you *all* the time. And I *thought* you liked him too. Maybe I shouldn't have, but . . . I sort of told him to go for it."

"What?" I exploded. "Why would you do that?"

"You don't understand. Eli used to have this girlfriend, Sarah. He was completely devoted to her. And then her family up and moved to Texas with, like, two weeks' warning. He was completely crushed."

"That's really heart-wrenching, but—"

"Let me finish," Emily insisted. "They tried to stay together long distance. He e-mailed her every day, sent letters once a week—he even he racked up this huge long-distance bill. But Texas was just too far away, and after a couple of months, it was clear that Sarah had moved on. Eli was so depressed over the whole thing I thought he'd never even *look* at another girl again. But then you show up and wham! He's gone. Totally head over heels."

"But he doesn't even *know* me."

"He says you're 'spunky.'"

" 'Spunky'? What the hell does that mean?"

She shrugged. "I can't explain *why* he likes you. I just know he *does*."

Even though I'd had my suspicions, having Emily confirm them really freaked me out. No wonder Eli had been trying to "candidly" take so many pictures of me. My armpits were sore from the number of times I'd reflexively thrown up my hands to shield my face from his prying lens.

"You really shouldn't have told Eli anything without talking to me first," I said.

Emily sighed. "You're right. And I'm sorry. But this wouldn't have happened if you hadn't been so . . . *private*. I mean, we've been hanging out for almost a month now and you never once mentioned any boyfriend."

"I told you, I have trouble getting close to people," I snapped.

"Well, since Sarah, so does Eli."

As if I needed the guilt.

Thankfully, Emily dropped the issue then, but if I know Emily—and actually, I'm starting to think I do—it won't be dropped for long.

The rest of the party passed uneventfully, save for Debbie Ackerman grinning at me every five seconds. Poor girl. She's about to get her heart broken too. Unless . . . maybe I really *could* get Deb and Eli together. Maybe all he needs is to see Debbie looking like a hotter, more confident version of herself.

A little voice in my head says, *Right. And maybe the real Evan Walsh will show up to take you to the homecoming dance.*

My God. How did this *happen*?

When I got home this afternoon, Trudy asked me how the party was. I thought about telling her the truth, but she already worries about me so much that I ended up saying, "It was fine," and retreating to my room.

After a "catnap" that lasted well over two hours, I picked up the phone and dialed Emily's cell. She answered on the second ring.

"Truth or dare?" I asked.

"What's up, Claudia?"

"Truth or dare?" I repeated.

"I don't get it."

"Come on, Emily—truth or dare?"

"Truth, I guess," she replied wearily.

ME: Why is it that you're so obsessed with your brother's love life?

EMILY: I'm not "obsessed."

ME: Okay, then. Overly concerned.

EMILY: I'm not—

ME: You know what I mean, Em.

EMILY (sighing): Eli's not just my brother, he's my best friend. But he's . . . I don't know. *Different.* I mean, don't get me wrong—he can fake it. The being social thing? But school Eli is completely different from home Eli. And there's something about you that makes him act more like home Eli. Honestly, Claud, he spends most of his time hiding behind that camera.

ME: Sort of how you hide behind all of your causes?

EMILY (bristling): What's that supposed to mean?

ME: You know exactly what I mean. Jesus, Em, you're like some kind of RoboTeen. Doesn't it ever get old? Don't you ever want to cut loose?

EMILY: That's so typical. Contrary to popular belief, my not drinking or smoking or sleeping around doesn't mean I'm some Miss Perfect. It just means that I'm part of a politician's family. And that my mom and dad both have pretty strong ideas about how I'm supposed to behave.

ME: I'm not talking about getting wasted or slutting it up. Trust me, I don't that do that shit either. Anymore. I'm talking about Emily the Untouchable. The straight-A student who never talks about boys or bands or trash TV. The girl who's more concerned about raising funds for the children's hospital than blowing her allowance on a frivolous pair of shoes she'll wear once a month maybe. You're always complaining about how I don't tell you stuff, but it's not like I know your deep dark secrets either. Hell, I don't even know what you want to be when you grow up!

EMILY: You think *I* know that? And for your information, I'm secretly hooking up with

Joey Harkus, I own every single CD the Barenaked Ladies have ever released, and I am addicted to *The Bachelor*. So there!

ME: Whoa. You hook up with *Joey*?

EMILY: At least once a week. Twice if his asthma's under control.

ME: I never would've known.

EMILY: That's right. You wouldn't have. Because I don't parade around, spilling my personal, private business to anyone in earshot. God, Claudia—you *know* the girls I hang out with. You know what they're like. Did you even listen to them bash that movie actress last night? They're ten times worse with people they actually know.

ME (slowly): So what you're saying is, you have a hard time letting people in too.

EMILY:

ME: Em? You still there?

EMILY: I've got to go. See you on Monday.

Ever since she hung up, I've just been sitting here, thinking about how ironic it is that Emily and I would turn out to have so much in common. There's way more to that girl than even I'd guessed. And I'm not just talking about that Joey Harkus thing (though I seriously need to find out more about that). It's this whole deal of having a public face versus a private one. Granted, the Whitmarsh twins didn't grow up in the tabloids, but it sounds like they work as hard as I always have to keep their real selves shielded from the scrutiny of the public eye.

Rafe, our pizza delivery dude, just rang the doorbell, which means dinner is here. Although now that I read that last sentence, I realize how sad and pathetic and not good for me (or my expanding waistline) it is to be on a first-name basis with the pizza guy.

Insert frustrated sigh here.

9/13

Dear Marissa,

Another sleepless Sunday night; another 3 a.m. letter to the only person on the planet who *truly* "gets" me. Is my mother even delivering these to you? Or is she reading them for her own personal pleasure and then feeding them to the incinerator? (MOM—if you *are* reading this, the Botox isn't working, and nobody believes you're only thirty!)

Do you remember that sitcom pilot you made a couple of years ago—the one where you played the girl with telekinesis who did things like help rig her dad's golf games? Duh, of course you remember. What *I* remember is how traumatized you were when the network made you sit behind the one-way glass and listen in on the focus groups bashing everything from the script to your hairstyle. And how at the time I couldn't understand *why* it was so traumatic, seeing as we'd grown up our whole lives having critics and tabloid reporters say way worse things than the dozens of nobodies who got paid in doughnuts and free tickets to *The Price Is Right*.

Well, I want to let you know that I finally understand.

Last night I went to this slumber party (long story) and

we watched the first part of *Girls on Top*, and for a solid hour I had to listen to a dozen girls talk trash about every aspect of my life: I'm a slut, I purchased my disgustingly large breasts, I broke Harlan Darly's heart. (I can't even describe the irony of that last one.) My point: it was thoroughly demoralizing. I mean, where do they get off judging me like that—these moderately wealthy white kids who live in the suburban bubble of protection their two-parent families provide? Seriously, these are girls whose biggest worry is that they won't have a date to the homecoming dance or that Johnny will break up with them if they don't let him get to third base by Christmas.

I don't mean to oversimplify their problems. I know that people like you and me grew up in a totally different world, and had we been born into "normal" families, we might be worried about the homecoming dance too. But we didn't grow up that way. While girls like Lauren Johnson are reading *Teen People* and dreaming about parties with J. Timberlake, girls like us are working fourteen-hour days, being sniped at by the director to lose another fifteen pounds because he can't see my hip bones clearly enough, and fending off the advances of a twenty-something co-star who wants me to give him a hummer in his trailer between takes. Never mind that I was all of fourteen. Never mind that he'd never learned the phrase "no means no."

God, I sound morbid. I actually went to bed at eleven but woke up two hours later from a really horrible nightmare. It's too creepy to even write it out, but I'll say it starred Harlan Darly and the sperm donor I call my father.

That's the other thing I've been thinking about lately: the

sperm donor. How I grew up blaming my mother for chasing him off, even though she told me a thousand times he dumped her the second she told him she was keeping the baby (i.e., me). How I never heard word one from him until *Star* printed that piece about me getting my first $1 million paycheck when I was ten. And how when he started calling not long after, I thought it was because he wanted to get to know me and be a part of my life, when all he really wanted was some money for an investment property in Boca (i.e., drug money to support the shithead's nasty habits, which I inherited).

I hate it when I can reduce my entire life story to a cliché.

I also hate it when I start to sound like The Victim, so I think I'll sign off and try to get some dream-free sleep in before my alarm starts bleating at 6 a.m.

Lots of love,

Morgan

Mother:

I'm overnighting yet another letter to Marissa. PLEASE make sure that she gets it. Oh, and I'll know if you've been reading these letters. Don't ask me how; I'll just know.

Morgan

P.S. Where's my allowance for this month?

9/13—*Later*

Here's a simple recipe for disaster:
- 0 hours of sleep
- $^1/_2$ of 1 cup of coffee
- 2 bites apple cinnamon Toaster Strudel

Toss ingredients into empty vessel of a girl suffering from severe PMS. Agitate with a completely unexpected geometry quiz. Let simmer for fifty minutes in guidance counselor's office. Add several handfuls of M&M's for garnish.

The first thing Ms. Janet Moore said to me this morning was, "You look like shit."

"Likewise," I replied, even though she looked just as Gap-tastic as ever. Seriously, there wasn't one flyaway hair on her whole head. (NOTE TO SELF: One day, when not pissed at JM, ask her which shine serum she uses.)

She smiled like I hadn't just insulted her and asked me why I hadn't been sleeping. Not "if," mind you—but "why."

"Why do you care?" I asked.

"Why are you so certain I don't?" she shot back.

I had to admit, it was a good question. We sat there and stared at each other for a few minutes. Then she said, "Have you ever been in therapy, Claudia?" I told her I'd been in and out of it since I was six. She nodded. "Then you know that whatever you say in here is confidential."

I sighed. "Nightmares," I said. "That's why I couldn't sleep last night."

She asked me what they were about. I said, "Just this guy I used to know." Janet nodded and waited for me to say more. "Someone mentioned his name the other day and it must've triggered something, that's all."

More silence. Eventually Janet asked, "What was your relationship with this boy?"

Insert the sound of me snorting.

"There wasn't one," I said. "That's the point."

She was taking down some shorthand notes on a junior

legal pad she rested on her lap. I craned my neck to see if I could read what she was writing. Janet handed me the pad. It read:

Claudia—9/13—no sleep/nightmare—boy.

"Those are some detailed notes there," I said as I handed it back to her.

She laughed. "They're my 'triggers,' so to speak. So I can remember what you and I talked about in today's session."

On her desk I could see the heart-shaped frame holding the picture of her and Sappey. An idea was born.

"I'll make you a deal," I said. "I'll answer your questions—in detail—but for every one you ask, I get to send one your way—about you and your boyfriend."

Her left eye twitched slightly. "Do you really think it's appropriate for me to tell you personal information about Mr. Sappey and myself?"

I shrugged. "At least that way I'd know I could trust you. You keep my secrets, I'll keep yours. It's a fair trade."

"I'm not exactly a fan of emotional blackmail, Claudia," Janet said slowly.

"Suit yourself."

After several more minutes of silence, she said, "One condition: I reserve the right to veto any questions I find inappropriate."

"Ditto," I said, surprised that she had caved so easily.

Janet held out her ever-present bowl of M&M's. "Tell me about the boy in the nightmares."

That's when it hit me: I'd caved pretty easily too. Why? Why would I do that? I've thought about it all day and what I've come up with is this:

Despite the fact that I'm almost always worried someone's

going to find me out, there's something oddly liberating about being somebody else 75 percent of the time. Like, as Morgan I couldn't talk about what happened with anyone. Not even with Marissa, and she's the one who knows me best. And at Crapplewood, I was bound by the shackles of being Morgan Carter—too guarded to share anything truly personal, not just in group but during the one-on-one counseling sessions, too.

But here I'm not me. Here I'm Claudia. And in some strange way, being Claudia gives me permission to acknowledge parts of myself that Morgan never could.

Anyway, after some hemming and hawing, here's how it went down:

ME: I was fourteen. He was about eight years older.

JANET: Go on.

ME: We flirted a lot in the beginning. Then he wanted to fool around. I'd never done anything before, but he was sort of insistent. And then one night we were at this party, and I got totally wasted, and the next thing I knew we had sex.

JANET : Was it consensual?

ME: I don't recall saying no. I don't recall saying yes, either, but . . .

JANET: How much did you have to drink that night?

ME: A lot. I was downing Cosmos like they were Kool-Aid. We'd smoked a little weed, too.

JANET (nodding): Let me get this straight: you think being wasted implies consent?

ME: When do I get to ask you a question?

JANET: Shoot.

ME: How long have you and Sappey been dating?

JANET: Since July. Did you go to a doctor afterward?

ME: Wait. Wait. Wait a second—I tell you the tragic story of how I lost my virginity and all I get in return is "since July"? I need details, Janet. Details.

JANET: We got to talking at our teachers' in-service day last summer. He asked me if I wanted to get dinner afterward. I was new in town, so I said yes, and one thing led to another.

ME: So you're dating him by default? Because he's the first eligible bachelor you met?

JANET (ignoring me): My turn. Why didn't you go see a doctor?

ME: Because they automatically run drug tests. There was probably more than pot in my bloodstream, and let's just say that's frowned upon in my line of work.

JANET (looking confused): Your line of work?

ME (panicking inwardly): Uhh, you know. Being a teenager.

JANET: I see.

ME: Back to you: what could you possibly see in that pretentious nut bag?

JANET: Keep in mind that you only get to see one side of Mr. Sappey.

ME: Yeah, the asshole side. What, is he really good in the sack?

JANET (clearing her throat): Unfortunately, our time is up for today.

ME: So it's true? He really *is* good in the sack? I don't know if I should high-five you or throw up in your garbage can.

JANET: See you next Monday, Claudia.

Then in English, Emily was babbling on about how sign-ups for the Very Involved Panthers club were down this year. Apparently even Eli isn't going to the meetings, but that's because Deb's got him working overtime at the yearbook (wink, wink). "You should join," she said. "It'll look great on your transcript."

I snickered in spite of myself. Transcript. As if I have to worry about that. "Sorry, Em—but I think my tolerance for dealing with the dork brigade pretty much crapped out at your dear friend Debbie's snooze of a slumber party last weekend."

Emily got this wounded-puppy look on her face, and it

took me a few beats to understand how she heard what I'd said. Not only had I slammed all of Emily's dorkster friends, I'd dubbed her President Dork. It was the kind of thing that, if I'd said it to Marissa, would have carried no weight whatsoever. But Em's like a thousand times more sensitive than me and my old crew; hence, the wounded puppy.

Sighing, I said, "I didn't mean it like that, Emily."

"Then how *did* you mean it?" she asked quietly.

When I didn't answer right away, Emily tucked the front strands of her hair behind her ears and said, "If my friends and I are such dorks, then why are you hanging out with us?"

"You don't like those girls any more than I do," I said. "You told me so yourself!"

Emily ignored me. "Do you really have to be such a snot around them? I mean, do you *really* think they haven't noticed how you roll your eyes at everything they say and do?"

I fought the urge to roll my eyes at that comment. Things would be so much easier if Emily would just agree that her friends are lame, but it seemed like that wasn't going to happen. If I wanted to keep Emily as a friend, I'd have to try to smooth things over. "I'm sorry. But you have to understand—things are very different where I come from."

"Oh, right," she said. "I forgot how hip those Pennsylvania Dutch are."

"Sure," I quipped. "Haven't you watched the new season of *Pimp My Buggy*?"

We stared at each other for a minute, barely blinking. Then Emily dissolved into laughter.

Yes. Score one for the washed-up movie star.

"So when are your meetings?" I heard myself ask.

Emily shook her head. "Don't do me any favors."

"No, really," I said. "I'm interested. I used to do quite a bit of charity work back home. And you're right—I could be a little less stuck-up. So, you know. Let me help."

And that is how I became the latest member of VIP.

Joy.

Then in film class, Sappey handed back our last essay. Guess who got a big fat D-plus? I suppose it's better than a plain D, but what really got me was what Sappey had scrawled across it in bright red ink: *Ms. Miller, if you spent as much time reading my assignment sheets as you do trying to choose subjects you think I'll dislike, you might get better grades in this class. Next time, FOLLOW INSTRUCTIONS.*

I whipped around to LaTanya and demanded to know what she'd gotten. It was another A. She'd written her essay on how films by definition must utilize the visual element—and then had gone on to prove how even though the *Spider-Man* movies are highly visual, they lack the emotional depth also requisite in true films.

As much as I hate to admit it, it was pretty damned good.

"Will you do me a favor?" I asked her. "Read through this and tell me what exactly I'm doing wrong." She gave me a look like, "Why is the hardheaded white girl asking me for help?" But then she said, "Fine. Meet me in the library during lunch tomorrow."

"Agreed."

Now my brain is a whirling pile of puke, and I'm still trying to figure out how Ms. Janet Moore got me to spill, and how Emily roped me into her dumb volunteer club, and how Sappey made me feel like a big fat idiot yet again. Even though deep down I know I'm right and he's wrong, his constant snarking isn't doing anything for my self-esteem.

It's only 8:30 p.m., but I'm going to bed.

9/14

It's 11:48 a.m., and I should be in English, but I'm actually at home, in my pj's, eating tapioca pudding from a big plastic bucket and bemoaning my entire existence.

Say good morning to my inner brat*grrl*.

I told Trudy I was taking a mental health day and she wigged out. She kept saying, "What's wrong? Are you okay? Should I stay home from work?" What she really wanted to ask was, "Do you need to call your sponsor?" I could see it on her face—she was convinced that the moment she left, I was going to dig into some secret stash and get bombed off my ass.

"Relax," I said. "I just need to get caught up on some sleep."

Finally, after much convincing, I got her out the door and went straight back to bed. I got about an hour of uninterrupted sleep before I bolted straight up. I don't know if I had another nightmare or what, but suddenly I was wide awake.

I've always been one of those people who hates being alone for more than an hour. Mostly because, growing up, I never actually got to be alone longer than a bathroom break. So waking up in an empty house, with virtually everyone I know either at work or at school or on a list of people I'm not allowed to contact under any circumstances, I picked up the phone and dialed my mother's cell.

Imagine my surprise when a very groggy-sounding man answered the phone.

"Hello?" the man said, through a barely muffled yawn.

I said, "I'm sorry—I'm trying to reach Bianca Carter. Is this the right number?"

"Yeah," he mumbled. "But she's sleeping."

"Who is this?" I demanded.

"This is her husband—who's this?"

I couldn't even respond. *Husband?* The last I heard, my mother wasn't even dating anyone. Was *this* why she hadn't returned any of my eight million calls?

After a long silence I croaked, "This is her daughter. I would like to speak with her, please."

"Oh, shit."

And in those two words—spoken in a clear, unmistakable voice—I knew exactly who had answered the phone:

My manager, Sam Rosenbaum.

"Oh my God!" I croaked into the phone. "Sam? Is this some kind of joke?"

There were some muffled sounds, like someone had buried the cell under a mountain of pillows. Eventually, Bianca came on the line.

"Morgan, darling—what's wrong? Shouldn't you be in school right now?"

"What's wrong?" I shouted. "What's *wrong*? Did you get *married*, Mother? Did you marry *Sam*?"

"Calm down, Morgan," she said, in her pseudo-soothing voice. Then she sighed. "This isn't how I wanted you to find out."

"How exactly did you want me to find out, Mother? And when? You got married without even telling me about it? *When did this happen?*"

"Hold on," she cooed. "Sam wants to talk to you."

"Morgan, baby," Sam said when he came on the line. "Don't be angry with us. We never meant to fall in love. It just happened."

I closed my eyes and tried to breathe normally. I couldn't help but think that I'd somehow managed to wake up in an episode of *The O.C.*

"This is bullshit," I said, tears pooling in the corners of my eyes. "How could she? How could *you*?"

I didn't wait for him to answer. Instead, I hung up the phone and turned off the ringer. Then I put my own cell on silent, grabbed the tub of tapioca, and had a good cry.

As much as all of this hurts, I'm glad I finally have a little clarity. I mean, my life makes so much more sense now. Sam didn't ship me off to Fort Lame as a tactic to revitalize my career; he sent me here so that he could marry my spoiled brat of a mother without me knowing. Why, though? Why would he do that? Is it possible that Sam Rosenbaum *actually* fell in love with Bianca? Or did Bianca pretend to fall in love with him to shore up her financial future once her meal ticket nearly OD'd? The minute I entered Crapplewood, I became more of a liability than an asset, and no way would Bianca have given up the comfortable existence I'd provided since I was a baby.

I've almost called Marissa half a dozen times since I hung up on Sam. The only thing stopping me is the fact that if I do talk to Marissa, I'll have to reveal my secret, and the last four weeks I've spent here will have been for nothing. I can't exactly publish a memoir titled *Morgan Carter: My Month in Hiding*.

If I called Trudy, she'd be here in a second, comforting me like the mom she's become. But the truth is, she's not my mother—she's not even my real aunt. She's just a lonely woman who was kind enough to take in her best friend's recovering addict daughter. Plus, I know if I called Trudy, she'd think I was in danger of falling off the wagon. And okay—I can't lie. It *has* crossed my mind. Fortunately I've thus far managed to remind myself that it's not the drink I really want, but the feeling I used to get when I drank.

Anyway, I can't believe this. Sam and my mom. Me, here, expelled from their lives. It's like my deepest fear being realized—that when it comes right down to it, it isn't me they love, it's what I do for them.

I am totally, utterly, completely *alone*.

9/14—*Later*

Emily called me the second school let out to ask me why I wasn't there today. I told her I was hosting a pity party (guest of honor: me) and she wasn't invited.

"But what about tutoring?" she asked.

"Why bother?" I said. "Even when I 'apply' myself, I end up with Ds."

"Is this because of Sappey?"

"The comment? Yes. My pity party? Not so much."

She sighed. "Do you want to talk about what's *really* bothering you?"

"Not especially."

"Too bad," she said. "I'm coming over." She hung up before I could protest.

I spent the next ten minutes scrambling around the house, making sure the house was a Claudia-friendly, Morgan-free zone. Then I realized that I was still wearing my pj's and that I had a huge blob of tapioca on my left boob. I was heading to my room to get changed when the doorbell rang.

Shit.

It was the first time Emily had come inside, but she wasn't one of those people who wanted a tour or who commented on the framed prints hanging on the wall. She didn't even make a face after seeing me in my tapioca-stained pj's.

"Should we work in the living room or at the table?" Em asked. "I was thinking we could start with chemistry today."

"I'm not really in the mood for a tutoring session," I said.

"Well," Emily replied, all business, "it's either tutoring or talking. And since you said you didn't want to talk about it—"

"You can't force me to be tutored!"

'Here," she said, reaching into her bag. "I brought you something." She handed me a chocolate bar from DeBrand. The label read, CHOCOLATE MAKES EVERYTHING BETTER.

I chuckled. "See?" I said. "You *do* know me."

We sat there quietly for a minute. Then Emily asked, "Are you okay?"

I wanted to say, "No. No, I am not. My manager married my mother in a secret ceremony I most certainly wasn't invited to, and frankly, it *sucks*."

But what I really said was, "I'll be fine. It's just, you know, that time of the month. Plus, Mercury is in retrograde, and apparently that screws with everyone."

Emily didn't look convinced—not that I can blame her. I could hear how lame an excuse it was even while I was saying it. I had to deflect.

Marissa's sage advice echoed in my head: *Turn the*

conversation. "Hey, Em—you never did tell me what's up with you and Joey Harkus."

She blushed. "Oh, *that*. It's . . . nothing."

"So in your world, 'nothing' means hooking up with a guy on a semi-regular basis? I mean, Jesus—why aren't the two of you at least *dating*?"

"Jesus," she replied.

"What?"

"Jesus is why we aren't dating."

Turns out that Joey Harkus doesn't think that Emily is a devout enough Christian to be his full-on girlfriend. He has no qualms, however, about feeling her up in the front seat of his daddy's truck on the weekends.

"What a loser," I said. "Why do you put up with that?"

She shrugged. "I'm too busy to have a real boyfriend."

This I could understand. I'd never actually had a real boyfriend myself.

"But that doesn't mean I don't need a little booty now and then," she continued, causing a swig of Diet Coke to escape through my nose.

"Did you just say 'booty'?" I asked, half laughing and half choking.

Emily turned slightly redder. "You know what I mean."

"Miss Whitmarsh!" I exclaimed. "I had no idea you were such a skank."

"I wouldn't go that far," she said smirking, "but I told you before—I'm not the girl you think I am."

"Prove it," I challenged.

She chewed on her bottom lip for a second, like she was actually considering how she could convince me she was a covert wild child. Then she started shoving her books into her messenger bag and said, "You're on, missy. Go get changed."

"Into what?"

"Doesn't matter," she said. "Just make sure you wear comfortable shoes."

I didn't know what to expect—"comfortable shoes" didn't indicate that we were headed on some wacky adventure—but I have to admit that I was surprised when Emily pulled up to Putt-Putt Golf & Games.

"It's like forty degrees out!" I said.

"Wuss. Besides, we're going inside."

I followed her into the stone building—home of fifty arcade games, as the sign declared. She walked right up to the change guy and handed him what looked like a twenty.

"Hey, Shorty," the guy said. "You in for your weekly fix?"

"You know it," Em shot back with a wink.

I followed her back toward the restrooms to this funky platform thing set up in front of a screen on which computer-generated homegirls were shaking their groove thang.

"What the hell kind of game is this?" I asked.

"DDR," she replied. "Dance Dance Revolution?"

"I repeat: what the hell kind of game is this?"

"I guess the phenomenon hasn't hit Amish country yet," she said, chuckling. She slipped three tokens into the slot, turned to me with this Catwoman look on her face, and said, "Watch and learn."

Apparently the point of the game is for the player to imitate the moves on the screen. It starts off kind of basic: step to the front, slide to the right. But then, as the music heats up, so does the dancing. Like, sometimes you have to land on the left and right arrows at the same time, then immediately return to neutral and hit the right arrow three times in a row. Emily's limbs were flying everywhere; her legs executed the steps with military precision, but her hips, arms, and head pop-rocked like she was Jenny from the Block. Every time she nailed a step the word *Perfect!* scrolled up the screen. At the end of the round, you get a grade—and Em got a triple A.

She whipped around to face me. "You want to try?"

I didn't, but I had a feeling we were "bonding," so I said okay.

Emily popped in six tokens total so that we could go head-to-head. A new song came on; about five moves in, I was already off track. Instead of scrolling *Perfect!*s, I was getting almost all *Boo!*s. My final score? The dreaded *E*. In DDR, *E* is the equivalent of *You failed, you big, rhythmless loser!*

I thought that would be the end of it, but Em kept egging me to join her. Round after round, I floundered, never scoring higher than a D (oh, but how I treasured those Ds). Emily, however, kicked major DDR ass. And oh—you want to talk about a workout? By the time Emily played her last token, I could barely breathe, and the sweat-soaked strands of my mud brown hair were plastered to my forehead, face, and neck.

"How long have you been playing that?" I asked her after I stopped panting.

"Year and a half. It's fun, isn't it?"

"Oh, yeah," I said, clutching the backs of my thighs, both of which burned like I'd just lathered up with napalm. "It's a *blast*."

"Great stress reliever, too."

"No doubt," I said. "You're a monster on that thing! Have you ever thought about going out for the dance team or something?"

She waved me off. "Oh, please. I don't do that in front of *people*."

"What about Joey Harkus?" I teased. "Haven't you ever shown him your milk shake?"

"Uh, oh. He'd say I was inviting the devil to boogie down or something."

"God. Tell me you're joking."

She shook her head earnestly. "I kid you not. I mean, my family goes to church every Sunday, but the Harkuses—it's a whole other thing for them. Their church hosts monthly revivals and stuff. I don't even want to think about what that's like." Then she went on, grinning. "I mean, can you picture it? The congregation swearing they are slain in the spirit, cripples being cured."

"Blind men being given sight," I added with a laugh. "Everyone talking in tongues and fainting."

"Stop." Emily giggled. "You're being so *bad*."

"Exactly," I told her. "And sometimes a little bad is good."

In the car, Em checked her cell and saw that she had a missed message from Eli asking her if she wanted to make a Munchies run. "What do you say?" she asked. "Time to refuel?"

I flipped down the visor and checked out my flushed face in the little mirror. Even Claudia had to have some pride, I thought, and politely declined the invitation. But Em wasn't taking no for an answer. She texted Eli to say we'd swing by and pick him up, started the car, and took off.

"So why don't you dance in front of 'people'?" I asked.

She didn't answer right away, and I was about to ask her again when she said, "Remember how I told you about the different versions of Eli? School Eli, home Eli—that sort of thing?"

"Sure," I said.

"Well, the same goes for me. There's the good-girl versions: school Emily, the one who gets straight As and runs clubs and all that, and home Emily, who gets her chores done on time and never breaks curfew. There's also twin Emily—"

"The Emily you are around Eli?"

She nodded. "And when I'm alone, there's Emily Emily. That's probably when I'm the most genuine." She peered at me out of the corner of her eye. "Then sometimes I forget to take my medication and home Emily tries to kill off twin Emily."

I laughed at her attempt to play it off like a joke. But at the same time I wanted to hug her, because I knew exactly how she felt. It was how I'd been feeling when I told Janet about Harlan Darly.

Em shot me a worried glance. "You must think I'm a freak. Right?"

"God, no," I said. "If anything, I'm flattered that you let me see Emily Emily. She's really much cooler than I gave her credit for."

The conversation died as we rolled up to the Whitmarsh house, but it was a natural death. And I had to give the girl credit—she'd gotten my mind off my mom and Sam.

"Where were you guys?" Eli asked as he hopped into the backseat.

Emily shot me a look. "At Claudia's house. I was helping her study for a chemistry test."

"Yeah," I said. "Chemistry."

Thankfully, something outside the window caught Eli's attention. He asked Emily to slow up a bit, rolled down his window, stuck his ever-present camera out, and with one hand grasping the telescopic lens took like fifty shots of something. When he pulled the camera back in the car and gave Em the okay to resume normal speed, I asked him what had caught his attention.

"Nothing in particular," he said.

"Liar," Emily said, grinning. "He just doesn't want to tell you in case the pictures don't turn out. Eli's a total perfectionist when it comes to film."

"It runs in the family," he shot back. "Right, Em?"

At Munchies, Emily asked the waiter for a triple order of Scooby Snacks. I asked him for a diet *pop*. Eli grinned and said, "You're a quick study."

"You don't know the half of it."

It was nice, actually. Sitting there with the two of them, talking about nothing important. For a little while I was able to forget that I was Morgan Carter, former child star, constantly worried that her mild-mannered alter-ego cover would get blown. Instead I felt like I really *was* Claudia Miller. For a little while, anyway.

While we ate, Eli really started opening up. It was like I was getting to know the side of him only Emily sees. In the span of our hour-long snack attack I learned that he (a) collects other people's family portraits—the really old sepia kind, where no one smiles because they had to hold the same pose for hours; (b) owns the first three seasons of *Dawson's Creek* on DVD because he used to have a big-time crush on Katie Holmes; and (c) is a whiz on the theremin, which is some kind of crazy electronic instrument you play without actually touching anything. Eli tried to explain it to me—it has something to do with magnetic fields and the player's hands manipulating sound waves through pitch and volume—and he says they were used to make sound tracks for the cheesy sci-fi flicks of the 1950s and early 1960s.

In other words, he's a geek—but he's a very *interesting* geek.

"How does one decide to become a master theremin player?" I asked.

"I go to a lot of flea markets and stuff, looking for old photographs," he explained. "A couple of years ago I saw a vendor demonstrating one to a potential buyer. I couldn't afford it—he was asking three thousand—but I found a kit on the Internet for a pretty good price."

"Wait a minute—you built your own?"

"Yeah," he affirmed. "It wasn't that hard."

Emily rolled her eyes. "Don't listen to him. He slaved over it for weeks. And then it took him a full six months just to learn how to play 'Baa, Baa, Black Sheep.'"

"Unbelievable," I said. "You'll have to play for me sometime."

Eli nodded, and I watched his cheeks turn bright red. In all the friendly banter, I'd forgotten that he had a crush on me. There was an awkward silence before Eli excused himself to use the men's room.

"I'm sorry," I whispered to Em, once I thought Eli was out of earshot. "I didn't mean—"

She waved me off. "Don't worry. He's fine."

I wasted no time in jumping back to our earlier conversation: "Now, about this DDR obsession—"

Emily shushed me. "Not here—Eli doesn't know about that. And I'd rather he not find out, okay?"

"I didn't think you were the type to keep secrets from your brother."

"Like I said, people tend to surprise you. You know, once you stop making snap judgments based on their fashion sense. Once you drop the crap and really become *friends* with them."

Then it was my turn to blush. I hadn't realized my shallowness was so apparent. But also, I was starting to feel guilty about not being honest with the twins. Especially Emily, after she'd been so open with me.

I got home around five, a full hour before Trudy got off work. Unfortunately, I was done just long enough to rip me out of my Claudia Miller fantasy world and remind myself that Morgan Carter's life has spun completely out of control (no doubt evidenced by her habit of referring to herself in the third person).

My point is that by the time Trudy made it home, I was once again a soggy, tearstained mess. When she asked me what was wrong, all I could say was, "I feel sad." I wasn't ready to tell her the truth. Not tonight, anyway.

I've been writing in this thing for hours. I think I've cut off the circulation in my thumb and three fingers. Time for a hot shower and a good night's sleep!

9/15

I woke up this morning feeling completely exhausted, so much so that I considered extending my mental health break by another day. But Trudy looked way too concerned for me to even bother trying. Plus, I had Emily's VIP meeting to attend after school, and I knew it was sort of a big deal to her that I go. Also, I knew if I stayed home, I'd spend the day watching trash TV and waiting for my mother to call and patch things up (not a likely occurrence, considering the level of communication she'd exhibited thus far). Besides, I didn't want to give her the satisfaction of her knowing I'd waited around for her call. So, off to Snider I went!

In homeroom Mr. Pickles handed me a note from Ms. Janet Moore. It was a pass for me to report to her office ASAP. I scooped up my backpack and headed down the hall.

"What's up?" I asked from the doorway.

I knew I was in trouble when she asked me to close the door behind me.

"You need to get back to your classes, so I'll make this quick," Janet said. "Your guardian called me yesterday. She's worried about you, Claudia."

"Yeah, well, maybe *I'm* worried about me too," I shot back.

She asked me what was going on, and I hesitated for maybe twenty seconds before plopping down into her guest chair and telling her the whole sordid mess. Leaving out, of course, the part about my new stepfather being my old business manager. I skirted that issue by saying he was the father of an ex-boyfriend, which to me seemed almost as heinous as what had actually happened.

"That's a lot to deal with," Janet said.

Yeah, I thought. *No shit.*

JANET: Clarify something for me—when did you find out about your mother's marriage?

ME: Yesterday. Around noon.

JANET: So this was *after* you'd already decided to take the day off?

ME: Um, yeah.

JANET: And you haven't told your guardian about the phone call.

ME: Trudy, her name is Trudy. And no, I haven't.

JANET: Then why is it that she—that Trudy—was so concerned yesterday?

ME (blinking rapidly):

JANET: Claudia?

ME:

JANET: What else aren't you telling me?

Here's the thing about keeping secrets: once you spill one, you have this almost primal urge to spill them all. Now that she knew about Harlan Darly, I had to work really hard *not* to tell her the rest. About how humiliating it is to go from shooting *CosmoGirl!* covers to fading into the general obscurity of Snider High. About how much more difficult "one day at a time" is when you're no longer living in the protected walls of a high-cost treatment facility—when you're being forced to deal with your feelings on a daily basis instead of being able to numb them. About how sometimes I dream about drinking or getting high, and it seems so real that when I wake up and realize that I'm still here and that I'm still me, I feel the kind of sadness that lingers after someone dies.

About how maybe that someone is *me*.

JANET (sighing): I can't help you if you won't talk to me.

ME: I'm eight months sober.

JANET: As in . . . ?

ME: As in for real. Eight months off pills and coke and booze and all of it. I got my six-month chip a month before I moved here, but I don't carry it with me or anything.

JANET: Congratulations, Claudia. That's a wonderful achievement.

ME: Whatever.

JANET: I take it you're going to meetings.

ME: Once a week. Twice last week.

JANET: So when you told Trudy you wanted a mental health day . . .

ME: She probably thought I plotting ways to throw myself off the wagon.

JANET: It takes a while, you know. Earning back people's trust. But it does happen, Claudia. I promise you.

ME (indignantly): How the hell would you know? What, did they teach you that at guidance counselor school?

She didn't say anything, just reached into top drawer of her desk and pulled out a little velvet pouch, which she then tossed to me. Inside was a bronze-colored coin with a triangle and the number five on the front. I turned it over; sure enough, there was the Serenity Prayer, the one I said at the close of every meeting I'd ever attended. I looked up. Janet nodded.

"Five years," she said quietly, "as of last January."

No wonder she hadn't been shocked when I'd blurted out the length of my sobriety. Suddenly I felt very naked, like there wasn't much I could hide from Ms. Janet Moore. Her eyes were like lasers, cutting through my bullshit in a way that freaked the hell out of me. I quickly put the medallion back in its pouch, handed it to her, and said, "I want to go back to class now."

"Okay," she said. "But remember, Claudia—I'm here if you need anything. No matter what, no matter when. Deal?"

Shit. I've been writing this for the last three class periods—it pays to keep your journal in a college-ruled notebook!—but now Sappey's glaring at me from across the room. He must know I'm not recording every precious word he says.

Now he's handing out another stupid assignment sheet

for another stupid paper. (Double shit—I totally forgot I was supposed to meet LaTanya in the library yesterday during lunch. No *wonder* she was giving me the freeze before class!)

More later.

9/15—*Later*

The hits just keep on coming!

I went to Em's Very Involved Panthers meeting directly after Sappey's class. She wasn't kidding when she said the VIPs had gone MIA! Besides me and Emily, there were only four other Panthers in attendance: Lauren Johnson (the chick from Deb's slumber party who's all about Harlan Darly), Meadow Forrester (very voluptuous redhead from my gym class; is biologically incapable of sweating), Colin McAfee (who I'm fairly certain plays Will to Meadow's Grace), and—no joke!—LaTanya Samuels.

"What are you doing here?" she asked.

"What are *you* doing here?" I shot back.

"Well," she deadpanned, "I'm a very involved panther."

I laughed. "Better than a marginally invested chipmunk, I guess."

"I'm still waiting for my apology," she said. "What happened to you yesterday?"

"Mental health day," I explained. "I'm really sorry. I totally forgot."

"Obviously."

She reached into her bag and pulled out my paper, which looked like it was bleeding red ink. "I think I figured out your problem," she said, handing it back to me.

"Yeah? What is it?"

"First of all," she said, "you referred to Soderbergh as 'Steven.'"

"So? That's what I call him!"

It wasn't until LaTanya asked who else in Hollywood I was on a first-name basis with that I realized what a stupid mistake I'd just made.

"You know what I mean," I said, trying to recover. "Soderbergh is . . . too hard to spell?"

LaTanya frowned, not buying the dumb act. "I don't think so."

Lauren Johnson, who was sitting a desk away, leaned in toward LaTanya and said, "Ask her what her boyfriend's name is."

I am going to kill Lauren Johnson.

LaTanya cocked her head to one side. "You got a boyfriend? Who?"

"Evan Walsh," Lauren cried triumphantly. "Her boyfriend's name is supposedly *Evan freaking Walsh*."

"Yo, hold up," LaTanya said. "You're dating *the* Evan Walsh? Aren't you, like, from Amish country or something?"

I sighed, trying to keep calm. "His name is Evan, but he's not *the* Evan. And yes, I'm from Lancaster, but I'm not Amish. And," I added, falling back on my patented defense mechanism—insult, "if Lauren Johnson doesn't butt out of my conversation right this section, I'm going to tell the entire school that her cup size is the result of gel inserts she wears in her Wonderbra and not the gift of mother nature as she'd like everyone to believe."

Lauren turned away.

Works every time.

"Still," LaTanya said, "that's a weird coincidence. . . ."

It would have been tough to explain . . . if Em hadn't picked that moment to call the VIPs to order.

After the meeting, which lasted forty-five minutes (not that I remember a single thing that was said), Emily had a couple of financial things to take care of. She tossed me the car keys and asked me to check in on Eli, to see if he was ready to go. I walked down to the yearbook room, but it was empty. So I hightailed it to the other side of the building, where the photo lab was. Sure enough, the red security light was on. I waited for about a minute for it to go off, but when it didn't, I knocked anyway.

Finally, the light went dead and the door opened about three inches. I took this as an invitation and stepped inside the room. There, drying on the line, were about seventeen pairs of eyes staring back at me And they weren't just anybody's eyes. They were *my* eyes.

"Eli," I said slowly. "What the hell is this?"

He smiled. "It's just a . . . you know . . . *project*."

I studied the photos. There I was—sitting in the cafeteria, making my way across the quad, talking on my cell phone, sipping a cup of coffee; there was even a picture of me reading in the library. In every picture I was completely unaware that anyone was even looking at me, much less snapping my photo. I couldn't even recognize where most of them had been taken. Despite all the times I'd ducked out of the frame or covered my face with my arm, Eli had managed to get several clear shots—all extreme close-ups in which the resemblance between Claudia and Morgan was intensified. They were exactly the kind of shots that would bring in a pretty penny, if the right buyer were found.

"It's a project?" I spat. "A project for profit. Right?"

Before Eli could respond, I started ripping the damp prints from the line. No way could I let anyone else see his handiwork.

"Claudia!" he exclaimed. "What are you doing?"

Ignoring him, I tore each picture in half, then quarters, then eighths; I tore until they were confetti. Then I shoved the remnants into the garbage.

"Jesus," he said. "What is *wrong* with you?"

I held out my palm. "Give me the negatives."

Eli frowned, stepping away from me. "No way."

"Seriously," I said. "Give them to me now."

"No," Eli said again. "They're not from one roll of film. And some of them aren't even mine—they're the year-book's."

"You really don't expect me to believe that, do you?"

Eli folded his arms across his chest.

"Who are they for?" I demanded. "Did Fuller call you? How much is she offering?"

"I don't know who 'Fuller' is." He threw up his hands in frustration. "These were for Ms. Gibson. She gave us a class assignment. A candid portraits project. You seemed like . . . I don't know. A good subject. I thought you might even be flattered. Trust me—I won't make that mistake again."

Then he turned away in a huff, dug into his backpack, and pulled out a crumpled sheet of paper. "The assignment," he explained. Sure enough, there it was, in black and white. My hands started shaking just a bit; all I could think about was how psycho I must've looked, tearing those pictures to shreds before bothering to ask why he'd taken them. I needed to fix things—fast.

"Oh my God," I said. "Eli, I'm so sorry. Let me explain."

"Explain what?"

"I—I can't be photographed," I began.

"Right." He snorted. "What, are you some kind of wanted felon or something?"

"Not exactly."

Eli turned around slowly. I could tell I'd piqued his curiosity. Now I just had to nail the delivery.

"There's a lot you don't know about me," I began. "I told everyone that I moved here to make a fresh start, which is true. But it's only half the story."

"Go on," he encouraged.

I closed the door to the photo lab and locked it behind me, remembering to flick on the outside warning light. "You have to promise me you won't tell a soul," I said, my voice barely above a whisper. "Not even Emily . . ."

He nodded.

"I'm here because I'm in hiding. Sort of. It's complicated."

"Hiding from what?" he asked.

I swallowed hard. Telling him the story could be a huge gamble, but not telling him might be a bigger one.

"My father is crazy," I blurted. "Really crazy. And violent. He used to hit me and my mom. One time he shattered my nose. That's why she left him."

"Oh my God," Eli said, his brow furrowed with concern. "That's horrible."

"The judge gave her full custody, but my dad didn't care. He started following me around, like to school and stuff, and he'd say horrible things to me about how if I didn't tell him I loved him, he'd hurt me worse. My mother got a restraining order on him, but he wouldn't stop."

Eli sat down on a nearby stool, a dazed look on his face. "I can't believe it."

I nodded. "There's more. I used to have this dog named Muppet. She was a cross between a shih tzu and a poodle. One day she disappeared. A week later we found her on our doorstep. Her neck had been broken. We couldn't prove that it was my dad who did it, but . . ."

Even as I said it, I feared the dog bit would be too over the top. So unbelievable that Eli would know it was all a lie.

Feeding him the plotline from a Lifetime Original Movie I'd made three years ago was risky, but I also I knew the odds of Eli being familiar with *You're Not My Father Anymore* were slim to none. I forced two crocodile tears down my cheeks and prayed he'd buy my story.

He did.

Eli, who already looked horrified beyond belief, reached out and touched my arm. "Claudia, I am so sorry. I can't even imagine what you've been through. I—I'm sorry."

I smiled the small, brave smile of a girl who'd overcome great tragedy. And now, the final sale . . .

"That's why I'm here. My mom thought it would best to send me somewhere safe. Somewhere he wouldn't think to look. I know it must seem stupid to you, but that's why I'm so paranoid about having my picture taken. It's a safety thing. He can't ever know where I am. There can't be any record of me anywhere, because there's always a chance that he could find me."

I was crying really hard now, mostly fake tears, but still.

"Oh, Claudia," Eli said softly. "I'm so, so, so sorry."

I forced my shoulders to tremble as the tears flowed more freely. Eli gently slipped his arms around me. I could feel his heart beating wildly in his chest. Poor guy. I'd probably just given him a heart attack, first with that outburst and then with my super-sad sob story. I hated the idea of manipulating him this way, but what else could I do? I *could not* blow my cover, and acting came so naturally.

Still, it was hard not to notice how Eli smelled, sort of like Old Spice deodorant mixed with photo chemicals, a combination that was oddly comforting.

There was pounding on the lab door, and we pulled away from each other. "Eli, are you in there?" Emily asked from the other side.

I wiped at my eyes while Eli unlatched the door and turned on the fluorescents overhead. Emily took one look at me and stopped dead in her tracks. "Claudia, are you crying?" she asked.

"Of course not," Eli said, covering for me. "It's the chemicals. They're irritating her eyes."

"Oh. Well, let's go, then," Emily said impatiently. "I've got a ton of work to do."

I didn't say much on the drive home, not even when Emily thanked me for volunteering to be her co-chair on the haunted house project. (Wait—when exactly had I done this?) My body felt exhausted. First I'd unloaded a huge weight by confessing to Janet that I was a recovering addict. Then I'd added an even heavier one with my whopper of a lie. Eli had looked so upset, like he was ready to track down my fictional father and kill the bastard himself.

Maybe I shouldn't have gone so far. Eli was too nice a guy to simply brush off what I'd told him. No, he'd carry it with him almost as much as I would.

I am a complete ass.

Trudy's not due home for another hour. I can't think about this anymore. Maybe I'll go take a nap.

9/15—*Much later*

My "nap" lasted until 8 p.m., when a very worried Trudy shook me out of sleep.

"Morgan," she said, her voice quavering, "I need to know what's going on. You've been staying up all night, sleeping all day . . . and why are your eyes so puffy?"

"I've been crying," I said. I sat up, still groggy. "But I haven't been using, if that's what you're asking."

She sighed heavily and sat on the edge of my bed. "Are you *that* unhappy here? I thought . . . I don't know. I thought things were getting better. I thought you and I were doing okay."

"It's not you," I told her. "It's . . . everything else."

I told Trudy the whole story then—why I'd been having nightmares about Harlan Darly, how Sam answered Bianca's phone yesterday, what I'd ended up telling Eli in the photo lab. The only part I left out was Janet showing me her sobriety chip. That was a secret I'd never spill. They don't call it Alcoholics Anonymous for nothing.

By the end, even Trudy was crying.

"Morgan, why didn't you ever tell anyone about that Harlan Darly?" she asked, sniffling.

I shrugged. "I was fourteen. I used to get embarrassed buying tampons. No way was I equipped to tell anyone that some twenty-two-year-old sleazeball boned me in his beach-side bachelor pad."

When Trudy's tears had dried up, anger took over. "I

can't believe your mother," she said through gritted teeth. "What was she *thinking*?"

"What's she ever thinking?" I said. "She's Bianca—she's beyond rational thought."

We laughed then. It was the first time I'd laughed in I don't know how long.

"I have an idea," Trudy said after a while. "Let's *both* take the day off tomorrow. There was another inappropriately large check from your mom in today's mail. I say we cash it and blow the whole damned thing on stuff we don't need."

"What about Janet?" I asked.

"The guidance counselor?"

"Yeah. She'll be worried if I'm not in tomorrow."

"Well," Trudy said, "I'll leave her a message tonight. Let her know this is all my idea." She kissed my forehead then, and it was such a tender gesture that I almost started blubbering all over again. Instead, I pulled myself together and said, "What do we want on tonight's pizza?"

After ordering a large ham and pineapple, Trudy called every number she's had for my mom in the past six years and ended up leaving something like ten messages, each one issuing quite the smackdown. Then she made me give her all of Sam's numbers and she repeated the process.

Needless to say, neither of them called back.

9/16

I'd forgotten how delicious retail therapy can feel.

The only ground rule that Trudy and I set was that anything I bought for myself had to be in the price range of a normal teenager and/or her parents—sensible, considering the nature of my disguise. So we started at Target, filling up two carts with everything from prepster argyle cardigans to fuzzy, faux-Birkenstock-style clogs. Oh, it was a beautiful thing. Crystal-tipped hair pins! Vampire-red lip stains! And just for fun, matching bottles of Glow by J.Lo perfume!

Two hours and $600 later, we headed to Saigon, a small Vietnamese restaurant that served amazing pork fried rice, for a quick lunch. Then it was over to Old Navy, Claudia Miller's second-favorite store, where we purchased even more clothes and cute accessories. To feed our brains we made a stop at Barnes & Noble, where Trudy got *The South Beach Diet* and *The South Beach Diet Cookbook* and I picked up *The Drama of the Gifted Child* and *Children of the Self-Absorbed*. (Guess I couldn't totally get Mama Bianca off my mind.) After snagging extra-large caramel macchiatos, we ducked into one of those Asian nail places for twenty-minute pedicures. Trudy, bold bitch that she is, opted for a daring shade of lime green instead of her super-safe ballerina pink. I went with a more classic red.

When we were too exhausted to spend any more money, we headed home. Sitting on the front stoop, looking chilly and dejected, was none other than Eli Whitmarsh. The sight of him brought my guilty feelings flooding back. At the same time I was strangely happy to discover him there, waiting for me.

"Hey, Eli," I said, trying to sound casual. "What's up?"

He thrust a sealed brown envelope at me. "I needed to give you these."

I dropped the shopping bags I was carrying, took the envelope, and jimmied it open with a freshly painted pinky nail. Inside were more than a dozen strips of film, mixed in with some partials. I knew without asking they were the negatives I'd demanded from him yesterday.

"You didn't have to do this," I said quietly.

"Yes," he said, "I did."

Meanwhile, Trudy's standing there holding out the house key but unable to reach the door. So she said, "Hi, I'm Claudia's aunt Trudy. Would it be okay for us to move the party inside?"

Eli scrambled up and apologized for blocking her way. Then he introduced himself and, ever the gentleman, grabbed the bags I'd dropped plus one Trudy was losing her grip on and took them into the house.

"Impressive," he said. "The two of you must medal in shopping."

Tru and I exchanged glances. Then, slick as olive oil, she said, "I won a thousand dollars on a scratch ticket last night. I figured Claudia and I could use a day off, so I cashed it in and took us on a mini–shopping spree." Who knew Trudy could be such a cool liar? Now *that's* what I'd call impressive.

"I should get going," Eli said.

"So soon?" Trudy asked.

He smiled. "It's almost dinnertime."

"It's a shame you can't stay," Trudy said breezily. "We'd love to have you over for a meal. Your sister, too."

"Actually," Eli said, "Emily's helping my mom with some charity auction tonight, so I guess I *could* stay. I mean, if you want me to." That last bit was directed to me and me alone.

"Uh, sure," I said. "I'd like that." I was a little nervous— an extended visit sans Emily and plus Trudy—but I couldn't deal with the thought of him going home to an empty house and eating alone. It was just a meal, right?

Eli excused himself to call home and leave a message for his dad. After he hung up the phone, he asked, "So, what are we cooking?" Trudy and I both laughed. I explained that we ate out so often that the only groceries we kept in the house were of the breakfast and/or snack variety.

This did not deter young Eli, though. He went through the fridge and the pantry and within five minutes was cooking up the great American meal: Kraft macaroni 'n' cheese, Bush's baked beans, and Ball Park franks with yellow mustard. Eli did all of the work, right down to setting the table with paper plates and artfully folded paper towels that doubled as napkins.

"Now *I'm* impressed," Trudy said as we sat down to eat.

Eli blushed a little. "Me and Em do a lot of the cooking at home," he explained. "Dad has meetings and functions and things he has to go to at night, and Mom usually goes with him. Last spring, during tax season, it got worse. Em and I even started TiVo'ing *30 Minute Meals* on the Food Network."

"Ooh, I love that show!" Trudy squealed. "Rachel Ray makes meat loaf look like fun."

"Did you see the one where she made a three-course meal using nothing but squash and tomatoes?" Eli asked. "She's, like, the MacGyver of produce."

Thanks to Tru's awesome conversational skills, dinner wasn't nearly as painful as it could've been. I'd say something like, "Eli is a photographer for the yearbook," and then Trudy would take over and ask him twenty questions about what that entailed. One thing I've noticed about Eli recently is that he gets really animated when he's carried away in conversation. Like, he never looked bored or annoyed by Tru's questions. You know, how I was when his parents were grilling me. Nope, Trudy and Eli had an actual *dialogue*. For example, he asked Trudy about her job, and I found out that she's a business relationship manager for Bank One, which means she's sort of like an ambassador between the bank and some of its small-business clientele. I knew she worked at a bank, but for some reason, I'd never bothered to find out exactly what she did.

When we were finished, Trudy went into the kitchen to wash the dishes—really just three pans and some silverware.

"Are you feeling better?" Eli asked.

"Better than what?"

"Well," he said, "when you weren't at school today, I thought maybe it had something to do with . . . you know. What we talked about yesterday."

"Not really," I said. "Just, you know—taking a little shopping break."

"Oh."

He still looked really concerned, which compounded the guilt I was already feeling. "Listen," I said, "I shouldn't have unloaded on you like that. I'm fine. Really."

Eli didn't respond. I tried again.

"I was really upset yesterday. But honestly, it's not as bad as I made it seem."

"Claudia," he said slowly, "the guy killed your *dog*. I'd say that was pretty bad."

I winced. I'd known that Muppet bit would come back to bite me in the ass.

"Please—can you just forget I said anything? I'm really okay."

"I was thinking," Eli continued anyway, "that my dad has a lot of . . . connections. Maybe he could help. I'm not sure how, but . . ."

Yes, that's exactly what I need. A former DA digging into my past. Without even thinking about the consequences, I grabbed Eli's hand and squeezed. "Thank you for worrying about me," I said softly. "But don't worry too much, because then I'll be worried about you worrying about me."

Eli cleared his throat. His hand felt slightly damp in mine. Why is it that I never remember Eli's crush on me until *after* I've done something to encourage it? The last thing I needed was some kind of romantic entanglement. I was having enough trouble keeping my lies straight as it was.

"I was wondering," he said, still holding my hand, "are you going to Johnny Appleseed this weekend?"

"Am I going to *where*?"

He chuckled. "The Johnny Appleseed Festival. The city hosts it every year. There are these war reenactments and, uh, blacksmith demonstrations."

"Blacksmith demonstrations?" I repeated. "Sounds . . ."

"Boring," he finished for me. "I know, but it's actually not. There are all kinds of entertainers and bands and stuff, too. Like a Renaissance festival, only set in the early 1800s and with whole lot of food made out of apples."

I've never been to a Renaissance festival, and to be frank, this incarnation sounded equally boring. But all I could focus on was the fact that Eli was still holding my hand. I knew I could pull away from him, but in a metaphorical sense, he wasn't about to let go. Not unless I could find him a Claudia replacement to get psyched about.

Then it hit me: I could use this apple fest as an opportunity to fix Eli up with a new and improved version of Debbie Ackerman. She'd asked me after lunch yesterday when we'd be doing her makeover. I pictured the carnival at the end of *Grease*, when Sandy debuts her new look in front of the fun house. Debbie could be the one Eli wants!

"Sure!" I said. "That sounds great!"

"Really?" he said.

"Definitely," I assured him. "I'm totally into it."

"Cool." He stood up. "I hate to eat and run, but I actually have a lot of work to do. I kind of need to reshoot that assignment."

"You mean, the one I destroyed?" I asked.

"It's no big deal," he said. "But it's due on Friday."

Hello! Is this guy for real?

The problem with Eli Whitmarsh is that he's too damned nice. I don't know what makes a good guy like him want to have anything to do with a jackass like me.

Of course, he doesn't know I'm a jackass.

Then I wondered—what it would be like if I really *was* Claudia Miller. Would Claudia want Eli Whitmarsh to be *her* boyfriend? Of course she would. Maybe Eli dressed like a dork and was shy around large groups of people. But the guy had heart. Claudia could do way worse than him.

I walked Eli out to his car. We said goodbye, but before he climbed in, he leaned over and kissed me on my forehead. His face turned bright red, but he didn't try to hide it. "If you need anything, you know where I am," he said. Then he got in and drove away so fast he left a little rubber behind.

I stood there, blinking, as he drove away. Could anyone *actually* be that good? A few weeks ago I would have said no way. But now . . .

Back in the house, I hollered Trudy's name, but she didn't answer. I wandered around until I found her in her bedroom, sitting at the foot of the bed, having an angry phone conversation with someone.

That someone turned out to be my mother.

Trudy shooed me out the door and closed it behind me. It's been two hours and she's *still* talking to her.

I should be catching up on my class assignments, but I'm not. Do you have any idea how hard it is to get any work done when you're trying to eavesdrop on other people's conversations? Not to mention trying to figure out why a tiny kiss from Eli Whitmarsh made you slightly weak in the knees?

Yeah, didn't think so.

Oh my God. I've started talking to myself inside my own journal. This can't be a good sign.

9/16—*Later*

I am such an idiot!

No sooner did Trudy hang up with my mother than the phone rang again. This time it was Emily, and she sounded annoyed.

"Why did you do it?" she asked.

"Do what?"

"Agree to go on a date with my brother!"

"I—" I started, shocked. Then I realized: of course he would think we'd made a date. Of course.

"Oh, Em—I thought we were all going together," I explained. "Like a group hang."

"Well, that's not what Eli thinks," she said.

"I'm sorry," I said. "I told him I'd go because I thought I could try to fix him up that night."

"With who?"

"Debbie."

"Debbie *Ackerman*?"

"Duh," I said. "She's totally in love with him. If we give her a makeover, we can turn her into someone Eli could fall for. Then . . . he'll stop crushing on me, and no one will get hurt."

Emily sighed. "He knows that Debbie likes him, Claudia. He just—he wants *you* to like him."

"I do like him," I said. "Just . . . not in that way."

[Insert extended period of silence here.]

Eventually Emily said, "Claudia, I need to ask you something." I told her to go for it. She hemmed and hawed for a minute. Then this:

"I don't think you have a real boyfriend," she said quietly. "I think you said that because you're not supposed to be in any kind of relationship right now. Because it's part of this twelve-step-program thing. Right?"

I felt like someone had sucked all of the air out of my lungs. I couldn't even speak.

"Claudia?" Emily said. "It's okay. I won't tell anyone."

"How did you figure it—?"

"My mother," she cut in. "She saw you leaving a meeting a couple of weeks ago. She asked me if you'd mentioned anything to me about it, but I said no. I didn't even put it all together until after the party."

My voice came out all quavering. "Emily—you really, really can't tell a single soul. There's too much at stake here. Seriously, I can't even—"

"Claudia," she said softly, "I told you I'm a good listener. I promise you, I will never tell anyone, not even Eli."

That was a pretty big promise for her to make—especially the part about not telling her brother. I wanted to believe her, but how many people had lied to me in the past?

And now I'd put myself in a totally tight spot. Between the things that Emily knew and the story I'd spun to Eli . . . if news got out, there was a strong likelihood that people could put two and two together and figure out who I really was.

I needed time to think. To breathe.

"Uh, Emily? I have to go," I said. "I have to . . . uh . . . call my sponsor."

"Oh," she said gravely. "Right. Well, see you tomorrow?"

We made plans to hang out after school to "discuss the Debbie situation."

That taken care of, I bolted to Trudy's room. Only Trudy wasn't talking.

"Your mother is sending you a . . . special delivery," she said. "That's all I'm allowed to tell you."

"What?" I screeched. "You and I are supposed to be on the same team! That means you're supposed to tell me *everything*!"

"Trust me," Trudy said. "You're going to be very happy about this."

I was fuming. "What, does Bianca think that she can buy me off? And why is she talking to you but not to me? Why won't anyone tell *me* anything?"

Trudy looked like she was about to cry. "Morgan—please. Just . . . wait out the weekend, okay? Your mom says she's sending a letter along with the special delivery. The letter explains everything. You might not love the explanation, but . . . Bianca's heart is in the right place. I swear to you."

"I can't believe this," I said, shaking. "I can't believe you. She's got you totally snowed."

I stormed out of her room and into my own, locking the door behind me. She knocked a couple of times, but I refused to answer. I didn't even bother to tackle any of my homework. Everything's already late anyway—what's the harm in waiting another day?

9/17

In homeroom, Mr. Pickles handed me another note from Ms. Janet Moore: *SEE ME ASAP*. This time the *ASAP* was underlined three times.

"You must really miss me," I said to her when I reached the office.

"Sit down," she instructed.

I asked her if she'd gotten Trudy's message. She said she had, but it wasn't why she called me in. Turns out that next week is ISTEP+ testing. Apparently, every high school student in Indiana has to pass this Graduation Qualifying Exam. It's given during sophomore year, but since I transferred in as a junior, the administration decided I needed to take it this year.

"Are you kidding me?" I asked. "I've never taken a standardized test in my entire life."

"Well," Janet said, smiling, "there's a first time for everything."

The good news is that I get to miss a bunch more classes. The bad news is that I'll have twice the amount of work to make up in a very short time.

Janet switched our usual Monday morning session to

seventh period to accommodate for the testing. She had a twinkle in her eye when she told me, so I knew she'd purposely changed it to that time so I could skip Sappey's class.

As I was leaving, she said, "How are you holding up? I have some free time after school if you'd like to talk again."

"Thanks," I said. "But I've already got plans."

This made her smile. I guess I earned points for having a semi-normal social life.

In English Emily passed me a note. It read, *Broke up w/ JH. You were right, he is an ass!*

I wrote back, *Good 4 U! U R 2 good 4 him.*

At lunch Debbie Ackerman pounced on me before I could reach our usual table. I told her to relax, that Emily and I would pick her up around six tonight and take care of everything. This made her beam rainbows.

Emily, however, wasn't nearly as psyched. This despite the fact that Joey Harkus had relocated to a different lunch table. She pulled me aside as I was rushing off to chemistry and said, "You're not going to go through with this Debbie thing, are you?"

"Well, yeah," I said. "*We* kind of have to, don't we?"

Emily stamped her foot lightly, which was kind of funny for someone who always seemed so mature. "You know he doesn't like her. A makeover isn't going to change that. You're just giving her false hope!"

"Look," I said, "Debbie could use an infusion of confidence regardless of Eli. If we can help her get it, then we're doing our good deed for the day. Right?

"What's with this 'we'?" Em asked. "*I* never agreed to this."

"True. But you know I don't drive, and outside of Eli, she's *your* best friend."

"No, she's not," Emily said. "You are."

A couple of weeks ago, that Hallmark moment might have made me gag. But right then, standing outside the cafeteria, I had the sudden urge to give Emily a big fat hug. Let's just say I didn't fight it.

"Fine," she said when I let go. "I'll help you. But you know how I feel about this."

Chemistry was horrible, per usual. Despite the fact that An-Yi verbally abuses me whenever I try to help out with lab assignments, she apparently missed me yesterday. I know this because she spent the first half of the period berating me for not having been there to assist her with some litmus paper experiment. Unbelievable. I cannot win with this girl! When I couldn't stand her squawk any longer, I said, "Don't you ever shut up, you pompous, know-it-all bitch?"

She stared at me, not blinking. "I can't believe you just called me a *bitch*," she said. Then she turned away and added, "You are a very mean girl."

In film, LaTanya was all, "Girl, where you been?" and I was all, "Girl, where *haven't* I been?" This made LaTanya laugh. LaTanya, I should note, is ranked third in our class and by most accounts is the smartest girl in the school. I suppose that's why I find it hilarious when she starts talking like Li'l Kim.

"Sappy was talking some trash about you yesterday," she said. "Asked me if I knew why you were only coming to class every other day."

Sure enough, Sappey picked that moment to acknowledge my presence. "Ms. Miller," he said, "so nice of you to join us today!" He used that snarky, condescending voice of his, too. I wanted to scream several expletives at him that would've surely landed me in detention, but I didn't. Instead, I packed up my bag and walked out of his room without another word. My destination? The office of Ms. Janet Moore.

"Your boyfriend hates me," I said glumly, slumping into one of her "guest" chairs. "Got any candy?"

Janet handed over the bowl of M&M's. "I'm sure you're wrong about that, Claudia."

"Whatever," I said, rolling my eyes. "Can you write me a pass saying I was supposed to be here during this period? Otherwise my ass is fried."

She shook her head at me in that mom sort of way. "Just for today," she said. "But you can't run in here every time you don't want to be out there."

"You offered!" I reminded her. "This morning—remember?"

"I offered," she said, "to have another session with you. *After* school. I don't remember suggesting that my office could be your new hideout."

"What happened to whatever, whenever?"

Janet shook her head. "Don't pull that BS with me, Claudia. You know exactly what I meant by that."

"Fine," I growled. "I'll go back to class."

Except I didn't. I snuck into the library and spent the period scribbling in this notebook. (What else is new?)

Just heard the dismissal bell—better pack up my stuff and go meet Em.

9/17—Later

I'm sitting in the lobby of Eden Salon & Spa with Em, waiting for Debbie Ackerman to get her hair chemically straightened.

She's under the delusion that doing this will make her a sex goddess that even Eli wouldn't be able to resist. I've tried to explain to her that it's not so much about over-processed hair as it is about feeling cute and having attitude. She totally didn't believe me.

It's been a long afternoon. First Emily and I had our super-secret meeting to formulate "the plan." Actually, I didn't see the need for any sort of plan, but Emily insisted we have a course of action. Typical Em. Even her to-do lists have to-do lists. Problem was, her idea of a "plan" entailed me telling Eli that I'd had a boyfriend back home (presumably Evan Walsh, except not *the* Evan Walsh), but that he just dumped me. I asked her how she thought this was going to be helpful.

"Because," she explained impatiently, "you're lying about the boyfriend. This way, you can correct the lie. Plus, Eli will think that you've just had your heart broken and that you'll need plenty of time to heal before he can ask you out. When the requisite waiting period has passed, you'll either be ready to date someone and consider Eli a viable possibility, or Eli will have moved on. See? Everybody wins."

I told her she sounded like a bad self-help book and she sighed. "You're missing the point, Claudia," she said. "I've run a bunch of scenarios and this is the only one that keeps your secret safe *and* spares my brother in the process."

As much as I hated to admit it, she was right. Assuming, of course, that Eli didn't question why I'd confessed my deepest, darkest secrets to him without mentioning any boyfriend whatsoever. Begrudgingly, I told her I was "in." This produced an enormous smile on Emily's face—for about thirty seconds. Then she remembered: we still had Debbie Ackerman to contend with.

We got to Debbie's house earlier than expected, and her mother insisted on fixing us a snack before we went shopping. Only, Mrs. Ackerman's version of "snack" is more like my idea of lunch. We each had half a grilled cheese sandwich, a cup of homemade chicken noodle soup, apple wedges, and a glass of milk. No wonder Deb was plump. Her mother never stopped feeding her!

While we ate, we talked about Operation Debbie. I wanted to hit Glenbrook Square Mall and pick out a cute outfit for her to wear to the Johnny Appleseed Festival tomorrow—including shoes and accessories. Afterward we'd hit the cosmetics department of Marshall Field's to find out what colors looked good on Debbie and then go to Rite Aid or Target to buy affordable counterparts.

So Emily drove us over to the mall. Our first stop was Delia's, where I picked out this adorable black mini with a drawstring waist and ruffled hem. Since Debbie's short, it fell just above her knee. It camouflaged both her butt *and* the thighs she so desperately hated. I paired it with a short-sleeved white shirt made out of some stretchy fabric that narrowed at the waist, giving her more definition, and a gray argyle sweater with a pumpkin-colored pattern running through it. Very "fall."

Debbie, of course, hated it.

"It's so . . . schoolgirl," she whined.

"It worked for Britney Spears," I shot back.

"In case you've failed to notice, I don't exactly share Britney's physique."

"So what?" I said. "You look good in this. Doesn't she look good, Em?"

Emily shrugged.

"Thank you," Debbie said to her, and retreated to the dressing room.

I told Emily that if her intention was to sabotage my makeover, then she was succeeding. But all she said was, "I'm just the chauffeur, remember?"

Meanwhile, Debbie kept picking up all of the wrong things. She went nuts for this high-necked, horizontal-striped sweater that was a size too small. It hugged every pudge roll she had and made her boobs look like two blimps trying to take flight. And she insisted on searching for a pair of boot-cut jeans, even though all of the ones she tried on made her hips and ass seem twice their actual size. The girl couldn't have gravitated to less-flattering clothes if she *tried*. It was actually comical.

So I decided to mess with her a bit. I started picking out the *least*-flattering things. Needless to say, Debbie thought they'd look great on her. It was hilarious: the girl's taste ran from trendy-ten-minutes-ago to downright tacky. In the end, I had her wearing a pink ruffled micromini and a white faux-angora turtleneck sweater with a circle of pink, red, and purple pansies embroidered across her chest. She absolutely loved it.

"Now, that's what I'm talking about," she said. "This is the kind of outfit boys notice."

"You're right," I said, totally egging her on. "It's fabulous. You *so* have to buy that."

Emily stifled a giggle. When Debbie went into the dressing room to change into her own clothes, Em whispered, "And you accused *me* of trying to sabotage the mission."

I shrugged. "I give up. That girl clearly knows nothing about fashion. What else can I do?"

Emily grabbed this gaudy red beret with a purple pleather band around the bottom. She waved it in front of me and said, "Bet you can't convince her she'll look hot in this, too."

"Oh, I *so* can."

"Prove it," Em said. "Winner buys the next round of Scoobys."

"You're on."

When Debbie reemerged, I walked right up to her, placed the hat on her head, tilted it to the right, and said, "Oh my God. Look at you. You were born to wear this beret."

"Really?" Deb asked. "You think?"

I nodded emphatically, and sure enough, she agreed.

I whispered to Em, "Don't think I won't collect."

As Deb proceeded to the cashier, I was struck by the sheer meanness of the situation. This girl was about to spend her life savings on the most hideous clothes ever made. As much as I liked my little joke, I couldn't let her go through with it.

"Um, Debbie . . . wait!" I called after her. "On second thought, maybe I'm wrong about the sweater, and the skirt too . . . and, yeah. That hat? So last season."

"What are you talking about?" Debbie snapped. "You said the outfit looked great on me!"

"Well, what I mean," I said mumbling, "is, ah, there's probably a sale happening at Target and we're going later anyway, so why not shop around? No harm in shopping around, right?"

Debbie laid her hand on my shoulder. "You've been a big help, Claudia. Really. But I think I know what looks best on me."

If that was the case, then why had she wanted me to take her shopping to begin with? I fought back the urge to deliver some sarcastic comment designed to wound.

"Debbie, wait. I was just—"

"Claudia, I'm not putting back this outfit. It's the one I want and I'm buying it," Debbie said firmly, handing the items to the cashier.

"Fine," I conceded. "Just put the hat back. I just remembered that I saw my math teacher wearing the same one."

"Okay," she agreed, after a pause, "I wasn't that into the hat anyway."

The cashier deducted the amount of the hat from her total. I turned to Emily, who was standing behind me, her mouth open in shock.

I shrugged. Emily frowned. It was an expression that said, "Nice work, dumbass. *Now* what are we going to do?"

The truth was, I had no idea.

At Payless, Debbie picked out a pair of calf-high leather boots in burgundy. Yeah, that's exactly what a girl with stubby legs should go for, especially when paired with a skirt so short it barely covered her panties. I tried to stop her, but it seemed Debbie was through listening. We trooped over to Claire's, and I halfheartedly tried to steer Debbie toward classic pearl studs. Instead, she found this pair of hot pink feather earrings. Of course, she fell instantly in love.

This is when the hair issue reared its ugly head (no pun intended). Debbie started freaking out about her frizzy curls, and suddenly she was all, "Let's go to the salon!" Nothing would deter her from this mission, not even the assurance that a relaxing hair balm and a ceramic straightening iron could achieve the same effect without being permanent.

So that's how Emily and I ended up here, camped out next to a koi pond in the Eden's lobby. We've been waiting here for an hour and a half, and the grilled cheese sandwich wore off ages ago. I was going to insist our next stop be dinner, but seeing as how I want to throttle Debbie and how Emily wants to throttle me, it doesn't seem like the smartest idea.

9/18

I just had the weirdest dream. It must've been because I spent so much time yesterday prepping Debbie for her fake date with Eli. I simply can't acknowledge any other reason why my subconscious mind would script that particular plot.

Because last night I dreamed that I was making out with Eli Whitmarsh. Not only that, I was *liking it*!

The twins will be here in less than an hour and I haven't even showered yet, so I best get moving.

9/18—*Later*

The special delivery Mama Bianca told Trudy she was sending arrived today. In fact, she's in my bathroom right now, taking one of her marathon showers.

That's because my "special delivery" was none other than Marissa Dahl herself.

My best friend! Marissa! Here! In Fort Wayne!

I still can't believe she's really in the next room. We'd been at the festival for most of the day when Trudy brought her over. Her "disguise" consisted of denim overalls, a white tee, brown shit-kickers, and a University of Indiana baseball cap, under which her hair was piled and pinned. Not to mention an obnoxious pair of Harry Potter–esque glasses and, strangest of all, some kind of retainer that flashed silver across her teeth. If I hadn't been one of six people in the world who's ever seen Marissa sans makeup, I never would've known it was her.

But first I should probably hit the rewind button, because a bunch of stuff happened even *before* Marissa arrived.

When the twins picked me up, I was given shotgun. It would've been fine, but Eli kept smiling at me, and I kept remembering my dream. Then at Debbie's house I made my move to the backseat, which wiped Eli's smile clean. Debbie got into the car, her face flushed with anticipation, and Eli didn't say word one about her "miraculous" transformation. By the time we got to the Johnny Appleseed Festival, Debbie was shooting daggers at me.

I know. *Fun.*

It could've been a disaster of a day except for the fact that the festival is actually sort of cool. I mean, okay—it's a little hokey, what with the people roaming around in period costumes and crafty grannies selling plastic tissue boxes embroidered with (you guessed it!) apples. And I honestly don't believe there's anyone in the world who is better off having tasted "fresh-fried apple scrapple."

That said, the minute you get to the fairgrounds, you can hear the bagpipes. The musicians march pretty steadily, winding their way through the crowd—and when I say "crowd," I mean it's like the entire population of the Glenbrook Square Mall (on a Saturday!) dumped into a space one-tenth the size. And the smells—incredible! Everything from roasted turkey legs to caramel kettle corn, and, of course, all things apple.

I let Eli steer me toward a cider booth, where he was gentlemanly enough to order four smalls instead of the two I knew he wished he was getting. He passed them around until each of us had one. Then we just stood there, not talking, the silence broken only by our loud slurping noises.

Debbie, who has soured enough to be declared a Granny Smith, wouldn't stop glaring at me. The worst part was, I could tell that even through the anger she was fighting back tears. Eli hadn't shown the tiniest bit of interest in her. I'm not sure he even noticed her new clothes and hair.

My fault, obviously, as I was the one who made her think she had a shot with Eli to begin with. So I decided to toss her a bone.

"Hey, Eli," I said, poking his arm. "Doesn't Debbie's hair look awesome?"

"Um, yeah," he replied. "Really great."

But he'd given her no more than a cursory glance before staring off into the distance.

So I tried a different tactic.

"Whoa," I said, pointing at a semi-hot boy in a Snider Panthers football jersey who was standing in line at the apple-burger booth. "That guy was totally scamming on you, Deb."

She craned her neck. "Who? What guy?"

"Come on," I said. "We'll go walk by."

I guided her away from the twins and said in a low voice, "What's going on with you?"

She snorted. "I could ask you the same thing."

When we'd put enough distance between us and the Whitmarshes, I said, "Look, the only reason Eli responds to me is because I actually talk to him. You have to stop getting so nervous around him. It doesn't matter how hot you look—if you can't hold a conversation, you'll never hook a guy like Eli."

Debbie smiled shyly. "You think I look hot?"

I surveyed the results of yesterday's makeover. It really should've been more of a makeunder, but what could I do about it now? If only she hadn't gotten rid of her curls. Clothes are easy to replace, and a damp tissue would take off most of that hot pink blush. But her stick-straight hair was permanent, at least until it grew out, and it made her moon face seem even moonier. So I did the only thing I could possibly do in the situation: I lied.

"Yes," I said, squeezing her elbow. "You look way hot. Now you just have to make sure Eli can actually *see* you."

She nodded like I'd just issued her a military order. Then she adjusted her miniskirt and said, "Let's do this thing."

Debbie turned up the charm, which was not good, considering the girl knew nothing about how to flirt properly. She ended up doing some strange version of TV sitcom flirting—lots of hair tossing, high-pitched giggles, putting on fake pouts, and poking Eli's side with her fingernail. It was like watching a train wreck.

Debbie Ackerman is to flirting what Jessica Simpson is to acting. In other words, truly horrible.

If that weren't bad enough, Eli kept looking at *me*. So intensely, like he wasn't seeing my dyed-to-dull brown hair, horn-rimmed glasses, and cheap chain store clothing. It was like he was looking into my *soul*.

Oh God, that looks even lamer on paper than it sounded in my head. But I can't think of how else to describe it. While he kept his eyes locked on me in a penetrating stare, he asked me all sorts of questions, and not necessarily personal ones. It was more like he wanted to know what I thought about certain things. For example, when we were watching one of the Civil War reenactments, he said, "I wonder if, a hundred years from now, there will be entire leagues of people devoted to reenacting battles from, say, the Vietnam War."

"Of course not," I said. "We only like to relive the wars where we did something good, like win freedom for the slaves or liberate the Jews. Plus, there's the whole television thing."

He asked me what I meant and I started talking about how Vietnam was the first war that got TV time and how once viewers could see the horrors of what was going on over there, war ceased to be glamorous. Then we ended up in this whole big discussion about war and the media in general, and whether if the American Revolution had been televised, we (as in, society) would still have the same view of it.

It was interesting—the conversation, I mean. I used to talk about stuff like this all the time, but no one really listened to what I had to say or took it seriously, except maybe Sam. Even Marissa, who knows me best of all, used to get bored when I'd get going on history. She couldn't make it through an entire episode of *Band of Brothers* without glazing over.

Then I noticed Debbie Ackerman trying to microwave me with her eyes, and my end of the conversation dried right up.

Debbie goes, "Oh my God, I'm *starving*. Let's go get lunch." It had been part of my early coaching, seeing as I know how Eli hates it when girls pick at their food. Only Debbie, in true Debbie fashion, took it to the wrong extreme. She ordered a large bowl of chicken corn chowder, an apple burger, a side of ham and beans, cornbread, *and* an oversized apple fritter—all of which she wolfed down and chased with an extra-large helping of apple blossom iced tea. I kept thinking she was going to go all Violet Beauregarde, only instead of turning into a giant blueberry, she'd morph into a Macintosh.

Needless to say, Eli was not enchanted.

We finished lunch and went to watch the Old Time Medicine Show. That's when I spotted Trudy. When I realized who was with her, I choked so hard that my own iced tea shot out my nose.

"Hello, darlin'," the disguised Marissa drawled, in this fake, indistinguishable accent that I think was a cross between southern and *Fargo*. "Livin' out here has done nothin' to improve yer table manners, don't ya know."

I thrust what was left of my drink at Eli, who was standing next to me, and threw my arms around Marissa in a hug, practically squealing with happiness. I kept saying stuff like, "Oh my God, I can't believe you're here, how did you find me?"

Then I realized that my Fort Wayne posse was standing there, staring at this uncharacteristic display of affection.

"Sorry," I said. "This is my best friend from back home. She's . . . unexpected. But in a good way."

"Yes," Trudy said, trying to catch my eye. "She's very early. And she *insisted* on coming here right away to surprise you."

Eli was the first to introduce himself, extending his hand. "And you are . . . ?"

"Daisy," Marissa replied. "Daisy Du—"

"—chovny," I finished for her, giving her a warning look. "Daisy Duchovny."

Debbie frowned. "Like that guy from *X-Files*?"

"Yes," I said. "But they're no relation."

"That's weird," Deb mused.

"What?" I asked.

"Your best friend and your boyfriend both have famous people's names."

"Boyfriend?" Eli repeated.

"Boyfriend?" Marissa-as-Daisy echoed. "Which *boyfriend* is this?"

"Evan," I said tightly.

Marissa wouldn't let up. "Surely you don't mean Evan *Walsh*? *My* ex-boyfriend?"

I laughed nervously. "Come on, *Daisy*. That was years and years ago. Besides, I told you that he just dumped me, remember? Now he's my ex-boyfriend too."

"Oh . . . *right*," Marissa purred, clearly amused. And then, as if she suddenly remembered her accent, she said, "Would this young gentleman here be willing to get a lady a fresh cuppa apple cider and a corn dawg?"

Eli dispatched himself immediately; Trudy went with him, though I wasn't sure why. I guess because they'd bonded the other night over dinner? I quickly told the other girls that "Daisy" and I would be right back and dragged Marissa out of earshot.

"Oh my God! What are you doing here?" I asked.

"Bianca sent me," she said. "It was all her idea. She said you were feeling a little 'lost' and could I please go cheer you up? Considering the company you've been keeping, I'm not surprised." Marissa snort-laughed. "I can't believe they stashed you here," she continued. "For God's sake, Morgan, look at this place!"

"Shut up!" I growled. "I'm Claudia—*at all times*."

Marissa fumbled through her pockets until she located a

semi-crushed pack of Marlboro Reds. "I know," she said, lighting one. "Mama B made me sign this confidentiality agreement before she'd hand over the plane ticket. If I 'out' you—accidentally or otherwise—I am legally bound to pay you more than five mil in damages."

Leave it to Bianca. "Money" should have been her middle name.

Marissa shook her head, amazed. "This . . . country festival. It is so obviously the place where tacky came to die. Can we get out of here? Please?" I told her not yet and she whined, "Why not?"

"Because," I said. "You sent Eli to buy you food, remember? And we definitely can't leave without Trudy."

"*Her,*" Marissa growled. "It took me over an hour to convince her to bring me here. She's so . . . I don't know. Rigid? Someone needs to remove that stick up her ass and show her a truly good time."

Her snap judgment of Trudy made the hairs on my neck bristle. "Be nice," I warned her. "You have no idea how good to me she's been."

But Marissa just rolled her eyes.

I led her back to where I'd left Em and Debbie. "Remember," I said as we walked, "I'm *Claudia*. Beyond that, try not to say anything. We'll go home as soon as possible, I promise."

Eli and Trudy had already returned, and when we rejoined the group, Eli handed Marissa her treats. She took one bite off the corn dog and made a gagging sound. "I don't think I can eat this. Here," she said, thrusting it in Debbie's direction. "You look like the kind of girl who enjoys a good dog."

Debbie flashed me a look of helplessness, but I guess my

earlier coaching had ingrained itself in her brain. "Sure," she said weakly. "Thanks."

"So, what's next, y'all?" Marissa asked the group. "Is it time to go flirt with the farm boys or do the Electric Slide?"

Again, I bristled. I realized the Fort Wayneans weren't exactly the epitome of cool, but did Marissa have to mock them so blatantly?

Two bites into the dog Deb started turning green. "I don't think I can finish this," she said, handing it off to Em. "I feel like I'm going to—"

Before she could finish her sentence, puke spewed from her mouth—and went ALL OVER MARISSA.

A steady stream of curses passed through Marissa's lips. I couldn't help it; I felt myself struggling to resist a smile. Where was Eli's camera when you needed it? The image of a horrified, vomit-covered Marissa was too classic. Luckily, Debbie's hurling also provided a viable excuse for us to bug out early—something we desperately needed to do.

Eli insisted on walking us to Trudy's car, even though I told him he didn't have to. Emily stayed behind, nursing Debbie, and Tru took Marissa to a nearby Porta Potti to get cleaned up. For a moment, we stood by the Saturn all alone.

"I can't believe Debbie threw up on your friend," he said.

"Me either."

"Before that, though," he continued. "I had a really great time. Maybe . . . I mean . . . do you think we might be able to go out again sometime?"

I couldn't stop myself from blurting out, "What about my boyfriend?"

He looked confused. "I thought you said you broke up with him."

"I did," I said. "Recently. I mean, like *really* recently. So recently that I haven't told anybody but Ma—" I stopped myself just in time. "My Daisy," I finished. "She's the only one who knows. Well, except for you and your sister and Debbie."

"Oh. Yeah, I understand," he said, but the naked disappointment in his voice led me to believe otherwise.

If I hadn't had that dream, and if Eli hadn't been so nice to me, it would've stopped there. But it didn't.

I put my hands on Eli's deceptively strong shoulders, stood on my tippy toes, and gave him a quick kiss flat on his mouth. "Thank you for today," I said. "I had a lot of fun. I just . . . need a little more time."

The weirdest thing? It wasn't completely a lie.

Eli chuckled. "Know what? You look normal, but really? You're so *weird*. Someday I'll figure you out, Claudia Miller. Someday."

Of course, that's exactly what I'm afraid of.

Trudy got me and Marissa back to the house, safe and still in disguise. There was so much I wanted to say, but Marissa insisted on cleaning up before we settled in for some girl talk.

Holy crap! I just looked at the clock—Marissa has been in the bathroom for almost two whole hours. I better go check up on her and make sure everything's okay.

9/18—*Much later*

Some things never change.

Marissa was still in the bathroom, all right—talking to the newest boyfriend on her cell. She was sitting on the counter, wrapped in fluffy white towels that she must've brought herself, a bad-girl smile painted across her lips. She held up her pointer finger and mouthed, "One sec," and I was practically jumping up and down, dying to know with whom she's really been canoodling.

Finally, she purred, " 'Bye, baby," and hung up.

"Who?" I demanded, hands on hips.

Marissa raised one eyebrow, looking a little like Madonna, and said, "You couldn't handle it."

"Try me."

Eventually she confessed the name of her latest lover man, but I will not put it in writing. Not to protect the not-so-innocent, but because it wouldn't be fair to Marissa. Especially not after she signed that confidentiality agreement Bianca had drafted.

If you must have a mental image, think middle-aged, Oscar-winning actor who, despite being married to a certi-fied babe—with whom he has four children—still likes to date young girls on the side.

My jaw dropped to my knees.

"Told you," Marissa said, grinning wickedly. "But hey— we can talk about my sordid affairs later. Let me get a good look at you!"

She jumped off the vanity, stood back, and cocked her towel-turbaned head. In a former life I would've vamped it up for her, doing fake supermodel poses, but the second Marissa's baby blues lasered in on me, I became even more self-conscious about the weight I'd put on.

After what felt like several uncomfortable minutes, Marissa nodded. "You got curves, woman." My breath stopped dead in my lungs. Then she added, "Me likey."

I did the standard girl thing and shrugged off the compliment. "I look like a pig."

"Oh, *whatever*," she said. "That hair I'm not so crazy about. But the bod—it's smokin', Morgan. Like Kate Winslet with better boobs. Seriously."

This time, I didn't protest, but I rolled my eyes to let her know I still wasn't buying it.

I wanted to ask her so many things—did she know about my mom and Sam? What had our mutual friends been up to? Was anyone spreading crazy rumors about my "disappearance"? But before I could spring a single question, Marissa squealed and said, "I almost forgot—I brought you prezzies!"

Still wearing nothing but the towels, she shooed me toward her luggage—three full-sized pieces, all hot pink Diane von Furstenberg (how long was she planning on staying, anyway?)—and pulled out a gift-wrapped box that looked like it came from Neiman's.

"You didn't have to buy me anything," I said. "The fact that you're here is present enough."

"Oh, gag," she replied. "Of course I did. It's practically your birthday."

"Not for, like, two more weeks," I reminded her.

"Shut up," she said, "and open it."

Inside was an Ugg backpack in baby pink sheepskin and suede. Marissa beamed. "It's for school," she said. "To dress up the books." It was such a cute bag, but I didn't have the heart to tell her that (a) I'd need four of them to fit all of my books inside and (b) "Claudia Miller" couldn't go to class sporting designer anything.

"Look inside," she said. "There's more."

The package inside the backpack revealed a small, long-but-skinny Kate Spade purse, also in pale pink. I squealed, even though I'd have to stash it with the Ugg. "It's gorgeous," I gushed. "You're way too generous."

"Keep going," she said again.

"There's more?"

"More."

Inside the purse was a matching Kate Spade wallet, a Chanel Glossimer in Cry Baby, and a mini-bottle of my favorite Marc Jacobs perfume. I couldn't help myself; I immediately opened the atomizer and spritzed my neck. It smelled heavenly.

"Marissa!" I exclaimed. "Why did you do all this?"

"Because," she said, "you deserve it. But don't stop now—you've got other pockets to go through."

I shook my head. "No. This is already completely insane."

But sure enough, there were more goodies in the front flap of the Ugg: a camera phone covered in pink Swarovski crystals—just like Sarah Jessica Parker's from *Sex & the City*, a pair of pink plastic Gucci sunglasses with pink-tinted frames, and a shimmery pink iPod mini.

I looked at all of the pink spread across my bed and laughed. "I feel so *Legally Blonde*."

Marissa laughed too, clearly pleased with herself. "I thought, if Morgan has to be stuck in a dreary public high school, the least I could do is give her a few simple essentials to brighten up her days."

"You're too much."

And it *was* too much—all of it, really—but as shallow as this sounds, there was something so comforting about being surrounded by such pretty, expensive things. It felt like the old days, before I was branded a washed-up addict—before I'd all but killed my career.

Then I realized, in the old days, we would've celebrated Marissa's shopping spree with a coordinated drink—say, pink champagne or super-strong cosmos. We'd sit at the bar, crossing our legs so that our miniskirts showed maximum thigh, tricking old men into buying us more drinks by tying knots in our cherry stems using only our tongues.

And then I flashed forward to today. Now my idea of a good time is hanging out with the twins at the Johnny Appleseed Festival and nursing a chilled sassafras tea. I wanted to ask, "How did I get here from there?" but I already knew the answer.

"Smile," Marissa said, breaking my train of thought. "Presents are supposed to make you happy!"

"I'm happy you're here," I said.

She nodded in agreement. "Me too."

By this time it was going on seven and I was starting to get hungry. I ticked through a list of restaurants Trudy and I had checked out since I moved in, trying to think of a place Marissa might like. Then it hit me: let me show her something distinctly Fort Wayne. To me, that meant Munchies. I told her to get dressed (as Daisy, of course) so we could go grab some grub.

But the minute we opened our menus, I knew it was the worst-possible place I could've taken her. It had been a really long time since I'd looked at the world as pre-rehab Morgan Carter—the Morgan Carter who would've died rather than choke down fried potatoes in public. I could see Marissa's frown as she scanned the fat- and carb-rich items that were standard Munchie fare.

When the waiter arrived, Marissa ordered Perrier and a small salad, hold the carrots and with the fat-free vinaigrette dressing on the side. I came *this close* to saying, "I'll have the same," when I realized I didn't want to have what she was having. My rabbit-feeding days were over (for now). Besides, hadn't Marissa just complimented my curves?

So I ordered the usual—Scooby Snacks with extra Munchie dip and a Diet Coke. I added a cup of corn chowder on the side, just because I could.

I felt really pleased with myself until I saw that Marissa's frown had deepened. "What is it?" I asked. "Do you want to go somewhere else?"

She shook her head. "It's just—wow."

"What's 'wow'?" I didn't like where this was going.

"It's nothing," Marissa said. "Except—"

"Go on," I urged. "Spill it."

She sighed lightly. "Come on, Morgan. Corn chowder? Why didn't you just order a side of 'heart attack'?"

I knew her comment came from "a place of concern," but it pissed me off anyway. This was the first time I'd seen Marissa in almost a year. I'd barely even talked to her the whole time I was in Crapplewood. She shows up for five minutes and suddenly she's an expert on me and my life? Yes, I know I'm stuck in Fort Lame, but despite all of the shit that came along with this move, I'm actually doing okay. No drugs. No alcohol. No boys. So what if I have a fetish for cream-based soups?

ME: I like corn chowder.
MARISSA: You used to like acid, too, but I don't see you dropping it every chance you get.

ME: Ouch.

MARISSA: I'm sorry. It's just that . . . well, Morgan, do you *ever* plan on working again?

ME: Of course. That's why I'm here, remember?

MARISSA (rolling her eyes): This place is a joke. You'd have been better off hiring a personal trainer and doing off-off-Broadway theater until you could, like, snag a part in the latest Aaron Spelling series.

ME: You said I looked good like this.

MARISSA (with an exasperated sigh): You're missing my point.

ME: Well, what *is* your point?

MARISSA: My point is that you shouldn't be here. This town—it has no culture. No anything! Look at this restaurant, for God's sake. Everything looks so *dingy*. I know you, Morgan. Every day you spend here, you're going to wither just a little bit more.

ME (in a quavering voice): Excuse me, but you *don't* know me anymore, Marissa. You don't have the faintest idea what I've been through. Hell, you never even bothered to visit me in rehab!

MARISSA: I read your letters. The ones you sent then and the ones you've been sending me now.

ME: Oh. Well. It's so admirable of you to take the time to read your personal correspondence.

MARISSA: Enough with the sarcasm, okay?

ME: No. Not okay. Because if you want to boil it down to the simplest of parts, it's like this: one day I was your favorite party girl, and then the next I almost died. You couldn't handle that, so you just cut me loose.

MARISSA: That's not fair, Morgan.

ME: Yeah, tell me about it.

MARISSA: Maybe I wasn't there for you in the way you needed me to be. But watching you OD that night—it was hard for me too. Christ, I was almost as high as you were. It could've been me! You don't know how long it took me to get rid of that fear. Not to mention the guilt.

ME: Well, I'm sorry, Marissa. I guess I forgot everything is about *you*.

MARISSA: Damn it! If you want to be pissed at me, that's fine—but at least be pissed for the right reasons.

ME: Oh? What are those?

MARISSA: Me not knowing how bad things had gotten for you. Or how much you were using. And you're right—I should've visited you when you were at that . . . that place. More importantly, I never, ever should've never let them stash you away somewhere. I should've insisted you come live with me instead of the country folk they've got you mixed up with.

ME: Country folk? Marissa, what movie did you wake up in today?

MARISSA: Oh, come off it! I read your letters, Morgan. Do you really think that Billy Joe and Skippy Sue are a positive influence on you? What, do you help them milk their cows and go to church with them every Sunday?

ME: I cannot believe you said that. The Whitmarsh twins are good people. They do volunteer work—not because it's a photo op or PR stunt, but because they honestly give a shit about something. And "Skippy Sue"—do you know she tutors me for free? She and her brother are always driving me around places. They even took me to a baseball game! With their parents!

MARISSA: Oh my God. Are you telling me you actually *like* these local yokels?

ME: Stop calling them names! Jesus—when did you become such a heartless *bitch*?

Of course "bitch" was our waiter's cue to deliver Marissa's plate of lettuce and my steaming Scooby Snacks. I tried to flash the guy a silent apology, but Marissa barked, "What the hell are you looking at? *And where's my goddamned Perrier?*"

And then her face went blank, and she said, "Excuse me. I need to use the ladies' room." I watched her walk right past the restrooms and out the front door. For a second I wondered if she was just going to leave me there, but that's not Marissa's style. She probably needed a break to cool off. So did I, for that matter.

The food smelled good, but I was no longer hungry. Not because of Marissa's snarky comments, either. It was because I simply felt sick inside. How long had I been dying for even five minutes of girl time with Marissa? Now she was here, and there was a part of me that just wanted her to go away.

I tried to imagine what I must look like to her after all this time. I'm not talking about the physical stuff, necessarily. I'm talking about my *life*. It was inconceivable to Marissa that I could feel anything but disdain for Indiana, but the minute she started criticizing Fort Wayne, Trudy, and the twins, I felt hot. Angry. Who was she to judge?

But hadn't I done the exact same thing? From the very minute I stepped off the puddle jumper? So how could I be angry with Marissa? But I was. Am. Was.

I'm so confused. I thought seeing Marissa would remind me of who I am. But really, it's only reminding me of who I used to be. The gap between the two is wider than I thought. I'm not sure I'm ready to deal with that, either.

Eventually Marissa came back to the table. She apologized, as did I, but we mostly picked at our food in silence. Then Marissa said, "You want to get out of here?"

I said I did and flagged the waiter for our check. Marissa insisted on paying and I didn't fight her, though I probably should have. We didn't talk the whole way back to the house.

Before we went in, Marissa grabbed my wrist. "Morgan—wait."

"What is it?" I asked.

Her eyes were half filled with tears. "I really am sorry."

I told her I was too and she nodded, but then she started to cry. I asked her what was wrong, but she kept shaking me off. Finally, she sat down on the front stoop and waited for the sobs to subside.

"I was really terrified that night at the Viper Room. All I could think about were all the people who died there—wondering if we were going to have to add your name to the list. But I was also angry with you for doing so many drugs and for being stupid enough to mix them like you did.

"I swore to God that if you lived, I'd go completely clean. And I did, for a while. No alcohol or anything. I still haven't touched any drugs—not even pot—but I drink once in a while. Not like we used to. But, you know, some champagne here, some whiskey there. It makes me feel guilty, though. Like I'm backing out on my promise."

It felt like a lot for her to lay on me, especially after our heated dinner discussion. But I could see that she was being sincere, so I said, "I feel guilty too, you know."

"Why?" she asked.

"The obvious reasons," I replied. "Scaring my friends. Bianca. Throwing away everything we'd ever worked for. But also I keep thinking that a lot of people's livelihoods depended on me. I'm not saying that Sam Rosenbaum's eating out of trash cans because I'm no longer a working client. But still, I was income. When I lost my job, they lost a piece of theirs."

Marissa laughed and wiped some remaining tears from her swollen eyes. "I never would've thought of it like that," she said. "But it's so typical of you, Morgan—you've always seen yourself as someone else's dollar sign."

Before her words could fully sink in, she gasped. "I almost forgot! Wait right here," she instructed. She ran over to the rental car and fished around the trunk for a minute.

When she returned, she was carrying a business-sized envelope.

"From your mother," she said.

I could spend fifty pages writing about all the things I felt while reading the letter, but in the end, I think Bianca's words speak for themselves. So, I'm pasting the letter here in my journal instead.

Dear Morgan,

I know you're angry with me. I can't say I blame you. We should've told you about us before you left L.A., but Sam was concerned that you'd think he suggested the high school plan as a means of "getting rid" of you. Morgan, you have to believe me when I tell you that is the last thing either of us would want to do. Sam has always thought of you as his daughter, and we both love you very much.

But I would be lying if I said we didn't have any ulterior motives in sending you to stay with Trudy. The truth is, Morgan, we were afraid you couldn't continue your recovery here. It's not that we didn't trust you; it's everybody else. The friends you partied with. The dealers who'd find your phone number, no matter how many times we changed it. Too many temptations and too much free time.

The part about Sam not being able to find you work—that was true, Morgan. I wish it wasn't, because I know how important your career is to you. Sam spent a lot of time trying to figure out a way to get things back on track. I know you think it's the "plot of a bad movie," and I admit, it's extreme. But sweetheart—for the first time in your life, you're allowed to be a normal girl. It's an experience that money cannot buy you, and I hope you're taking advantage of the opportunity—maybe even enjoying it.

As for me and Sam . . . we fell in love while you were staying at the facility. It's exactly how you might imagine it—me seeking comfort from him, him seeking solace from me. Both of us blamed ourselves for your "problems." Me because I think, on some level, I always knew what you were doing. I knew that whatever it was made you look fragile and unhealthy. My weakness was that I didn't know how to stop it, so I pretended it didn't exist.

When Sam confessed to me that he had firsthand knowledge of your "problems," I was so angry at him. How could he know and not tell *me*, your own mother? Then I realized that he carried as much guilt as I did and that whatever secrets he kept for you were to protect *me* from the truth.

It doesn't excuse what we did—or didn't do—for you. You will never know how sorry I am, Morgan. But I can't apologize for falling in love with Sam, because he's the second-best thing that ever happened to me, right after *you*.

I'd like it if you'd consider meeting Sam and me in the Fiji Islands for your winter break. I think it would give us all a chance to heal and become a real family.

Your loving mother,
Bianca

9/19

Today Marissa and I drove about fifty miles south to Fairmount to visit James Dean's grave. The place was like a dead zone (no pun intended). It was just a normal, pink marble headstone with a couple of flowers and a candle resting on it. For some reason, Marissa thought there'd be more people at his grave—"Like with Elvis!" she said—but

Fairmount has a population of three thousand and it looks like the kind of town that time forgot (and not necessarily in a good way). Also, as a kind elderly lady informed us, next weekend is the James Dean Festival, which is when his admiring fans make the yearly pilgrimage to his grave.

"Great," I said. "Now what?"

We consulted the road map we'd picked up during the drive down—Marissa saw the signs for Gas Town and thought it would be funny for us to get gas there, even though the tank was mostly full—and we figured out that Indianapolis wasn't that much farther away.

"Let's go see if we can find some culture," Marissa said, and sped off.

On the way we saw a sign advertising the Museum of Miniature Houses, which Marissa insisted we had to visit. So we made another stop, this time in Carmel. I have to admit, the craftsmanship that goes into the models is impressive, but they're not something you can stare at long-term. We whipped through the museum and its adjoining gift shop in under an hour.

As we strapped our seat belts back on, I turned to Marissa and said, "What are we doing?"

"What do you mean?" she asked. "We're seeing the sights!"

I rolled my eyes. "Be real," I said. "What we're really doing is trying to avoid a repeat of yesterday. Right? Numbing our brains to avoid another awkward outpouring of emotion."

Marissa sighed, pushed her black Oliver Peoples sunglasses onto her head, and looked straight at me. "Look—I'm sorry this trip is such a bust. I thought we'd spend the weekend hanging out, staying up late so we could talk about boys and clothes and everything we don't get to talk about anymore."

"Me too!" I said. "Every time I wished you were here, that's all I wanted. Just to talk and be silly and have fun."

"But there's all this . . . *stuff* between us. It feels too—"

"Heavy," I cut in. "So let's get rid of it! We'll wipe it all clean. You be you, and I'll be me, and we'll just enjoy the time we have until you fly back. Okay?"

"Do you think you can do that?" she asked. "You seemed pretty angry with me yesterday. For a lot of things."

I nodded. "I'm sorry I exploded at you like that. It's just—"

"What?" she prompted.

"I'm building this new life here," I said. "And it's hard. Like, harder than rehab, in some ways. But I'm doing it. And then you waltzed in and started criticizing everything, including the only people in Fort Wayne who don't treat me like some sort of social pariah. . . . I just felt like, 'Who are you to judge them? To judge *me*?'"

Marissa's nose wrinkled in that I'm-trying-not-to-cry position. "I didn't mean to hurt your feelings," she said, "or insult your friends. From your letters . . . you seemed really unhappy here. I thought you needed a bitch session. That's all."

She reached out and squeezed my hand. Then she said, "Look, I know I can be a real selfish asshole. But you're my best friend, Morgan—you're like my *sister*. And I love you, even if sometimes I suck at showing it."

We hugged. It felt good.

"Come on," Marissa said. "Let's get you home."

Back in the Fort, we swung by Doc Rickers and Marissa bought six pints of Ben & Jerry's because she couldn't decide which flavor she'd like best (typical). Then we went home and changed into pj's and set up camp in the living room, dishing about boys and work (Marissa) and school (me).

"So tell me about your secret lover man," I said.

Marissa rolled her eyes. "What's to tell? It's almost over, anyway."

"Over? When did it start?"

"About three months ago," she said, through a mouthful of Cookie Dough. "I met him at P. Diddy's birthday party. He was one of the oldest guys there, so of course I was immediately attracted to him."

"You and your father complex," I mused.

"I know, right?" Marissa ran the spoon around the edges of the carton like we always did, to get the melty bits. "This one might have cured me, though. Old guys these days are getting more and more insecure. Who wants to spend their Friday nights stroking somebody's ego?"

I laughed. "Bet that's not all you're stroking."

"Dirty girl," Marissa said. "What about you? Have you been getting any hot farm boy action?"

I shook my head. "Standard first-year-of-recovery rules: no lust allowed."

"But, darlin'," she said in her Daisy voice, "lust is what keeps us *alive*."

For a minute I considered telling her about Eli's crush on me. But I knew she'd just make a lot of crude jokes about church pews and tractor seats, so I held my tongue. Instead I regaled her with tales of Mr. Sappey's snottiness.

"And the worst part is," I said, "my next paper is supposed to be a 'cultural reading of a film that has great emotional resonance.' Translation: some elitist Jim Jarmusch joint that has no discernible plotline whatsoever."

"You said 'joint.'" Marissa snickered. She grabbed my

pint of Chunky Monkey and stabbed her spoon into it. "You know, that's not a bad idea."

"Jim Jarmusch?"

"No," she said. "A Spike Lee joint. Like *Do the Right Thing* or—I know! *Malcolm X*. Talk about how he cast Denzel in the title role."

It took me a minute to see where she was going, but then something clicked. "Because Denzel is America's favorite black actor," I began.

"Except for Will Smith," she cut in.

"Right," I said. "But Denzel has more range, and he's one of the only people who could've gotten away with playing such a radical figure. If they'd put, say, Ice-T in the role, it wouldn't have worked. It had to be Denzel."

Marissa rang an imaginary bell with her spoon. "Perzactly."

"You, my dear, are a genius," I said. "There's no way Sappey can fail me with that as my premise."

"Well, there's that. Or you could, you know, slip him a benjamin."

Marissa crapped out around 2 a.m. and is snoring softly in my room. I can't sleep. Not that that's so unusual for me. Except the reason I can't sleep tonight is that I feel too damned good. Marissa and I had a great time, and no alcohol was needed. It's a totally different kind of high, and I'm just hoping it lasts even after Marissa is gone.

I should try to go to sleep soon, though, or I don't know how I'll make it through school tomorrow.

Week
SIX

9/20

I've been kidnapped!

Well, not exactly. I'm writing this from the deluxe executive suite at the Ritz-Carlton in Chicago. More specifically, from a plush velvet chair the color of Dijon mustard, and I'm wearing nothing but a cream-colored, spa-quality Turkish terry bathrobe and complimentary black lace thong, inhaling the intoxicating scent of fresh-baked chocolate croissants and French-pressed café au lait. God, I'd honestly forgotten how much I love overpriced hotel rooms—especially ones outfitted with not one but two full-sized bathrooms and a separate dressing area complete with an Italian marble vanity.

Yeah. That's what I'm talking about.

I'm not supposed to be here, of course. I'm supposed to be at Snider High School, taking that stupid standardized test and meeting with Ms. Janet Moore just so I can skip my best friend Mr. Sappey's film class hell. But Marissa made me an offer I simply couldn't refuse.

It happened like this:

Because we went to bed so late last night, Trudy had a really hard time waking me up this morning and I missed the bus. She was going to drive me to school herself, but then Marissa said she was on her way to the airport anyway, so she might as well drive me. Trudy looked a little dubious—in fact, when she hugged me goodbye, the last thing she said was, "Morgan, *please* don't skip school again. Okay?" I said I wouldn't, which at the time wasn't a lie because I wasn't planning on skipping anything.

So then I got ready for school and Marissa got ready for the airport, and we loaded her bags into the rental and took off for Snider. When she pulled up to the curb, I said, "This sucks. I feel like we just caught up and now you're taking off again."

That's when she said, "I have an idea."

I knew that skipping school—especially after promising Trudy I wouldn't—was a bad idea. But right then, with Marissa giving me her patented let's-be-bad-girls face, I didn't care about being good.

At that moment, being good was boring.

So Marissa called the airline to change her departure date, and we drove to Chicago.

The drive itself was pretty horrible. Lots of flat land that looked like nobody had loved it in a long time. I got excited when I realized we had to drive through Gary, Indiana, on the way, because Gary is the hometown of the Jackson 5 (one of my all-time favorite bands) and the subject of a song from *The Music Man* (one of the all-time great musicals). Sadly, it turns out that Gary is like the bleakest, most desolate-looking place on earth. Everything in it is industrial. Definitely a disappointment.

Then we hit Chicago, and Marissa rolled up to the Ritz. Two valet guys took our bags and another took the car keys, and all I could think was, This *is where I belong*. Marissa checked herself in as Betty Rubble (her favorite hotel alias) and I used my old standby, Angela Chase (protagonist from the classic teen drama *My So-Called Life*). Later I wondered if that was such a good idea, because I'm pretty sure there are some paparazzi and media types who know I used to use that name. But then I realized—no one's looking for me in Chicago, if they're looking for me at all.

It was almost noon when we finally settled into our suite. Marissa dialed room service and ordered us egg-white-and-veggie omelets and a basket of assorted croissants. ("They'll cancel each other out," she assured me.) Then she retreated to her bathroom, cell phone in hand, and I haven't seen her since. Which is fine by me because right now I feel so completely *relaxed*.

Now that I'm all caught up on journaling, I think I'll go take a dip in the Jacuzzi tub myself. Hopefully by the time I'm done, Marissa will be ready to rock. We have big, big plans for today. Marissa thinks we should try to stalk Oprah while we boutique-shop our way around the city.

Love Marissa! *Love* her!

9/20—*Later*

If shopping were an Olympic sport, Marissa would be a five-time gold medalist. Seriously, that girl can spend money like nobody's business. But the best part is, she knows exactly how to justify completely unnecessary purchases, so you end up feeling really good that you just spent $157 plus tax on a pair of Seven jeans that make your ass look like it was custom-sculpted by one of the top plastic surgeons in L.A.

Technically the $157 plus tax is Marissa's money, since Bianca took away my plastic before I came here. But Marissa gave me a Visa and said, "Get whatever you want—I'll bill your mom later." From that point on I went a little crazy.

THE DAMAGE:

- The aforementioned Seven "Rocker" straight-legged jeans—$157
- Black Betsey Johnson velvet coat with embroidered pink flowers—$335
- Marc by Marc Jacobs silk charmeuse cami in pink—$188
- Lacoste short-sleeved stretch piqué polo in white—$72
- Free People slouchy striped trousers in gray—$92
- Juicy Couture smocked velour tube dress in raspberry—$92
- Sweat Pea poncho in pale pink with detachable mesh flower—$72
- Dr. Scholl's old-school sandals with rainbow strap—$40
- Kate Spade floral-printed ankle-strap pumps—$265
- Michael by Michael Kors classic flap-style suede purse in leaf green—$168
- Fresh Flowers chandelier earrings in brass and multi-colored Swarovski crystals—$60
- Le Mystère bra with removable straps in buttercream—$58
- Le Mystère low-rise thong, also in buttercream—$18

GRAND TOTAL SPENT (including tax): $1,762.53

Of course the grand total doesn't cover all the stuff Marissa declared "on her." Like the body wraps, hot glove manicures, and whirlpool pedicures we got at Channing's Day Spa. Then, feeling pampered beyond belief, we caught a cab over to the Sephora on Michigan Avenue, where Marissa proceeded to play stylist. At first I was almost insulted—I mean, I've been doing my own makeup almost as long as she has—but then I realized there's a million new products I'd yet to be introduced to.

I was having so much fun that I didn't stop to think that I might possibly be recognized. But as the day wore on, I gradually realized that Marissa was dressed in typical "undercover celebrity" garb—worn jeans and a plain T-shirt paired with a fitted blazer and very expensive shoes (in Marissa's case, an exquisite pair of bottle green Jimmy Choo heels), a baseball cap worn low, and the darkest possible pair of sunglasses. As for me, I was dressed for a typical day at Snider High, but between the two of us and the many, many bags we were carting around, it wasn't hard to tell we could be somebodies.

Marissa must've sensed my discomfort, because she said it was time to go back to our suite and rest up so that we'd be fresh for dinner. It was maybe four o'clock, and I knew I didn't have much time before Trudy found out about my truancy. So while Marissa got changed into her napping outfit—and yes, she actually does have a pair of pajamas specifically for napping—I took out my new cell phone and dialed home.

Surprisingly, Trudy answered.

"Hey," I said, "why aren't you at work?"

"Are you kidding me?" she growled. "Where the hell are *you*?"

Long story short, when Mr. Pickles submitted the absentee

list to the office, I got flagged because I was supposed to be taking my ISTEP+ qualifying exam. Can we say, "Oops"? So the secretary called my guardian (aka Trudy) to ask why I wasn't at school. Trudy called both the house and my cell (the old one that I left at home), and when I didn't answer either, she feared the worst. She'd been on the phone with everyone from Ms. Janet Moore to Bianca ever since. Trudy had even called my sponsor, who was extra concerned because she hadn't seen me at a meeting recently. Gaby got Tru so worked up that she was convinced I was doing whippits in a ditch somewhere.

"I'm fine," I said. "I'm with Marissa."

"Well, I knew that," she snapped. "Where exactly are you and the Hollywood hussy?"

I told her and she went ballistic. "This is unacceptable, Morgan," she fumed. "How am I supposed to trust you when you lie to me point-blank? You promised you'd go to school."

I tried to explain that it hadn't been an intentional lie, but Trudy wasn't calm enough to fully comprehend. I don't think it would've mattered anyway. She was livid, and I was in big, big trouble.

"You tell that girl to take you to the bus station and buy you a ticket home. I want you in your bed by midnight, do you hear me?"

I heard her, but I didn't want to. We had plans. Dinner. Late-night dancing. Finding a cool, all-night diner for break-fast at 3 a.m. Like the good old days.

"That's not possible," I said, trying to sound calm.

Trudy didn't respond right away; at first I thought she might not have heard me. Then, out of nowhere, a stream of obscenities like I'd never heard before—not from Trudy, not from anyone.

"Now, Morgan!" she was screaming. "You get your lying ass home right this minute!"

I waited until she calmed down some. Then I said, "Look, today has been fun. Today I didn't have to be Claudia Miller. But I wasn't Morgan Carter, either. I was just this nameless, faceless person hanging out with my best friend in the whole world."

"And running up her Visa bill!" Marissa chimed in from across the room.

"Shhh!" I hissed. Then to Trudy I said, "I'll be home by tomorrow night, I promise."

"Your promises aren't worth shit," Trudy spat. I'd never heard her so angry, not even with Bianca.

"I'm safe," I said. "I'm sober. I'm just . . . trying to have a good time."

Trudy let out a loud, exasperated sigh. "I can't even talk to you right now, Morgan. And I can't even begin to tell you how deeply disappointed I am. Maybe this whole arrangement was a bad idea. It's one thing to scare the piss out of your mother—it's another to throw that burden on me."

With that, she hung up.

I was stunned. No, I was beyond stunned. I was speechless.

"Ooh, are you grounded?" Marissa quipped, looking more than amused.

"Not funny," I said. "Maybe I should go back now. Trudy is way mad."

But Marissa wasn't having any of that. "Bullshit! You're here, you're having fun, and in another twenty-four hours we're going to be living in different time zones again. I'm not ready to say goodbye yet, and I don't think you are either."

She was right, but I still felt terrible.

"Listen, Morgan," Marissa said. "Fort Wank isn't your real life. Trudy isn't your mom. In less than a year you're going to be back in L.A., back to being a working adult. Trudy should remember that. *You* should remember that."

So . . . much to chew over. Marissa's alarm is about to go off and I haven't napped at all. My stomach is in knots. How am I supposed to enjoy tonight when all I can think about is how angry and disappointed Trudy is?

I would do just about anything for half a Xanax right now.

I'm only half kidding.

9/21

I'm on the same puddle jumper that flew me from Chicago into Fort Wayne a month and a half ago. I know this because it smells the same—like bologna soaked in orange juice. It's got the same rattle, too. The only difference is that this time, I'm prepared.

Last night was all kinds of crazy fun. Just getting dressed to go out was a total blast. Marissa put on a pair of Pucci pants that were sherbet orange with swirls of hot pink, lilac, lemon, and white. So Austin Powers. For a top she chose a white, sleeveless Armani turtleneck that was just short enough to show off a bit of belly. The kicker, though, was the black pageboy wig, super-furry false eye lashes, and cat-eye rhinestone glasses that made up the rest of her costume du jour.

As for me, I slipped into my new Juicy tube dress and ass-flattering Seven jeans. The Kate Spade pumps, green suede purse, and flowered chandelier earrings completed my own look, which was way hott. That's right—two *t*'s worth of *hot*. I couldn't stop staring at myself. I'd just spent the past six weeks dressing down—trying to wear anything that would make me melt into the crowd—and I can't tell you how good it felt to pour myself into pretty-girl clothes for a change. To be safe, I tucked my dyed-brown hair into a messy French twist and borrowed a pair of super-dark sunglasses from Marissa. Even though I knew I shouldn't be going out in such party clothes, I made sure I looked anonymous enough that no one would ID me as Morgan Carter. And, as Marissa said, "It's Chicago on a Monday night. Who do you think we're going to run into?"

Our first stop was Butterfield 8, a semi-chichi restaurant famed for its retro dinner menu. We started with the oysters Rockefeller and two bowls of Binyon's World Famous Turtle Soup, which was a first for me. (For the record, turtle *does* taste like chicken!) As an entrée, Marissa got the beef Wellington, while I opted for the chicken Kiev. We spent the night downing ultra-virgin drinks—Shirley Temples—and almost ordered the baked Alaska for dessert before our very cute, very gay waiter suggested we check out Sugar, which was supposedly this ultra-hip dessert bar over on West Kinzie.

As soon as we stepped out into the cool air, though, I knew I needed to dance. Hard. We were waiting for a cab when I spotted Katie Holmes walking toward us. Instinctively I ducked behind Marissa, using her as a human shield and dragging both of us behind a streetlight.

"What is *wrong* with you?" she asked, wiggling away from me.

"That's Katie Holmes!" I whispered hoarsely. "What the hell is Katie Holmes doing in Chicago?"

"Filming the new Batman movie with Christian Bale," she replied, with a bitter tang. "I was up for that part, you know. They said I was too 'young.'"

I buried my face as close to her turtleneck as possible without actually making contact. (Even in my panic I knew that it's nearly impossible to get heavy makeup off white cotton.)

Marissa laughed. "Girl, you are a nervous wreck!" she exclaimed. "Relax—there's no way she'll recognize us. No one knows that either of us is here, okay?"

I waited until I was certain that Katie was far enough away and that she *hadn't* recognized us before I came out of hiding. Marissa was right—I was a nervous wreck. For a second I wondered if maybe I should've gone home when Trudy demanded it, but then Marissa linked her arm through mine and said, "Let's go make some magic." Her energy, totally infectious, helped wipe the guilty thoughts from my mind. Or at least put them on hold for a little while.

We ended up at the Hunt Club, which is owned by Cindy Crawford's husband and, according to Marissa, has a very excellent VIP room. Not that I'd know—I told Marissa that there was no way in hell she could drop her own name while she was with me. It was way too risky. In fact, the whole night suddenly seemed like the most asinine idea ever—one false move and everything would be ruined. Maybe if I had downed a couple glasses of liquid courage, I would have been able to relax. Instead, I gnawed away at my new manicure until a couple of the cuticles started to bleed.

Marissa was acting pissy over my no-VIP edict, which I guess I could understand. I mean, both of us are used to using our celebrity as an all-access pass. When the bouncer asked Marissa for the $10 cover charge, she glared at me. I was just glad we weren't being carded.

Inside, the DJ was mashing up mad hits—like mixing the Carpenters' "We've Only Just Begun" into a classic Biggie Smalls cut—and it was at that decibel where sound registers in your body more than your ears. I hadn't been out dancing since . . . well, since the night at the Viper Room, and even then, I think I was too high to do more than sway to the music.

But oh—me and Marissa on the dance floor is something to see. I don't mean that in a perverted way, either, like we were freaking each other or pretending to make out. I've always hated club girls who do that sort of thing—like they're so desperate for male attention, they degrade themselves just to give the boys a cheap thrill.

No, the two of us actually *dance*. Like Janet Jackson after her robot phase but before the J. Timberlake/nipple-flashing Super Bowl incident. Or like a pre-"Dirrty" Christina Aguilera.

Suddenly, the image of Emily working her DDR magic popped into my head, and I felt a deep pang. How cool would it have been if she could've been at the club too? In an alternate universe, we might have been the Three Musketeers instead of the Dynamic Duo.

Marissa and I worked up a sweat within minutes. It must've released some kind of pheromone thing, because almost right away guys were swarming us like flies on honey. I even made out with one of them—this really cute redhead who looked like Eric Stoltz circa *Some Kind of Wonderful*. He wasn't that great a kisser, but he tasted good—like champagne.

Marissa fished my new camera phone out of my purse and started taking snapshots of me and the Stoltz clone. Then, later, when Marissa was doing her trademark table dance—completely sober, mind you—I got some ransom-worthy snapshots of her vamping it up in a less-than-flattering way.

And it all would've been fine, if only faux-Eric would've stopped asking if he could buy me a drink. Why is it that boys don't understand the concept of "no means no"? I declined his offer four or five times before I could no longer remember why I was saying no to begin with. I mean, it was just champagne. I could manage a glass of that, right?

Right?

So the next time he asked about buying me that drink, I squeaked, "Sure, whatever," and clung to his waist as he made his way over to the bar.

Faux Eric ordered another magnum of champagne and handed me a tall crystal flute. I could taste the crisp bubbles just by smelling the stuff. I swirled it around in my glass a bit, putting off what I was sure was inevitable: me taking that drink. Throwing away my many months of sobriety. Proving to the tabloids I really was a wild-child loser more worthy of scorn than respect.

But could it really be all *that* bad—just taking a sip?

My lips had barely brushed the rim when it happened: Chicago's own John Cusack and Jeremy Piven made their way into the club. They looked fully boss, and each had a blonde on his arm.

Unfortunately, J & J also brought the paparazzi with them. Suddenly, the whole club was filled with flashes from oversized digital cameras. I dropped the champagne flute, entering full-on panic mode. Even if the hacks didn't recognize us at that moment, I could end up on anybody's roll of film. And once they had my picture, they could put two and two together. Game over.

Once again I used Marissa as a human shield and tore ass out of there. We hopped into the first cab we saw and sank back into the cracked leather seats, trying to catch our collective breath. Then she started laughing really loud. I joined in, but only to cover up the way I was shaking.

I'd almost done it. Taken that sip. How could I have come so close to ruining everything?

It was time to go home.

As if she could read my mind, Marissa asked, "When do you get to come home? I mean, to L.A. For good."

I shrugged. "June, I guess. That's when I'll get out of school."

"I don't get it," she said as we boarded the elevator up to our suite. "You should leave *now*. You can move in with me! And every night will be like this really fantastic slumber party."

It was a good offer, and I can't say I hadn't thought about it before. But when I tried to picture myself back in L.A., all I could see was this sad, out-of-work-actress-turned-high-school-dropout who was too mortified to show her face in front of some snotty rich kids who thought they were semi-famous because they got invited to Jessica Biel's last birthday party.

Truth time: I am more than relieved to be on this stupid, shaky, death trap of a puddle-jumping airplane, heading back to Fort Wayne. I know I'm going to have to pay for skipping school, blowing off that test, and running off to Chicago with Marissa. That part won't be fun. But the past couple of days have been exhausting. Maybe it's because I had to wear so many different personas, or maybe it's because Marissa is so high energy and it takes a lot just to keep up.

Or maybe it's because I almost took that drink. How could I have come so close to ruining my life a second time? I'm not safe anymore in Marissa's world. And let's face it: it is *her* world now, not mine.

No, my world is in Fort Wayne . . . at least for now.

I can't explain it, but part of me is really looking forward to feeling empowered by Ms. Kwan's feminist lectures and eating M&M's with Ms. Janet Moore in her tiny box of an office. Plus, there's a new aerobic pole-dancing class starting up at the Y soon that has Trudy's and my names written all over it. And yeah, I'm even starting to miss the twins. I can't wait to catch up with them.

Time to fasten my seat belt and prepare for landing.

9/21—*Later*

Unbelievable! Trudy refused to pick me up from the airport. "You got yourself there—you can get yourself home." *Okay, I get it*, I thought. *Let's cut out the hardass routine.* But no. She was serious.

I don't have enough cash for a shuttle, and of course my "temporary" Visa is safely in Marissa's pocket. So my options are (a) hitch a ride home with a total stranger or (b) call Emily, ask her for a ride and make up a plausible excuse for why I'm at the airport at 3 p.m. on a Tuesday.

And to think, twenty minutes ago I was actually looking forward to being back in Fort Wayne.

9/21—*Much later*

This day just keeps getting better.

I tried to call Em and I got as far as hello before my cell died. Died! Can I just say how completely demoralizing it is to have to beg for quarters just so you can make a phone call? I finally got some change from a nice old woman waiting for her daughter and new grandbaby to arrive from Detroit, but then I had to look at pictures of the little whippersnapper for twenty minutes or so. It was the ugliest baby I'd ever seen.

Beyond that, I had to pee the entire time.

So I go find the ladies' room and then I track down a pay phone and try Em again. Only instead of dialing her cell I end up calling the landline, and guess who answers the phone? Eli. Em's not home, he tells me. Just my luck. So I suck it up and tell him that I'm stranded at the airport and he says, "Go wait at the Hertz rental booth. I'll be right there." No questions asked.

There's a comfy padded bench near the Hertz booth, which Eli must've known about or else why would he have had me wait at such a random place? I was so exhausted that I passed out cold. When I woke up, Eli Whitmarsh was standing over me, a slightly amused look on his face.

"Hey, little girl," he said. "Were you trying to run away from home?"

I sat up, yawning and stretching. "More like I was trying to run away *to* home."

He nodded as if what I'd said made perfect sense and said, "Here, let me get your bags."

Fortunately, the "bags" to which he was referring were these two black cheapy nylon things that Marissa and I picked up at the drugstore on our way to O'Hare. Originally I was just going to cart home my purchases in a big shopping bag, but the handle started ripping as we checked out from the hotel. Thank God it did—I don't know how I could've explained all that loot to Eli, especially not after he surprised me and Trudy coming back from that other low-rent spree a few days ago.

"So where's Em?" I asked as we load into the car.

"She's at a planning meeting," he said.

"For?"

"For the haunted house. Today's the day she's meeting with the guys from the Fort Wayne Youtheatre."

"Shit!" I said, smacking myself on the forehead. "I was supposed to be there!"

"I know. Em was a little upset that you weren't in school today."

I sighed. "Aren't you going to ask me where I was?"

"If you wanted me to know, you would've told me," he said. "Right?"

I wasn't sure how to respond, so I didn't. Then Eli said, "Is everything okay?"

"Sure," I said. "Everything's fine."

But it wasn't fine. Running off to Chicago with Marissa hadn't fixed any of my problems. They were all still there. I was failing most of my classes. My mom was still married to Sam. I'd made Trudy so angry she was willing to let me rot at the airport and, worse, seemed ready to throw me out on my fat ass. I'd missed yet another session with Janet, not to mention that ISTEP+ test thing, and I hadn't talked to my sponsor or been to a meeting in I can't even remember how long. Pretty stupid of me, considering how close I'd come to taking a drink . . .

I hadn't realized I was crying until Eli eased the car off the road and into a breakdown lane. He reached across me to the glove compartment and pulled out a travel pack of tissues. Wordlessly, he handed me one. I wiped my cheeks and blew my nose, feeling like a class-A freak show.

"I'm sorry," I said. "I don't know why I'm such a mess."

Eli smiled and told me I didn't have to apologize. His kindness made me feel worse. Especially when I remembered that his charity was based on a tremendous lie.

When we got to the house, Eli insisted on carrying my bags inside. Always the gentleman. I thanked him for giving me a ride home. "Seriously," I said, "I don't know what I would've done if you hadn't answered the phone."

"No problem," he said. "That's what friends are for, right?"

Right. Friends.

Eli hesitated a bit by the door. He looked like he wanted to ask me something, so I said, "What's up?"

"Nothing," he said. "I'll guess I'll see you in school tomorrow?"

I nodded. "Definitely."

"Listen, I was thinking—what are you doing tomorrow night?"

I laughed bitterly. "My guess is I'll be grounded. Why?"

"No reason," he said. "Except . . . if you're not grounded, do you maybe want to come over for dinner? I can show you my theremin."

Without even thinking, I quipped, "Is that what the kids are calling it these days?"

Eli looked stricken. I feel awful thinking about it. There he was, finally getting the courage to make a move, and I was cracking jokes at his expense.

"Kidding," I offered. "Can I let you know at lunch?"

"Sure."

It stayed awkward for another beat or two before Eli shuffled out.

It's now going on 6:30 p.m. and Trudy still isn't home. Is this her idea of punishment? Working late?

9/21—*Much, much later*

Get this: I really am grounded.

Me! Grounded!

Except, being grounded isn't that different from not being grounded. I don't drive, so Trudy couldn't take away my car privileges. I don't have a boyfriend, so it's not like I'm bummed that I can't make out with Johnny Sunshine down at Lover's Point. I don't even have much of a social life to speak of, because half the time that I'm with the twins we're doing schoolwork!

So basically, my "grounding" consists of me having to come home directly after school—except on Wednesdays, when I have my VIP meetings—rejecting all phone calls that aren't homework-related, and no TV for two weeks.

The only black spot is that when I asked Trudy if I could

have dinner at Eli's tomorrow night, she said no. A flat-out, non-negotiating *no*. Which sort of sucks, because I don't want Eli to take it personally. And hell, I kind of did want to check out his theremin thingamabob.

Even without the grounding, this isn't a great situation. In some ways, Trudy was my best friend here in the Fort, and now she can't even look at me. I mean, she's really that mad. She told me she's shocked and appalled that I'm so selfish, and how could I make her worry like that? She told me that she's been getting all sorts of phone calls, too, like from the principal and Ms. Janet Moore. She told me that Janet thinks I should start coming in early, before school starts, for my sessions, because I've already missed so many classes. Oh, and I'm required to see her three times a week until I've gotten "back on track."

Waking up at 4:30 a.m.? Now, *that's* a punishment.

She gave me crap about the shopping spree with Marissa, too. At first I thought she was going to take everything away from me, but then she said, "No, keep it. And every time you look at one of those things, remember the true cost. I'm not talking about money, Morgan, but I gather you already knew that."

For someone who's never been a mother, she's sure got that guilt thing down pat.

I poured myself a bowl of Lucky Charms for dinner (I guess part of my grounding includes Trudy not eating with me anymore) and am now hiding out in my bedroom, feeling just a little bit sorry for myself. Twenty-four hours ago I was putting on pretty clothes and eating chicken Kiev in one of Chicago's finest restaurants. Now this. What a difference a day makes!

There is a pile of books by my bed that need cracking, but I can't bear to do a lick of homework. Not tonight, anyway.

9/22

I can't believe I overslept! I set the alarm on my phone in addition to the clock radio on my nightstand, and I *still* overslept. Worse, Trudy didn't even bother to wake me up! If Ms. Janet Moore hadn't called the house to yell at me for missing my before-school meeting, I might be sleeping this very second.

Instead, I'm sitting in the waiting room of the principal's office, missing even more school. However, right now I should be in gym, so I'm not too brokenhearted.

I'm not exactly sure what this meeting is supposed to be about, but it's a pretty safe guess that it has something to do with my truancy. Better steel myself for more yelling.

9/22—*Later*

IT WAS AN INTERVENTION! A GODDAMNED ACADEMIC INTERVENTION!

I cannot believe this! Principal Barke (and yes, that's his real name) actually assembled a whole team of my teachers—plus one Ms. Janet Moore—in his office to talk to me about my "case." Lucky for me (and yes, that's sarcasm), several of them have free periods around the same time, including Mrs. Chappelle, Mr. Garrett, Mr. Pinzer, and everyone's favorite, the contemptible Mr. Sappey.

In other words, teachers from all of the classes I'm *failing* (minus Ms. Vineyard, who was probably making her students practice their serves in the gym).

The kicker? Ms. Kwan, the one teacher I truly like and the one teacher who could truthfully say that I'm not an idiot, couldn't be there to defend me, because the intervention took place during the period I have her class.

It was beyond awful. First, Principal Barke was all, "Miss Miller, we've called you in here because we're concerned. You've already missed four days of classes and it's not even October. According to most of your teachers, you're currently making Ds and Fs. And I can't even begin to understand why you thought it was acceptable to skip out on a standardized test you were told you needed to graduate."

While he's saying this, all of the teachers are standing there, concerned frowns creasing their faces, nodding in agreement. I could literally feel myself shrink into the cheap striped fabric of my chair.

Then he goes, "The thing that puzzles us, Miss Miller, is why you're performing so poorly. The transcript from your old high school lists you as making straight As. Is there some reason you're purposely sabotaging your performance here at Snider?"

After stifling my urge to snicker at the word *performance*—if only he knew!—I asked to see my supposedly stellar transcript. Barke reluctantly handed it over and, sure enough, it listed me as having a 4.0 GPA. Then I noticed the cover letter attached. It was signed by a principal named Samuel Rose.

Samuel Rose = Sam Rosenbaum = creator of phony transcript.

"I know you've been meeting with Ms. Moore weekly to discuss certain . . . issues," Barke continued. Here he paused and gave Janet a squinty-eyed look, like he was trying to let everyone in the room know just how effective he thought her counseling had been thus far. "I assume that your sessions with her are to ease your transition to Snider High School," Barke continued. He was the kind of guy who used the long *u* in *assume*, so it sounded like *us-youm*. It made me dislike him even more. "Am I correct in that assumption, Miss Miller?"

"Sure," I said. "Why not?"

I saw Janet close her eyes and draw a deep breath, so I think I knew that was the wrong answer even before Barke jumped up in my grill: "Miss Miller, I don't think you understand the seriousness of this meeting. If you don't pull up your averages soon, you will have much difficulty passing the eleventh grade. And if you don't start attending class on a regular basis, you'll automatically fail, regardless of your former GPA."

Now I'd *really* pissed him off. As a consequence, the other teachers' frowns deepened—all except for Mr. Sappey, who—swear to God!—looked like he was fighting off a smile.

I apologized for sounding flip, but it didn't have much of an effect on Barke. He made each of my teachers tell him directly where I was screwing up, one at a time, in a round-robin fashion. By the time Mr. Sappey spoke—"Claudia fails to read instructions thoroughly. As a result, she has yet to complete an assignment according to specification. In addition to this, her writing lacks an academic tone, so whatever valid ideas she may have get lost in the colloquial nature of her prose"—I felt like the world's biggest imbecile. If I couldn't make a comeback as an actress, I'd probably spend the rest of my days ringing up burgers at some fast-food haven, because that's about all I seem to be qualified for. (Then again, Mrs. Chappelle might disagree, as my geometry average is currently a 43.)

Mr. Garrett backed up Sappey's statements, saying that my paper on *Siddhartha* was original but poorly supported and lacking in "cohesion." Then he said, "Perhaps, Dr. Barke, you might arrange for Claudia to have some special-needs testing."

"Oh, for Christ's sake!" Janet exploded from her corner, shocking everyone (including me). "The girl doesn't have a learning disability! In fact, if any of you bothered to talk to her for five minutes, you'd realize she's quite intelligent."

Janet stood there, shaking. I wondered—was she just standing up to Barke, or did she really believe what she was saying?

Barke's face was bright red, though I'm still not sure if it was from anger or embarrassment. He coughed into his fist twice, then said, "Ms. Moore, I'd appreciate it if you would lower your voice. We all want what's best for Miss Miller."

"Oh, bullshit!" she cried, which was quickly followed by a round of gasps and Barke shouting, "Ms. Moore!"

"None of you know the first thing about this student," Janet continued, her shoulders rigid. "Claudia knows she needs improvement in certain areas. She's sought out tutoring—on her own, I might add—and will be meeting with me before school three times a week until she gets her grades up. I resent having to be a part of these . . . *proceedings*. They will do nothing to instill confidence in Claudia. If anything, they'll hinder the progress I've been making with her on my own."

"All right, Janet," Mr. Sappey said, voice dripping with condescension. "That's enough."

Her head jerked to attention. "Don't you dare take that tone with me, Bob!" she shrilled. "I deserve *respect*!"

And this began a verbal melee like nothing I'd ever seen. Sappey and Janet were going at it like they were the only two people in the room, and the others were already gossiping—"Can you believe she said that?" (Mr. Garrett) "I knew she was trouble when she showed up to our in-service day wearing a leather skirt" (Mrs. Chappelle). On top of that, Barke was turning even redder, trying (unsuccessfully) to get control of the situation. When he realized he couldn't, he turned to me and said, "Ms. Miller, perhaps you should go to your class now."

"No!" Janet roared. "I want to see her! *Now*."

It took me all of two seconds to swoop up my backpack and scurry into Janet's office. She followed shortly after, slamming the door behind her. I watched her stand there, staring at her shoes and smoothing her already wrinkle-free skirt. Then she picked up the heart-shaped photo frame of her and Sappey, slammed it facedown on the desk, and plopped onto her chair.

"*You*," she said, sounding slightly out of breath.

I froze. What do you say to a normally sane woman who's just flipped her lid? Janet was smoothing the sides of her hair (finally! A little frizz!) and taking really deep yoga breaths, all with her eyes closed. It was scary, actually. Especially now that I knew that Ms. Janet Moore wasn't someone you wanted to cross lightly.

"Well, Claudia," she began, digging out a handful of M&M's. "I just put my job on the line for you. What are you going to do for me?"

"Excuse me?" I asked.

"You heard me," she said. "What are *you* going to do for *me*?"

I was still a little shell-shocked, so at this point I was thinking she wanted me to, like, wax her car or pick up her dry cleaning or something. I was trying to work it out when she sighed impatiently and said, "Claudia! This isn't rocket science! *What are you going to do for me?*"

Suddenly it clicked. "Study," I said. "Bring my grades up."

Janet nodded. "And what else?"

"And come to school every day."

She nodded again. "And . . . ?"

I drew a blank. What else had I done wrong lately?

Fortunately, Janet took pity on me. She said, "You're also going to come to every scheduled meeting we have, and when you're in this room, we're going to do some real work. I meant what I said, Claudia—you keep screwing up and they're going to toss me out on my ass. Hell, they might do that anyway. So please don't make a fool of me. It's the least you could do."

She started filling out a late pass for me. I was still pretty frozen. She handed it to me and asked, "What are you doing after school?"

"Nothing. But that's because I'm grounded."

"Good," she said. "Grounded is good. However, I want to see you first thing tomorrow morning. If you are so much as a minute late, you will regret it. Got me? Now go."

I was on my way to Ms. Kwan's when the bell rang, so I changed direction and headed to Mr. Garrett's English class. I'd barely said hi to Emily when Garrett called me to his desk and handed me an envelope. "The work sheets you missed," he explained, avoiding my eyes. "I've put deadlines on each. If you don't get them in on time, you'll receive a zero." As I walked back to my desk, Emily mouthed, "What happened?" and I mouthed back, "Long story." Garrett then proceeded to spend the entire period looking at anyone who wasn't me. I just wanted class to hurry up and be over so I could talk to Em, but then she was the one who couldn't stay and chat: "Flu shot," she said as she ran out the door. "Gotta hurry or I won't be back in time for fifth!"

I knew it wasn't like Emily planned to get a flu shot at the exact moment I most wanted to talk to her, but I felt like she was ditching me anyway. If I'd been thinking on my feet, I would've offered to go with her—it wasn't like I was hungry for lunch anyway. Instead, I decided to go to the library and try to make a dent in some of my homework. Even before the stupid intervention I'd decided that I wanted to prove to Trudy and Janet that I could hack it as a normal high school student—that I was finally getting serious about changing. Not because Sam or Bianca wanted me to, and not because I was desperately trying to save my career. No, this time, I was doing it for *me*.

I caught Eli as he was heading into the caf and told him I was trading lunchtime for library time. He tugged on the sleeve of my shirt. "Hey, is everything okay?"

"Things could be better," I admitted. "But they could also be worse. Oh—and I can't come over tonight. It's a long story, but I'll fill you in later, okay?"

Then he did something very bold. Well, bold for Eli, anyway.

He hugged me.

Right there, on the threshold of the caf, with everyone watching.

Including Debbie Ackerman.

You know, I'm used to people being overly concerned

with every little detail of my life. But in the past it was always producers, directors, agents, and smarmy media types looking for a reason to trash me in the press. Now it's like I've got this whole circle of civilians worried about every move I make, not because it will improve their ratings, but because . . . well, just *because*. With the exception of Sappey, I get the really strange feeling that these guys actually care about what happens to me.

Or rather, what happens to Claudia Miller.

Gotta run—it's time for chemistry. I better make nice with An-Yi. Her brilliance is more crucial than ever.

9/22—*Much later*

Somehow I survived the day, even Sappey's class. He was even more evil to me than usual, calling on me every time he asked a question, even though I hadn't raised my hand, and then ridiculing my answers. It was so bad, LaTanya whispered over my shoulder, "Damn, girl—what did you do to him?"

Later, as I was heading toward the VIP meeting, I felt someone grab me by the bra strap. It snapped my back so hard I literally cried out in pain. I whirled around to see who the offender was.

Debbie Ackerman.

"You lied to me," she growled.

I rubbed the sore spot where the strap had hit. "What the hell are you talking about?"

"I saw him hug you," she said. "And I know he picked you up from the airport yesterday."

Of course, it was about Eli. With Debbie it's *always* about Eli.

"So?" I said. "What's your point?"

"Don't play dumb with me," she snarled. "You only pretended you wanted to hook me up with Eli so you could improve your own chances with him. Admit it."

I don't know why, but there's something about this girl that makes me want to be mean to her. Maybe it's because she's so outwardly bitchy herself? More likely it's that she keeps her ugly insecurities so close to the surface that I can't help but see them—and want to attack them. She's like . . . like a bulldog that unintentionally exposes his belly to a bigger, stronger, crueler beast (i.e., me). I always, always want to sink my teeth in.

So I said:

"Okay, so first of all? If I wanted Eli Whitmarsh, I would not have to worry about you being my competition." I tossed my hair for emphasis. "Second of all, you are the one who decided on that hideous outfit and who insisted on our little trip to the salon. And no one told you to order enough food to feed a family of five. So you don't you dare blame *me* for the fact that you made a fool out of yourself.

"Besides," I added, "I could've made you into the hottest girl in this school and Eli still wouldn't have gone out with you. He likes someone else. I guess I don't have to tell you who that is."

End scene.

Then at the VIP meeting, Emily was deep in conversation with Lauren Johnson, so I slipped into the desk next to LaTanya and said, "Put me out of my misery, will you?"

"Aw, why so glum?" she asked. "I mean, besides the fact that we've got another essay due for film tomorrow."

"Don't remind me." I groaned.

LaTanya leaned in close. In a low voice, she said, "So I

have it on good authority you were summoned to Barke's office this morning. Why?"

"Who told you that?"

"My girl Sheree is the student intern during that period. Go on, *dish*."

I gave her the quick-and-dirty version of what had happened during my scholastic intervention.

"Are you for real?" she asked. "That's crazy."

Then, without really thinking about it, I said, "If I'd known I would be in this much trouble, I never would've gone to Chicago."

Yeah. I said it. CHICAGO.

"Chicago?" LaTanya repeated. "What were you doing in Chicago?"

I scrambled to think of a plausible lie, but the truth—or rather, the almost truth—seemed the best route to take.

"My best friend from back home came in this weekend for a surprise visit. So, when she was going to fly back to L—Lancaster, I went to the airport with her."

"Oh. That's cool."

Crisis averted. I think.

After the meeting I went up to Em and apologized again for skipping out on her yesterday.

"So what's going on?" she asked. "One minute we're all hanging out at Johnny Appleseed and the next, you're just . . . gone. For, like, *days*. And I know Eli had to give you a ride home yesterday, but he wouldn't tell me from where."

I quickly filled her in on the bare-bones version of the story, leaving out the shopping spree, spa visit, and night-club excursion.

"It's weird," I concluded. "I'd been missing her—Daisy—for

189

so long that when she said I should skip school and go to Chicago, I didn't think twice. But then, once I was there . . ."

"Yeah?"

"I guess I wished you were there with us. We would've had a good time together, you know?"

"Wait a minute," she said. "You got into all of this trouble and you didn't even have a good time?"

"No, we had a good time," I clarified. "But it was a different kind of good time. Like, the sober version of the good times I used to have back home. But maybe my definition of a good time is changing? I don't know."

"Well," Em said in a semi-snarky voice, "it would've been nice if you could've answered at least *one* of my calls, but whatever."

"What? I didn't get any—" Then I remembered. "Oh, *duh*," I said. "I got a new phone." I pulled it out of my bag and showed it to her. "See? I didn't have a chance to give you the new number. That's all. Don't be mad, okay?"

"I'm not mad," Em said, sitting on top of a student desk. "I'm just totally stressed."

"Is it a DDR-curable kind of stress?"

She shot me a shut-up kind of look. "We don't talk about that here, remember?"

I laughed. "Sure thing, Agent Whitmarsh."

"It's this haunted house project," Em confessed, punctuating the sentence by gnawing on a cuticle. "It's a really big deal, Claud. Last year we raised more than fifteen thousand dollars. This year things are looking pretty dire. We have a quarter of the manpower, and because the economy is so bad, a lot of our suppliers are charging more. It's totally breaking the budget."

"So, we'll have a fund-raiser," I said.

Em shook her head. "The haunted house *is* a fund-raiser, remember?"

"Yeah, I know," I said. "We'll have a pre-fund-raiser fund-raiser. I told you, I'm really good at this raising-money thing. Put me to work already, will you?"

"Can you be at a planning meeting tomorrow night?" she asked.

"I don't know," I said. Emily raised one eyebrow in response. "I'm grounded," I explained. "But let me talk to my aunt. She let me to come to this meeting, so maybe all VIP activities are approved."

When Trudy got home from work, I told her about my dilemma. She agreed that I couldn't bag on Emily again. But her solution left a lot to be desired.

"You'll have the meeting here," she said. "Don't even try to fight me on it. The only way you can go is if I can keep an eye on you."

Fortunately, Emily didn't care where we had the meeting.

Oh my God. It's almost ten and I haven't even started my paper on *Malcolm X*.

More soon.

9/22—Much, much later

It's almost midnight and I have to be up at 4:30 a.m. to make my meeting with Janet. How did this happen? If I spent as much time on my geometry homework as I did writing in this journal, I'd be some kind of Pythagorean genius by now. At least Sappey's paper is done. I didn't spend nearly enough time on it, but it's not like my grade in that class could get much worse.

9/23—*Longest. Day. Ever.*

In my haste to appease Emily I forgot that on Thursday nights I have NA meetings, which starts at 7 p.m. So I told Em the VIP thing needed to wrap up at 6:30 sharp. She seemed concerned that we wouldn't have enough time, but I said that Trudy was the one making the rules and if she (Em) didn't like it, she (still Em) could go talk to my aunt. Emily didn't give me any grief after that.

Having the meeting at my house worked out okay. I did my usual pre-company sweep to make sure all Morgan-related items were clearly out of sight. Only three of the VIP members showed up, including Emily. Even LaTanya skipped, but that's because she had a debate team meet over in Auburn.

Eli, however, had decided to tag along. His official reason was that he wanted to take some pictures for the yearbook (but none of me, per our earlier agreement). His unofficial reason, I presumed, was that he'd get to see me.

We all gathered around the dining room table. Emily put on her best student government voice and outlined everything that needed to be done for the haunted house. She showed me pictures from years past. All I can say is, *lame*. From the looks of things, putting flashlights under their chins was as high-tech as these guys seemed to get. But where was the dry ice? The gelled lighting casting creepy shadows on everything? Wasn't there a theater troupe involved?

Plus, the "scenes" they'd set for each room were a total

snooze fest. Mostly ghouls and goblins hiding behind one-dimensional trees cut out from Luan and splattered with neon paint. Things that required no imagination whatsoever and weren't scary enough to give an easily spooked two-year-old the chills.

Emily said that in past years, small groups of people signed up to take on a room, and then they got to plan what they wanted to do themselves. Well, that explained why the whole thing was such an awkward mishmash. The only rule Em issued was that none of the actors could physically touch any of the patrons . . . for obvious reasons.

"Clearly," I said, "you need a theme."

"The theme is 'scary,'" Lauren Johnson said. "Duh."

I couldn't help but smirk at Lauren's simple-mindedness. "I mean a *unifying* theme," I said. "Something you could really advertise. Like, what if each room re-created a scene from one of the scariest horror movies of all time?"

Emily grinned and said, "Now you're talking."

We started to draw up a list of movies we could use for inspiration: *Psycho*, *The Shining*, *Friday the 13th*, *Nightmare on Elm Street*, *The Ring*. Lauren goes, "Don't forget about *Scary Movie*!" which proves (to me, anyway) that she really is clueless.

"That's a parody," I explained. "Like, the exact opposite of what we're trying to pull off."

I started sketching storyboards for each of the rooms, while Eli kept a running tally of what supplies would be needed. At one point Emily asked what we were going to do about the little kids. She said the haunted house had always been a family event, and the kind of spooky stuff we were planning might be too much for the *Dora-the-Explorer* set.

I had another flash of brilliance: Why stop at a house? They held the event on Mrs. Whitmarsh's friend's farm, in a converted barn that mostly stood empty the rest of the year. So my idea was that we expand. Add a hayride, a refreshment stand, and a kids' area, where they could do stuff like paint faces on little pumpkins.

"Oh my God, this is going to be the coolest!" Emily squealed. "I just hope we have enough *time*. We open in less than a month!"

"It'll be tough," I agreed. "But we still have weekends, and your parents know everyone who's anyone in Fort Wayne. We just need to get a lot more people involved."

The meeting adjourned later than I expected, so the minute everyone was gone Trudy raced me over to the church for my NA meeting. But instead of dropping me off, like she used to, Trudy walked me inside.

"This is sort of insulting," I said. "If I wanted to ditch, I could find a craftier way of doing it."

"I don't doubt that," Trudy said coolly. "But that's not why I'm here."

She marched straight up to Gaby and asked her if she'd mind driving me home afterward. "I think Claudia could use a little one-on-one time, if you don't mind."

Gaby didn't mind; in fact, after the meeting she suggested we go for coffee. Since all I had waiting for me at home was a huge mound of homework, I agreed.

Over pumpkin spice lattes she said, "I'm worried about you, Claudia. You're too new in recovery to be skipping meetings. I'd hate to see you backslide now."

"Trust me," I said, blowing on the foam. "I've been a total Girl Scout. I was even at a bar last weekend, and all I had were Shirley Temples." I left out the part about faux Eric and the champagne.

Her gasp was audible. "Claudia," she said slowly, "what were you doing in a *bar*?"

"Dancing," I said, feeling my cheeks grow hot. "But that's all. I mean, besides making out with this really cute guy I'll never see again."

It was like I had diarrhea of the mouth. Someone who hung out in bars, even if she stayed sober the whole time, was considered a dry alcoholic. And hooking up with anyone in the first year of recovery—albeit briefly—was definitely frowned upon.

"Claudia," Gaby said, her voice low and grave, "have you been working the steps? You need to work the steps."

"Of course," I lied. "One day at a time, right?"

She shook her head. "Why are you being so flippant? Have you somehow managed to forget how serious this is? It's a *disease*, Claudia. You'll always be an alcoholic. Always."

"Don't you think I know that?" I snapped, feeling two hot tears gather in the corners of my eyes. "God! I'm not even seventeen years old, but I feel like . . . like . . . like my life is already *over*."

"Why?" Gaby challenged me. "Because you can't ever get wasted again?"

"I don't want to get *wasted*," I mumbled. "I just—"

"Just what?"

"I want to be able to have a drink like a normal person! Just one! Maybe some wine with dinner or a glass of champagne to celebrate!"

"That's just it, Claudia," Gaby said. "With people like us, it's never 'just one' drink. You know—I know you know—that even the smallest sip from the tiniest glass could make the whole thing unravel. And then where would you be?"

"I didn't do it," I said, sniffling. "I almost did, but I didn't."

"Almost did what?"

Slowly, carefully, I told her about the drink faux Eric had bought me and how close I'd come to actually drinking it.

"And how do you feel now?" Gaby prompted.

"Scared," I said, my voice barely above a whisper.

"Good," she said. "You *should* be scared."

She told me she wanted me to go home and write out the story of my lowest point as an alcoholic.

"But I did that already," I said. "In rehab."

"Then do it again," she said tightly. "Fold it up and carry it with you, always. Then, whenever you so much as have the tiniest fragment of a thought about taking a drink, pull it out and read it. Remember why you got sober to begin with."

She stood up then and pulled me into a tight hug. "You've got to call me, Claudia. I'm your sponsor. I can help you be strong, okay?"

When I got home, I wanted to tell Trudy about what Gaby and I had talked about. But the minute I walked through the door, Tru picked up her mug of tea, said good night, and disappeared into her bedroom.

Now it's going on 11 p.m. and I feel thoroughly drained. But I've got to dive into this pile of homework, even if all I really want to dive into is my bed.

9/23—*Later*

It's no use. I'll never catch up. And no, I'm not exaggerating. Who would've thought that missing a couple of days of school could put a girl this far behind?

Maybe it's the lack of sleep, but lately I've been feeling extremely paranoid. There are days when I walk down the halls and feel like people are staring at me in a really weird way. Like they know my secret or, at the very least, they know I have one. Except these days I have more than one, and I can barely keep track of who knows what.

So, in geometry today I tuned out Chappelle's lecture on triangles and instead created a cheat sheet so I can keep track of all of my secrets and lies.

WHO	KNOWS	DOESN'T KNOW
Emily Whitmarsh	That I'm a recovering addict AND that I never had a boyfriend named Evan Walsh	Just about everything else
Eli Whitmarsh	That I can't have my picture taken AND that I moved here to hide from my past AND that my dad killed my dog Muppet (NOTE TO SELF: Tell less-complicated lies!)	My real identity OR that I'm a recovering addict OR that I might have a crush on him
Ms. Janet Moore	That I was raped and that I'm a recovering addict	Harlan Darly was my rapist OR my real identity
Debbie Ackerman	That I used to have a boyfriend named Evan Walsh AND that I supposedly have a friend named Daisy Duchovny AND that Eli Whitmarsh likes me	My real identity OR that I'm a recovering addict

LaTanya	I was in Chicago last weekend	Who I was with or why
Marissa	Everything	That despite the near-constant fear of being found out, I actually sort of like it here
Trudy	Everything . . .	. . . except that I miss us being close and that I really am sorry for disappointing her

Laying it all out like that was helpful, believe it or not. Because even if all of those people got together and compared stories (minus Marissa and Trudy, of course), then it would still take a real Morgan Carter aficionado to figure out Claudia Miller's secret identity.

After English, I broke down and asked Emily if she could help me with my unconquerable pile of homework.

"I wish I could," she said, "but I've got way too much going on this weekend."

"Yeah? Like what?"

"Just . . . you know. *Stuff.*"

She had this devilish little smile on her face and I knew she was keeping something from me. "God, Em—don't tell me you and Joey are at it again."

"Please!" Emily made a face like she'd just chugged a quart of sour milk. "Those days are *over*. But . . ."

"Go on," I urged. "Spill it."

"I can't," she said, blushing. "Not yet. I'll tell you Monday, okay? But why don't you ask Eli to help with the homework thing? I'm sure he'd be more than happy to."

I thought about it all through lunch. Asking Eli would be

easy; I knew he'd say yes. But that would mean spending more one-on-one time with him—Eli, who'd already kissed my forehead, not to mention hugged me in front of everyone. And oh, yeah—despite the fact that he's been kind enough to save my ass on several occasions, he's the one I've told the *biggest* lies. Hanging with him? Maybe not such a good idea.

But I'd made a promise to Janet that I'd get my grades up, and I knew I'd never get back into Trudy's good graces if I didn't buckle down and take school seriously.

"I need a favor," I told him as we were leaving the cafeteria. "A sort of big one."

"Shoot."

I told him about the backlog of schoolwork. "I wouldn't bother you at all, but Em says she's too busy and the situation has gotten really, really dire."

"Oh, I see," he said. "I'm sloppy seconds."

"Of course not. It's just—"

He grinned. "I'm kidding. You still grounded?"

I nodded.

"Okay, then," he said. "I'll come to you. How does six o'clock sound?"

Fortunately, when I called Trudy to "ask" if it was okay for Eli to come over, she said yes. She also said that she had a late-night meeting and that I shouldn't wait up. That job of hers is nuts. There have been a bunch of times she's had to work until ten or even eleven at night and then *still* has to be in by 7 a.m. sharp.

Oops—just looked at the clock. Eli will be here in less than an hour. Must go set up dining room table for study session. Also: see if there's anything in house I can cook for my newest BFF (Eli).

Somehow I managed to screw up boxed mac 'n' cheese AND microwaved hot dogs. Perhaps my idea to salvage both by cutting said dogs up and mixing them into the mac' n' cheese was not the smartest idea I'd ever had. Even so, Eli was nice enough to choke down a small bowl without once mentioning the soapy taste the noodles had somehow acquired.

Oh, but Eli? The boy is a total math *stud*. Not to mention an organizational genius! He helped me work out a plan of attack for this weekend that sees me entirely caught up by Monday night—which is good, because that's around the time I'd need to turn my attention to the haunted village project.

After we'd finished working, Eli told me he had a surprise for me. When he went out to his car to get it, I had no idea what it would be. Then he comes in carrying this thing that looks like a sophisticated rat trap. Turns out it's his THEREMIN.

He set it up on the dining room table and did some warm-ups with his hands. Then, his eyes closed, he proceeded to "wave out" Roy Orbison's "Pretty Woman."

When he finished, I clapped really loud. "You're such a rock star!"

"Eh," he said. "I do what I do."

"You do it well."

Eli offered to take me out for ice cream, but I was too pooped to scoop. And I was also grounded. Now the only thing left on my personal agenda for tonight is to have a long heart-to-heart with Trudy. It's about time we made up.

9/24—Much later

It's now almost midnight and Trudy still hasn't come home from work. Who works until midnight on a Friday? I tried to call her cell to make sure she was okay, but she'd turned it off. So I left a voice mail message and have been sitting by the phone ever since.

9/25

Trudy didn't come home last night!

I know, because I didn't fall asleep until almost 4 a.m., and when I got up at 7 a.m. to pee, I peeked in Trudy's room and she wasn't there. Her bed was perfectly made and everything. So I immediately dialed her cell and was relieved when she answered on the fourth ring.

"Where are you?" I asked. "I've been worried sick!"

"I'm at the grocery store." She yawned.

"*That's* your story? *Grocery shopping*?"

"Go back to bed," she instructed. "I'll be home soon."

But of course I couldn't sleep. I paced around the house until almost 10 a.m., when Trudy finally walked through the front door. Sure enough, there were exactly ZERO bags from Scott's Foods in her hands. Even less surprising was the fact that her cheeks were flushed and her lip gloss was smudged.

"You're dating someone!" I accused.

"Shhh," she said, like we were in a library or something.

"Don't shush me," I said. "You nearly gave me a heart attack last night. You made me tell you what *I* did when I disappeared, so spill it! I want *details*!"

Turns out the nights that I thought Trudy had been working late, she'd really been out having dinner with an attractive male coworker named Dave who had gone through his own divorce almost three years ago. "We bonded over French onion soup," she confessed, her face getting even redder.

I asked her why she hadn't brought him around yet and she said the "friendship" was still too new for something so formal. So then I asked her why, if she felt uncomfortable bringing him here, she didn't just stay at his place once in a while. That's when she told me about Ryan, Dave's six-year-old son, of whom he had sole custody.

"That definitely complicates things," I agreed. "But hey—how about once in a while I go over to Dave's to babysit Ryan, and then the two of you can a little privacy over here?"

"No," Trudy said. "Absolutely not."

At first I didn't understand why she was so opposed to the idea. Then it hit me: "You haven't slept with him yet, have you?"

"Morgan!" she cried. "We are *not* having this conversation."

"You haven't!" I repeated. "You stayed up all night talking, didn't you? God, Tru—have you even bothered to have sex with *anyone* since the divorce?"

But all she said was, "Go do your homework."

While I worked on the assignments slated for today, Trudy slept. And slept and slept and slept. She didn't even wake up when, at four-ish, Eli called to check in on me.

"How's it going?" he asked.

"Not bad," I said. "The schedule you made me is pretty specific. I love how you penciled in ten-minute bathroom breaks. And I see that you're calling at the start of my late-afternoon stretch."

He laughed. "It's not that bad, is it?"

"Of course not. I can't thank you enough, Eli. Seriously, I

don't know what I would've done without your help."

"Oh," he said softly, "I think you would've managed somehow. You're very brave, Claudia."

I flushed with pride, but then I had to wonder—was he saying that because of me or because of the "stalking dad" lies I'd told? My guess was the latter. Too bad Eli will never know the reasons I really *am* strong. Much stronger than I used to be, anyway.

Trudy woke up starving around six, so we decided to grab dinner at the Cork & Cleaver, which apparently is where Trudy and Dave had their first lunch date. I raised my water glass to her and said, "Congratulations on reentering the wonderful world of dating! May it not be too many moons before you and Dave consummate your affection."

"Oh, Morgan," she said. "You're too much."

She was smiling, though, a big, sparkly smile that let me know just how happy she really was. I figured then was as good a time as any to have our "talk."

"Listen, I need you to know that I'm really sorry I disappointed you and lied and all that stuff and I swear to God it will never happen again," I blurted out. Then, more slowly: "I miss you, Trudy. I hate that we don't talk anymore. What can I do to fix things?"

She nodded. "You're already doing it. Going to school, finishing your homework, going to meetings. Those are the things that matter. The rest of it just takes time." She reached across the table and squeezed my hand. "I know I was hard on you. But I have to be. Actions have consequences. I think that's something you're still beginning to learn."

It wasn't exactly the warm and fuzzy reconciliation I'd hoped for, but it was a start. At home the two of us got into our pj's and watched a rerun of Justin Timberlake on *Saturday*

Night Live. Trudy kept saying, "Can you please explain to me what girls find so appealing about that kid? I mean, look at him—he's barely out of puberty." It made me laugh.

9/26

Crap! It's almost six o'clock and I really need to get working. Since I stayed up late with Trudy, I didn't get up until almost eleven, which put me about two hours behind schedule. By the time I'd showered and eaten breakfast, I was so far off the homework chart, I decided I might as well enjoy my Sunday afternoon. So Trudy and I ended up watching a *Trading Spaces* marathon and making notes about things we want to do to the house once we have some time.

Anyway, here's a list of everything I'm supposed to do before bed:

• Complete twenty-five problem sets for geometry (2 hrs.)
• Read chapter 5 for U.S. history and study for makeup quiz (1 hr.)
• Read books I through X of *The Odyssey* and study for quiz (2 hrs.)
• Write up lab report for chemistry using An-Yi's notes, as Mr. Pinzer says I still have to do it even though I missed the experiment entirely (30 mins.)
• Write a one-paragraph "story" from a list of verbs and what tense they should be conjugated in for Spanish (20 mins. tops)

If I don't bother eating dinner or taking any bathroom breaks, I should be finished by midnight.

That's so . . . *wrong.*

ALSO: I've been thinking about how right before Marissa and I said goodbye in Chicago, she asked me when I'd be coming home to L.A. and how I said June. But lately, whenever I think of going back to L.A., I get this cold shiver of dread. It's not just avoidance, either. It's like . . . God, it's like when I think of "home," I think of *here*. This house. In Fort Lame.

When did *that* happen?

And then there's this: even if L.A. isn't my real home anymore, I can't leave it entirely behind. Because there's someone in L.A. who *is* real. Someone I'll have to deal with eventually—no matter how awkward or unpleasant the prospect seems.

9/26—*Later*

~~Dear Bianca,~~

Dear Mom,

It's late and I still have about two hours of homework left before I can go to sleep, but I can't stop thinking about what Trudy told me this morning over breakfast. She said you were upset that you hadn't heard from me. I thought it was odd, because I was feeling sort of the same way about you. But I guess you're having the same problem that I'm having, which is: I don't know what to say.

I'm angry that you went and married Sam without me knowing. I should point out that *without me knowing* are the key words here. It's not that you married my manager, although Sam doesn't strike me as your type. It's that you didn't think that I'd want to be there for the wedding. Is it that *you* didn't want me there? I'm your only daughter—

how could you do something so special without me present? And then not even tell me about it? I keep thinking that if I hadn't found out accidentally, you'd still be keeping your secret, and I'd still be in the dark.

But what's done is done, right? No sense in either of us wasting our collective energy feeling angry or guilty or regretful.

You mentioned in your letter to me that you want me to meet you and Sam in Fiji for Christmas break so that we can work on becoming a family. Well, I've been thinking about it, and I don't want to go. What I want is for us to all be in L.A., in our house, together. What I want is for the two of you to renew your vows with me standing by your side. No one else has to be there if you don't want them to. But I should've been there to begin with. Here's our chance to get it right.

I've been working really hard here, at least since I got back from Chicago. I'm all caught up on the work I missed, and I've even gotten involved with my friend Emily's charity project—a haunted house thing that benefits the children's hospital. I'm seeing Ms. Moore, the guidance counselor at school, three times a week, and I had coffee with my sponsor the other night. With the exception of my new addiction to caffeine, I'm completely sober.

It's really late and I should get to bed. Let me know what you and Sam think about my idea for Christmas.

~~Until then,~~

I love you always,

Morgan

Week
SEVEN

9/27

Sappey handed back our essays today, and—I still can't believe it!—my "reading" of Spike Lee's *Malcolm X* got me an A-minus. Let me repeat: SAPPY GAVE ME AN A-MINUS! Too bad I only got to enjoy it for about five seconds.

I was so excited that I immediately whipped around in my seat to tell LaTanya. Then I said, "Oh, Marissa's going to freak!"

It wasn't until LaTanya said, "Who?" that I realized what I'd done.

"Uhn-nobody," I stammered. "Just a friend of mine."

"The friend you went to Chicago with?" she asked, sounding suspicious.

I nodded weakly. "She helped me brainstorm ideas."

"Yeah?" LaTanya said. "I bet she's a real *doll*."

At first I thought it was a coincidence. Her calling Marissa Dahl "a real doll." But then, on her way out of class, LaTanya handed me her paper and said, "I think you might like to read this."

The title? "When Good Feminists Go Wrong: Gender Stereotyping in *Girls on Top*."

Oh my God. She *knew*!

The minute I hit the house, I dialed Sam's office. His secretary told me he was in a meeting. "I don't care," I told her. "This is an emergency!"

She wasn't easily swayed. Finally I said, "Tell him his stepdaughter's been shot. She's in the hospital and they need her insurance information."

That did the trick.

"Who is this?" Sam demanded. "What's going on?"

"It's me," I said. "I haven't been shot. But I really need to talk to you."

After Sam calmed down, screamed at me for the false alarm, and calmed down again, I told him about what LaTanya had said and how she'd given me her paper. Sam made me spell LaTanya's name for him and told me he was "on it."

"What do you mean, you're 'on it'?" I asked. "You sound like you're going to have her whacked or something."

He ignored the comment. "For Christ's sake, Morgan, you have *got* to be more careful. And after what happened in Chicago . . ."

I swallowed hard. "What do you mean?"

"You were photographed," he said flatly. "At the bar. *Holding a glass of champagne.* The hack IDed Marissa and faxed some photos to my office for confirmation that her companion was *you.* I somehow managed to convince him you were taking an extended spa vacation in Switzerland. It only took an additional fifty thou in hush money to make him go away. I'm just waiting for more of them to crawl out from under their rocks."

His words were like a punch to the gut. Here I was, thinking I was handling everything so beautifully when really I was screwing up all over the place and Sam was busy picking up the pieces. Just like old times.

"I didn't drink it," I said. "I swear to you."

"I can't even begin to go there, Morgan," he said. "After the hell you've been through? If you're stupid enough to start drinking and getting high again, then that's your deal. I love you too much to watch you destroy your life twice." He sighed heavily. "And let's forget that once they've got you on film, it doesn't matter what you really did or did not do. People believe pictures. Much more than they believe recovering addicts."

"I'm sorry," I whispered. "I'm so sorry."

"Don't," he said, his voice slightly softer. "I know this is rough. It's rough on all of us." After a short silence he continued. "Maybe this was a bad idea. Maybe you should just come home, and we'll figure out some other way to re-launch your career."

When the one person in the world who's always believed in you says he's ready to call it quits, it's the worst feeling in the world. Simply hearing the defeat in his voice broke my heart.

"No," I said firmly. "I am going to do this. I won't mess up again. I promise, Sam. Please, just give me another chance to make it right."

As if I wasn't already feeling ultra-low, it just occurred to me that in two days I will turn seventeen years old. I'd been sort of hoping I could actually celebrate my birthday, but now, with LaTanya knowing what I think she knows, I can't risk it. I may be a has-been, but if *Entertainment Tonight* still lists Lorenzo Lamas's birthday every year (and they do; I know, because it's also Sam's birthday), there's a strong likelihood that mine will be broadcast too. There's no way I can do anything that might possibly link Claudia Miller to Morgan Carter. Otherwise I might as well pack up my stuff and move back to L.A., like Sam said. And I *know* I'm not ready for that.

Trudy's out with Dave, so I can't even talk to her about any of this. I thought about calling Marissa, but now I'm afraid to even use my cell. What if someone is recording my calls? It's happened before. No doubt it could happen again.

In more normal news, I got Emily to spill a little about her weekend plans. I knew it was something big when she showed up at school wearing mascara and a little lip gloss.

"So who is he?" I asked her.

She couldn't hide her grin. "You don't know him."

"But I'm going to get to know him, right?"

"Maybe," she said. "Eventually."

"Do I at least get a *name*?"

Emily did the furtive looking-around-the-room thing to make sure no one was listening. "Caspar."

"Caspar?" I echoed. "As in, 'the friendly ghost'?"

Her eyes narrowed slightly. "As in, make that joke again and I won't tell you another thing about him, especially not that he's *already in college*."

"Whoa," I said. "College man. Nicely done."

I didn't get to find out more, though, because at that point, Garrett started yelling at the two of us for talking through the beginning of his lecture. "I'd expect this from Miss Miller," he said, "but *you*, Miss Whitmarsh? I assumed you had a little more *respect*."

Now it's really, really late and I should be asleep, but my nerves are buzzing too hard inside me. What I need is to talk to Trudy, but her cell is going directly to voice mail. Which means she's probably out with Dave. Which means I have no idea when she'll be home tonight or if she's even coming home at all.

9/28

Trudy finally got in around eleven; I pounced on her before she could even take off her jacket. I told her about LaTanya and my call to Sam and the revelation I'd had about my birthday. By the end, I was a sloppy, sobbing mess.

Trudy did her best to comfort me, but I could tell she was concerned. You know, I never stopped to think about it before, but by taking me in, Trudy made herself part of the story. If I was exposed, she'd be exposed too. While harboring an out-of-work actress isn't exactly a criminal offense, it was the kind of thing that would turn Trudy into a tabloid queen. Her home would be overrun with paparazzi, as would her office, and who knew how Divorced Dave would take the news.

My anxiety was out of control, increasing exponentially the closer it got to seventh period, when I knew I'd see LaTanya. I still didn't know if Sam had contacted her or what was up, but sure enough, she was waiting for me in Sappey's class-room. As soon as I sat down, she whispered, "Well? Are you going to tell me or what?"

I said, "I don't know what you're talking about."

I must've been real convincing, too, because LaTanya started laughing. I guessed she hadn't heard from Sam. "Come off it," she said, her voice still a whisper. "Tell me why."

"Why what?"

"Why Morgan Carter is hiding out in my high school."

Even though I kind of knew that she knew, hearing her say the words made me feel like I was going to throw up.

"Not here," I said. "Please—not here."

The dismissal bell rang too soon. LaTanya followed me out into the hallway, crammed with people going to their lockers, shouting out to one another, pushing by us because we were in the way. The noise thundered in my ears.

"Outside," I said. LaTanya nodded her agreement.

We walked to a far corner of campus and I dragged LaTanya behind a fairly secluded tree.

"Go on," she urged. "We're alone now. Give up the goods!"

I didn't know what to say. I was already kicking myself for not denying the accusation more forcefully.

"Ask me how I knew," LaTanya commanded. "Go on, ask."

She didn't wait for me to answer. Instead, she reached into her backpack and pulled out last week's *People* magazine. I could read the headline right away: IS CHICAGO THE NEW L.A.? There, on the top-right-hand corner of the page, was a semi-blurry picture of Marissa doing her table dance. I looked more closely. Standing behind and to the left of Marissa was none other than *me*.

"I had my suspicions when I was writing that paper. You know, about *Girls on Top*? I found some pictures of Morgan Carter—er, *you*—when you were younger, and I thought, 'Damn, Claudia *does* look like that actress.' And I found lots of articles about you and Marissa Dahl and all the trouble you two used to get into.

"So then I was at the dentist, right? And flipping through that issue of *People*. If you read it, you'll see it talks about

Marissa's breakup with Evan Walsh. That's when I remembered what Lauren Johnson said at the first VIP meeting, about you having a boyfriend named Evan Walsh."

She tossed her long dreadlocks over one shoulder and paused to take a breath. "By the time you mentioned you'd gone to Chicago," she continued, "I'd pretty much put it all together."

LaTanya smiled triumphantly, like I should pleased with her Nancy Drew impersonation. Instead, I thrust the *People* back at her. "This doesn't prove anything," I said defensively.

She waved me off. "People were already saying you looked like her. You. You looked like *you*. Whatever, you know what I mean."

"Who?" I asked. "Who was saying these things?"

"I gotta know," she said, ignoring my question. "What are you doing here? Researching a big movie role?"

I snorted. "Yeah, right. Like that ever happens."

She persisted, and eventually I relented, giving her the short-short version of how I'd landed myself in Fort Wayne. "Girl," LaTanya said, "now *that* is a story!"

I asked her how many people she'd told and she said none. "Why would I go spreading some crazy rumor before I even knew it was true?" she asked.

"Great," I said. "Now that you know, I guess everyone else will by tomorrow."

Her eyes narrowed. "Do you really think I would do that?"

I shrugged. "Why wouldn't you? *You* don't have anything at stake."

"But *you* do," she said. "So your secret is safe with me. Pinky swear."

Was she for real? I couldn't tell. I stared at her crooked pinky finger until she started shaking it in front of my face. "I pinky swear it," she repeated.

I linked my pinky through hers and she squeezed it lightly. Then she pulled me into a hug. "Poor thing," she said, patting my shoulder. "No wonder Sappey gets under your skin."

Then she told me she had to run. "But no worries," she said. She waved her pinky for emphasis.

Yeah. Easy for her to say. *Her* future didn't rest on the honor of *my* smallest digit.

Since I'd already missed my bus, I decided to drop in on Ms. Janet Moore. But by the time I got to her office, her key was already in the lock.

"I need to talk to you," I said.

She looked at her watch and frowned. "Can it wait until tomorrow morning?"

"Please," I begged. "I need to talk to you *now*."

She sighed heavily but unlocked the door anyway. As soon as we were in the room, I relocked it from inside. Then I sank into a chair and leaned back far enough that all I could see was ceiling.

"Come on, Claudia," Janet said. "What's going on?"

"Everything I say in here is confidential," I said. "Right?"

Janet nodded. I thought about how she'd torn into both Barke and Sappey at that intervention last week—how she'd leaped to my defense when no one else had. And how, even though she knew that I'd been raped and that I was a recovering addict, as far as I knew, she'd kept all that information to herself.

So I told her everything. Beginning from the time Sam

214

hatched this little plan straight on through to LaTanya confronting me after Sappey's class today.

It felt good, too.

The weirdest thing was that Janet didn't look the least bit shocked. I asked her if she already knew. "No," she said. "Of course not. But at least now I understand why you're having such a tough time adjusting to life at Snider."

"You swear you won't tell anyone," I said.

"Claud—*Morgan*," she corrected herself. "I doubt you would've told me if you didn't trust me. Am I right?"

I nodded.

"Good," she said. "Now I have to get going. But I want you here tomorrow morning at six-thirty sharp. We've got a lot to talk about. And don't think I've forgotten about those nightmares you were having."

It felt like a million years ago—the slumber party, Harlan Darly popping up in my dreams, spilling the whole sordid story to Janet in this very chair. Well, most of the sordid story. She still didn't know Harlan Darly was my rapist.

I asked Janet where she was headed. "I've got an appointment with my own therapist," she confessed. It wasn't the answer I'd been looking for.

"I, uh, meant which direction you were taking," I said. "I kind of need a ride home."

WHO	KNOWS	DOESN'T KNOW
Emily Whitmarsh	That I'm a recovering addict AND that I never had a boyfriend named Evan Walsh	Just about everything else

Eli Whitmarsh	That I can't have my picture taken AND that I moved here to hide from my past AND that my dad killed my dog Muppet (NOTE TO SELF: Tell less-complicated lies!)	My real identity OR that I'm a recovering addict OR that I might have a crush on him
Ms. Janet Moore	~~That I was raped and that I'm a recovering addict AND that I'm really Morgan Carter~~ Everything except that . . .	Harlan Darly was my rapist ~~OR my real identity~~
Debbie Ackerman	That I used to have a boyfriend named Evan Walsh AND that I supposedly have a friend named Daisy Duchovny AND that Eli Whitmarsh likes me	My real identity OR that I'm a recovering addict
LaTanya	~~I was in Chicago last weekend~~ EVERYTHING!!!	~~Who I was with or why~~
Marissa	Everything	That despite the near-constant fear of being found out, I actually sort of like it here
Trudy	Everything . . .	~~. . . except that I miss us being close and that I really am sorry for disappointing her~~

9/29

Happy birthday to me.

Happy birthday to me.

Happy birthday gimongous screwup loser girl,

Happy birthday to me.

9/29—Later

I dressed in all black today. I figured I might as well mourn what could very well be the worst birthday ever.

This time last year I and three hundred of my closest friends were packed into the Avalon for the fake prom I threw in honor of my birthday. I wore a fifties-style Betsey Johnson frothy pink strapless dress and the tiara Marissa had bought me as a present when she was in Paris. Orlando Bloom, dashing in his powder blue disco tux, did a body shot off my chest (if I remember correctly—I was pretty wasted) and *oh*. Yeah.

I'll never have fun like that again.

But get this: when I dragged my sorry ass into Janet's office this morning, she had a small tower of Krispy Kremes on a crystal plate, with five purple candles sticking out of the top one. She lit them as I closed and locked the door behind me, and then she sang me the birthday song, only instead of "gimongous screwup loser girl," she used my name. My real one. Morgan.

I asked her how she knew it was my birthday and she said, "I Googled you when I got home last night. I thought maybe it would help our sessions. Anyway, forget about that for now. You need to make a wish!"

I closed my eyes and tried to think of what I wanted most in the world. There were lots of things to choose from, but one was stubborn and kept pushing all of the other options aside. So I went with that one and blew out the flame. (What, like I'm really going to write my birthday wish in my diary? That's just as bad as telling people what you wished for!)

After we'd scarfed down a doughnut apiece, Janet asked me gently why I'd chosen to wear black on my birthday. I shrugged. "I guess because it doesn't feel like my birthday," I said. "I mean, this is great. Really. I wasn't expecting it at all. But . . ." I told her about the party I'd had last year and how I'd realized nothing would ever be the same.

"You're right," Janet said thoughtfully. "Now that you're sober, you'll probably remember more of your life. And if you do something really stupid, at least you'll be conscious of it. No more blackouts. No more hangovers."

"No more fun," I added.

"Morgan," she chastised, "that's not true and you know it."

I told her I didn't want to discuss my birthday anymore, so instead we talked a bit about how real school was different from on-set school. Janet wanted to know where I was having the most problems. I told her that most of my classes were boring and that I could not subscribe to the theory that my job as a student was to simply parrot back everything my teachers said.

"And then there's Sappey," I continued. "I mean, okay. He gave me an A-minus on my last paper. But before that he was, like, *punishing* me, because he thought I was making up these weird paper topics just trying to piss him off. I'm pretty sure I know what I'm talking about, you know, having been in the industry for most of my . . ."

As my voice trailed off I noticed that the heart-shaped

picture frame was no longer facedown on Janet Moore's desk—it was gone.

"Whoa," I said. "You didn't, like, *break up* with him or anything, did you?"

Her nostrils flared. "That's irrelevant. But I will say I understand where you're coming from. Mr. Sappey can be quite difficult . . . *hardheaded*, even . . . and yes, it's frustrating."

Ooh, *snap*! Take that, Sappey, you pretentious little snot bag!

Actually, something's a little different about Sappey lately. First there was that A-minus. Then today in class he didn't shoot me one disparaging glance. He even smiled at me once, and it looked fairly genuine. For Sappey, I mean. And the weirdest part? Discussion today focused on the different elements of moviemaking, and he asked the class what we thought was the most important component. LaTanya said it was the director, and this kid Angus said it had to be the writer, and some giggly girl whose name I can never remember said that actors were tops. I tried to hold myself back but couldn't help raising my hand.

"They're all instrumental to a film's success," I said. "But if you want to talk importance, I'd have to say the editor. A good editor can take a jumbled mess of footage and turn it into a decent film. A bad editor, on the other hand, can take the guts of what should be a great film and turn them into something that will go direct to DVD."

Sappey beamed at me. No fooling. "Excellent observations, Claudia!" he exclaimed. "It takes a sophisticated filmgoer to recognize how crucial a skilled editor is to the process."

!
?

It makes me wonder if he hit his head in the shower this morning. That, or maybe he's so bitter over whatever's going on between him and Janet, he doesn't have any poison available to spew onto me.

LaTanya didn't try to talk to me before or after class; if anything, she had this hard look on her face, like suddenly we weren't friends. I was grateful, actually, figuring it was best to keep my distance from her for a while.

I headed over to the VIP meeting after school and was surprised to see that membership had doubled in the past week. I vaguely remembered Emily telling me that LaTanya had snagged some kids from our film class who were into the whole horror movie theme. All I could think was, *Oh God—what if she* told?

Then an anxiety attack hit me with the force of a Mack truck. I could not fight the thought that they'd signed up because of me. That somehow everyone in school suddenly knew who I was. I started hyperventilating; sweat beaded on my temples. The logical part of me knew that Emily would be disappointed if I skipped the meeting, but the physiological part of me told me to *run*.

So I did. Straight into Eli Whitmarsh's arms.

He was in the yearbook room this time, his head bent over a light box. I said his name and it came out strangled.

"What is it?" he asked. "What's wrong?"

"Scared," I said. "I'm scared."

He held me wordlessly as I sobbed into the shoulder of his polo shirt. Then, when my breathing was semi-normal again, he said, "Come on, let's get out of here."

"Where are we going?" I hiccupped, but he didn't answer.

We made it as far as the twins' car. I started to put on

my seat belt, but Eli told me not to bother. Instead, he reached behind his seat and pulled out a squishy, shapeless mound wrapped in Tiffany-blue paper.

"I've been looking for the right time to give this to you," he said. "Here, open it."

It was like he knew without knowing. I worked a fingernail under the tape and gingerly pulled it apart. Inside was a stuffed puppy dog with glassy brown eyes.

"Oh, Eli," I breathed.

"I wanted to get you a real one," he said, "but I didn't know if your aunt would be too thrilled, so . . . I wasn't sure what color Muppet was, but I'm hoping—"

Before he could say another word, I pressed my mouth against his. Eli tensed up for a second before melting into me. I could feel his heart beating against my chest, could taste the salt of his tongue. It was the kind of kiss that made me forget how red and puffy I must've looked. The kind of kiss I never wanted to end.

A knock on the window took care of that, though. It was Emily, standing there, her jaw down to her knees. I couldn't even look her in the eye as I rolled down the window.

"Well," she said crisply. "Can I just you ask you one question?"

I nodded, bracing myself for the worst.

"What took the two of you so damned long? Eli, unlock the door, please. I'm *freezing*."

Now it was my turn for the jaw-to-the-knees bit. I couldn't say a word as Emily climbed into the backseat and started chatting on about the VIP meeting. When I tried to apologize for missing it, she wouldn't let me finish.

"No worries," Em said breezily. "But before I forget—

we're having another planning meeting this Friday, and everybody voted to have it at your house again. That way, you have to be there."

The thought of LaTanya inside my house gave me goose bumps. "I don't think that's such a good idea, Em," I said. "Can't we—"

"It's already settled," she said, cutting me off. "Friday, four-thirty."

Okay, then.

When they dropped me off, Emily got out so she could take the front seat. But before she did, she leaned in toward me and whispered, "Call me tonight; I want details. In exchange I'll tell you a *ghost* story or two." I was still feeling sort of dazed, so it took me a while to realize she meant Caspar, aka the new boy.

Trudy got off work a little early. She came home bearing gifts of helium balloons and takeout from Casa D'Angelo, including four different desserts. "I know it's not a birthday cake," she apologized.

"No," I said. "It's better."

After our celebration I started dialing Emily's number and then stopped. I knew she'd want to talk about what had happened with me and Eli, and I wasn't ready to discuss it yet, not with anybody. But also, even though part of me was dying to find out more about this Caspar cat, my head wasn't exactly in the right place for girl talk. So I hung up the phone and tried to keep busy working on geometry formulas.

Periodically, my fingers would fly up to my bottom lip, which was slightly bruised from earlier—but in a good way. Falling for Eli Whitmarsh had definitely not been part of my plan. And on a logical level I knew I shouldn't have kissed him. Things were complicated enough already. I couldn't so much as see my shadow anymore without thinking some burly photographer was going to jump out of the bushes and snap my picture. Plus the NA guidelines clearly state that I shouldn't get involved with anyone romantically. Even so, forget for a second that I'm still in my first year of recovery. There's still this whole issue of Eli not having the first clue who I really am.

Christ, *I* don't know who I am anymore!

Today I turned seventeen years old, but I feel at least seventy.

And I still haven't heard a single word from Bianca.

9/30

I floated through school today, a ghost in blue jeans. I know I went to all of my classes, but I can't remember a single thing I was supposed to learn.

Eli stopped me outside the caf and asked me if I wanted to sneak off campus for lunch. I was too worn out to say no, so I went. He drove to the nearest Starbucks so I could power-load on caffeine. "You look tired," he said.

"More than you know," I replied.

He made me eat a turkey wrap even though I wasn't hungry. "Coffee is acid on an empty stomach," he said. "Well, here it's always acid. But it's way worse if you don't have any food in you."

I was downing my second grande Sumatra when Eli gently placed his hand on my knee. I forced myself not to flinch. It wasn't that I didn't want his hand there, but I was still so confused as to what was right and what was wrong.

"Claudia," Eli said, "I need to ask you something."

"Okay."

"Yesterday . . . it was nice. And I was thinking . . . well, couldn't we maybe go out sometime? Just you and me. Like on a date. A real one."

I put the paper cup of coffee down. "I don't know, Eli."

He blinked several times, rapidly. Then, in a semi-squeaky voice he said, "Oh."

It was the *oh* that did me in. He sounded so hurt. I couldn't explain to him why I was hesitating. Doing that would mean telling him everything, and even though I had a feeling Eli Whitmarsh knew how to keep a secret, the burden of mine seemed too great to put on his shoulders, especially when I was barely holding it up on my own.

"You won't understand this," I said softly, "but if you ask me that same question a couple of months from now, I'll probably say yes. No, I'm pretty sure I will. But I can't right now, okay? So please—can we still be friends? Just until . . . until I figure everything out."

He nodded, but his eyes held that slightly stunned look, like he couldn't believe what he was hearing. I couldn't believe it either. But this was what was best, right? For him and for me.

Eli started to stand up from the table, but I impulsively grabbed his sleeve hard enough that he sat back down. His head was bowed slightly; a too-long shock of hair dipped into his eyes. I brushed it off his forehead and then, as if I were on automatic pilot, I leaned over into his space and kissed him again.

This one lasted much longer than the first, and when we finally pulled apart, I had trouble catching my breath. Eli touched the back of his hand to the side of my face and said,

"You kiss all your friends like that?" He meant it as a joke, but it landed like a punch to the stomach.

"We should go back," I said.

In the car Eli's hand crept over until it found mine, and he held it on the drive back to school. Neither of us said a word. Then, when he dropped me off at the front of the building, he asked me if he could call me tonight. I nodded dumbly and headed inside.

Later, in film, I found out what Sam had meant earlier when he'd said he was getting "on" the LaTanya situation. Turns out he did a background check on her, found out she was already eighteen, and dispatched a lawyer to make her sign another one of those confidentiality agreements. The cost? A full $100K.

I know this because I dared to talk to LaTanya after class today. She ignored me. I followed her to her locker, thinking at first I couldn't get her attention. Finally she whipped around and said, "Stop tailing me!"

"What are you talking about?" I asked. "I just wanted to say hi."

She shook her head at me, lips pursed tight. "Did you think I was going to be happy about your lawyer trying to buy me off? I gave you my word. But no. You had to send someone digging in my financial business—my *parents'* financial business—to see if I had a price. Well, I do. Happy now?"

"Wait," I said. "I don't understand."

"Right." She tossed her dreads and shifted her bag to her other shoulder. "I didn't want to take your money, *Claudia*, but Miami didn't give me enough financial aid to cover my tuition, as your daddy found out. That hundred grand might even get me through to grad school. So maybe I should be thanking you."

I stood there, jaw to the floor, as she sashayed away. This was Sam's master plan? Paying off that photographer and now LaTanya? I wondered who else he had made "agreements" with.

It struck me then that there was no way to win this situation. If my cover got blown, it could ruin everything I'd worked for to restore my former life. But even if I somehow miraculously lasted a full school year in Fort Wayne, when the truth came out, it would end up destroying everything I'd built here. And I couldn't see my friendship with the Whitmarsh twins surviving beyond either scenario, so in that respect, I was already screwed.

Seventeen has certainly gotten off to a great start.

10/1

I begged Trudy to let me stay home from school today, but she refused. "Morgan, you've just gotten caught up," she said. "Why would you mess that up now?"

I wanted to say, "Because everything else is already messed up anyway." Instead, I said, "Give me five minutes to get changed."

"It's for the best," Trudy said as we headed over to Snider. "Besides, aren't you having some meeting at the house tonight?"

Of course I'd forgotten all about that. It was no use trying to avoid the twins today; in a few short hours they *and* LaTanya would be invading the one safe space I had left.

Crap. Chappelle is passing out a pop quiz I'm completely unprepared for. More soon.

Hard to believe that earlier today I was sure things couldn't get any worse.

I was wrong.

The twins were the first to arrive at the VIP meeting. But I was beyond speechless to see who they'd brought along:

Debbie "I hate your guts" Ackerman.

"Hi, Claudia," she says, her voice all syrupy sweet. "When Emily told me you were helping out with her haunted house project, I just knew I had to be a part of it too."

"Great," I said. "The more the merrier."

We once again set up camp at the dining room table, Emily sat at one head, with Eli to her right and me to her left. Debbie smiled smugly as she claimed the chair next to Eli, like she'd just won part of the battle. If she'd been more boy savvy, she'd have realized that sitting across from the guy you're crushing on is way better than sitting next to him because if you're looking at each other, you can send all sorts of messages with your eyebrows alone.

Emily was annoyed because it took about half an hour for everyone to arrive, so we didn't even start the meeting until five. I was just relieved that LaTanya didn't show. I wonder if not entering my house was part of her confidentiality agreement. Anyway, Em is as insanely organized as her brother, and she had drawn up flowcharts on poster board that outlined each task that needed to be accomplished, when it needed to be done by, and how many people it would require. Then she passed out a separate chart she'd photocopied onto light orange paper that made suggestions as to who should sign up for what.

This turned out to be problematic, because Emily forgot

to factor in that most of the crew had other outside obliga- tions. The scheduling conflicts are too numerous to list here, but suffice it to say that negotiations went on for quite a while.

As everyone argued over who would get to do what, Debbie excused herself to use the bathroom and I headed into the kitchen to get refills on everyone's drinks. Twenty min- utes later, Emily had mapped out a plan that accommodated everyone, but by that time everyone was so exhausted that she called for a ten-minute bathroom break.

That was when I realized that the bathroom was free, but Debbie hadn't returned to the table. I leaped up and practically sprinted to my bedroom, where, sure enough, Debbie Ackerman was sitting on the end of my bed, flipping through the latest issue of *Entertainment Weekly*. My pink crystal-encrusted cell phone was sitting in plain view on my nightstand just a foot away.

"What are you doing in here?" I asked too sharply.

She shrugged. "I just wanted to see your room. You've seen mine, remember?"

"I thought I'd closed the door."

"Oh," she said, "you had. But I thought it was the bath- room, so I opened it." She nodded toward my cell. "That's a pretty phone. Kind of bling-bling, isn't it?"

"It was a present," I said tightly. "From a friend."

She smiled sweetly. "That's what I figured."

Before I headed out, I swiped the phone and jammed it into my pocket. Then, while Emily called the meeting back to order, I ducked into the bathroom myself to see what kind of incriminating evidence might have been stored on my cell. Luckily I didn't have any messages—incoming or outgoing—saved. I scrolled through my contacts, but when Marissa had programmed her number in, she'd done it under the name "Daisy," so even if Debbie *had* gone trolling through the list, she wouldn't have seen anything suspicious.

Still, I felt completely jittery the rest of the meeting, the kind of shakes I used to get thirty seconds after I'd snorted something. And as much as I tried to cover it, I knew it must be showing, because Eli's smiles morphed into concerned semi-frowns, and his twinkly eyes got seriously sober. When I went to refresh my soda—excuse me, my *pop*—for the fourth time, he followed me into the kitchen.

"Everything okay?" he asked. "You look a little weirded out."

He was standing just a little too close to me—you know, where the space between us was so small I could feel the static electricity from his shirt. It would've been so easy for me to slam him against the counter and kiss him hard.

I backed away from him—said I thought I was coming down with a cold and I didn't want him to catch it.

"I don't mind," he said.

"But I do." I fake coughed into my hand. "See what I mean?" I scrambled back to the table before he could say anything further.

The twins (and Debbie) were the last to leave. Before she headed out, Emily asked if I could help her run the big organizational meeting, which was going to be held at the theater next Wednesday night. "Sure," I said listlessly. "Why not?"

I was standing in the doorway waving goodbye when Debbie turned around and trotted back. "I forgot my sweater," she said. "Can you let me in?"

"You brought a sweater?"

She shut the door behind us. Then she said, "So I have to know, Claudia—why did you steal the one boy I cared about who might actually have cared about me?"

And then, just like that, I was tired of playing games. So I said, "I know this isn't what you want to hear, but I actually have feelings for Eli. I'm sorry about that. Really, I wish things were different. But they're not, and you can't keep punishing me for something that's out of my control."

"*Out of your control?*" she echoed. "You knew I liked him, and you went after him anyway. Fine. Whatever. But someday this will come back on you. Just watch."

Before I could respond—or determine whether or not she'd issued me a genuine threat—Debbie was already gone.

Another anxiety attack swept over me. I locked the front door and ran back to my bedroom. Everything seemed to be in place, and with the exception of the cell phone, nothing personal had been left out. I'd even had the foresight to hide this journal in my laundry basket (the only drawback to that ingenious move is that all the pages now smell like feet). I checked the closet too, but besides a couple of designer labels that I'm pretty sure Debbie Ackerman wouldn't recognize, it was free of any identifying items.

Debbie didn't know anything except for the fact that the boy she was in love with preferred me instead.

I have got to stop being so paranoid. Even though there are now two people in Snider who know my secret, both are legally bound to keep it. And honestly, if Sam hadn't bothered to pay LaTanya off, I still don't think she would've sold me out. It's just not her style.

How is this all going to end?

When is this all going to end?
I wish I knew.

10/3

Dear Marissa,

How would you like a new roommate for Christmas?

I've been thinking over your offer and how maybe I should take you up on it. Is it still good? The reason I ask is because I've screwed up pretty bad. I spent most of the weekend hunkered down in my room, trying to figure out how I can clean up all the messes I've made, but I don't think it's possible. I'm not sure why I ever thought this plan would work to begin with.

A week ago Sam suggested I give up and go back to L.A. At the time I was like, "No way," but now . . . maybe he's right. Maybe there is where I'm supposed to be.

Do you remember how you asked me if I'd gotten any "hot farm boy action"? Well, I wouldn't exactly call him "hot" or "a farm boy," but that guy Eli—the one who bought you the cider?—he's had a thing for me practically since I moved here. I'm not sure how it happened, but I'm starting to fall for him too. I can't explain it, Marissa. He's just so . . . *nice*. And I mean that in a good way. I feel like he knows me a hundred times better than anyone I've ever hooked up with, which is really sort of ironic, since he thinks I'm Claudia Miller, teenager on the run from her psychotic, dog-murdering father. (Don't ask.)

See what a pretty mess I've made?

Shamefully yours,

Morgan

Week
EIGHT

10/4

This morning's meeting with Janet was really good, despite the fact that I had to talk myself into going. She asked me why I looked so depressed and I filled her in on all the missing pieces, including the letter I wrote to Marissa last night.

"I feel sick to my stomach," I told her. "There's, like, *danger* everywhere I look. It's like all I'm doing is waiting for this thing to blow up in my face."

"That's one way of dealing with it," Janet said thoughtfully. "Or you could say to yourself, 'If it blows up, it blows up.' Then, instead of worrying all the time about something over which you have no real control, you might be able to enjoy the good stuff once in a while. Like Eli. He sounds good."

"Except you know I'm not supposed to be dating."

She sighed patiently. "Morgan, rules are made to be broken. You've been sober now what? Almost nine months? If you like this guy, and he makes you feel good about yourself, and you're not in danger of ruining your sobriety, then what's the harm?"

Before I left, she made me promise to make a list in my journal of five things I liked today. I'm supposed to do this each night before I go to bed so I can start focusing more on the positives than the negatives. So, here goes:

~~Five~~ Three Things I Liked about Today

1. Ms. Vineyard had to have emergency foot surgery over the weekend, so we won't have real gym class for at least a week.
2. Debbie Ackerman has some kind of twenty-four-hour flu and stayed home from school.
3. Sappey was also absent, and our sub was a nice woman named Mary Beth who actually knew what she was talking about.

I wonder if I should be concerned that my level of happiness increased forty times over just because I didn't have to see those three people today.

Or maybe I should, as Janet says, simply enjoy the goodness while I can.

10/5

~~Three~~ Five Things I Liked about Today

1. Eli brought me a grande Sumatra this morning in homeroom. Starbucks coffee is the bomb: even if you only got four and a half hours of sleep, you can still function like a normal person if you drink enough of it.
2. I got a 68 on my geometry quiz. That's almost a C!!!
3. Both Debbie and Sappey were absent again today.
4. LaTanya's cold shoulder has gotten warmer. She even smiled at me as she left class today. At first I didn't know why she was so mad, but I'm pretty sure that Sam's

234

lawyer's offer bruised her pride. I hope she realizes that nobody's thinking that she's some charity case.

5. Eli called about an hour ago just to say good night. But instead of saying " 'bye" he said, "Sweet dreams, you." It made me melt just a little inside.

Speaking of Eli, I spent the afternoon with him and Em, getting ready for tomorrow's big meeting. This entailed making visits to friends of Mr. and Mrs. Whitmarsh who were helping out in some way. Tom, who runs a pumpkin patch, agreed to donate a ton of baby-size specimens, so for $2.50, anyone who wants to can purchase a mini-gourd and, using the paint donated by Christine, who runs an art supply store, make their very own take-home jack-o'-lantern. For the littlest of little kids, Sheila, the librarian, agreed to organize a read-aloud of Halloween-themed books. And a whole posse of Ladies Who Lunch that Mrs. W. knows from various political dinners and charity fund-raisers is going to head up refreshments. We suggested a booth, but they told us we were thinking too small, so now there's going to be a full-on tent with tons of seating—and they swear they can get everything donated, so none of it will cost us a single penny.

I couldn't believe how much Emily had gotten accomplished while I was hibernating. Even before that, too. The movie theme was my idea, but the execution has been all Emily's. She never ceases to amaze me.

Our final stop of the day was to see Billy Jack Jones (and yes, that's his real name), who runs a lumberyard. According to the sketches we had Mr. Cart, the shop teacher, draw up for us, the project will use about three times the amount of wood we have left over from last year. Since whatever money we have in our budget has to be earmarked for special effects, our plan was to beg B. J. for a ton of stuff.

He wasn't as easily swayed by the whole charity aspect as the others were. I couldn't believe that a year ago, people like Donatella Versace were throwing designer gowns at me, just on the off chance I might wear one to, like, the Emmys or something. That's when I realized we were wasting a valuable resource.

"We can give you free advertising," I said. "We'll have a huge sign at the entrance that reads, 'B. J. Jones Lumber Presents the Haunted Halloween Village.'"

This gave Billy Jack pause. "How big'll the sign be?"

"Depends," I replied. "How much wood are you going to give us?"

Worked like a charm.

Must run through my own lists for tomorrow. So much to do, so little time.

10/6

This is too much. It is now day THREE of Snider High School operating without its gym teacher, its film teacher, and its yearbook editor. There aren't a lot of other people who've completely disappeared, so I can't blame it on some contagious-cold thing.

Blame my paranoia, but I think something odd is going on.

I just hope it has absolutely nothing to do with me.

The meeting was a rousing success! (And by "meeting" I mean the Halloween Village planning meeting and not my NA meeting, which isn't until tomorrow night.) ANYWAY, the theater was practically filled to capacity with volunteers who were either willing or roped into the project by Mr. and Mrs. Whitmarsh. The twins' parents were even in attendance, although Mr. W. had to leave early for another meeting of his own.

Mr. Cart came, saying he was offering his shop guys major extra credit if they came to the farm after school and helped raise the structure. He'd brought his good friend, Mr. Aronson, who runs the largest independent hardware store in the area, with him, and Mr. A. said he'd donate all the latex paint and supplies we'd need, provided we didn't mind using some of the returns that he'd re-tint for us.

It all came together so beautifully, and even the theater people jumped on board. The volunteer actors were way stoked about the chance to play Freddie and Jason and Norman Bates. They even had *more* great ideas, especially this girl named Satchel, who was some kind of genius with lighting and started spouting off about scrims and gels and stuff. We organized the theater people into teams by room, and then they went off in batches to the prop closet to see what they could borrow for the haunted house.

I feel so . . . exhilarated! Like, finally I'm doing something I'm good at—something people can see I'm good at—and I'm even having fun while I'm doing it. It's like . . . yeah. *Awesome.*

I think I'm going to try to do tomorrow's homework tonight, because after school the twins and I are going to help Mr. Cart's guys and maybe start the painting. I'll have to leave before sundown so that I can make my other meeting on time, but if I can work ahead, I'll have tomorrow night free to make more calls and check in to see that everything's running smoothly.

No list for tonight—besides, there were more than five things I liked about today. (Paranoia notwithstanding.)

10/7

Weirdest. Day. Ever.

Vineyard's finally back, her foot all bandaged up. The surgery didn't affect her cigarette-smoky growl of a voice, and she worked us extra hard in class today—double the normal number of indoor laps. I got violently sweaty and looked just awful, a fact that didn't go unnoticed by Debbie Ackerman, who was sitting primly at our lunch table for the first time all week. Her eyes were sparkling and her mouth was smiling, but her pores oozed pure evil. Something was up. I couldn't shake the image of her sitting on the edge of my bed, not twelve inches away from my cell phone. Had she dialed a number? No, because the call log had been clear too.

Fast-forward to film class, when Principal Barke made an appearance to tell us that Sappey would not be returning. Shocker! Apparently, he just up and quit over the weekend, without any warning, saying that he'd finally secured financing for his independent film (I knew it! I knew he was a wannabe!). I ran to Janet's office as soon as the final bell rang because I just had to see her reaction, but her door was locked and she was already gone. I have an appointment with her tomorrow morning, so I guess I'll have to wait until then.

Oh, but the weird(er) parts: I spent most of the day feeling like I was being followed. I know, I know. Most likely paranoia again. Still, I kept searching people's faces, wondering if I'd seen them before.

The twins and I did end up cracking open the paint at the farm site after school. Unfortunately, Emily was the only one who'd thought to brought a smock, so when Eli playfully started a late-afternoon paint fight, she came out unscathed while the two of us were covered head to toe. And then I didn't even have time to change clothes before my NA meeting, so I went to the church dripping white.

The meeting was fine, but I spent most of it making mental lists of what I'd need to do tomorrow and over the weekend. Anything to get my mind off Debbie and what she might or might not be planning. My head was still all clouded in thought when I left and headed to Trudy's car. I could've sworn I heard someone say, "Hey, Morgan!" and my head whipped around, but once again, no one was there.

Trudy was supposed to drop me off at home and then head back out to Dave's for a late dinner, but as I snapped my seat belt into place, she took quick stock of my mood.

"What's wrong?" she asked.

I said, "I think I'm being followed."

She frowned. "What? Why?"

I quickly explained the intense feeling I'd been unable to shake and how I thought I'd heard someone call my name.

"You probably think I'm crazy," I said. "But still . . ."

"I'll drive home a different way," Trudy insisted. "And I'll call Dave and cancel for tonight. I'd feel better if I was home with you."

239

"Are you sure?" I asked.

"Positive."

When we got back to the house, there was a brown paper package sitting on the front stoop. It was addressed to Claudia Miller; the return address was from a B. Rosenbaum (aka my mother).

I opened it inside the house and discovered a pair of Gucci sunglasses and a set of first-class airline tickets made out in my own name. There was a Post-it stuck to the sunglasses that read, *Hey, birthday girl—save these for Fiji! Love and misses, Mom.* I didn't care that the birthday present was over a week late or that she still hadn't returned any of my calls. What bothered me was that she still thought we were spending Christmas in Fiji. This meant that either she never got my letter to her or she did and decided to ignore it. Both were viable options.

Leaving the sunglasses and tickets in the box, I pulled out my cell to turn it back to normal (I always put it on silent when I'm at a meeting). That's when I saw the missed call from Eli. His message sounded urgent, so I called him back right away. Apparently there was this reporter guy who was hanging around the Haunted Village site today asking a lot of questions.

"He kept asking us about you in particular," Eli said. "But I told him you wouldn't want to have your picture taken—that he couldn't even put your name in the article."

"You didn't," I said, my voice barely above a whisper.

"Yeah, why?"

"I have to go," I told him. "I'll see you tomorrow."

Another panic attack washed over me. I tried to talk myself out of it.

Of course this reporter was asking about me, I reasoned.

I was an integral part of the Haunted Village planning committee. He was probably just looking for a quote.

But deep inside, the coincidences—and my weird feelings—were starting to stack up. I needed a second opinion. I tried calling Sam and my mom, but it was late. I didn't get an answer. I didn't leave a message.

I'm so tired, and worn out from all this worry I can't write another word.

I'll sleep now and get in touch with Sam tomorrow.

10/8

At least I know I'm not crazy.

I found out at school this morning—from Janet.

Or rather, from Janet pushing this morning's copy of the *Journal Gazette* (the *News-Sentinel*'s rival paper) in front of me about thirty seconds after I entered her office.

On the front page, an enormous, full-color picture of me, coming out of last night's meeting, hair stringy with dried gym class sweat and still streaked with Haunted Village paint.

The headline?

HOLLYWOOD STARLET "HIDING OUT" AT SNIDER HIGH.

Oh my freaking *God*.

I started shaking even before I'd finished reading the sentence. My breath got shallow, like there wasn't enough oxygen for my lungs. I felt like I was in one of those fight sequences from *The Matrix*, where time slows down exponentially, yet you're still conscious of everything around you. I kept reading the words over and over: *HOLLYWOOD STARLET "HIDING OUT" AT SNIDER HIGH.*

Before I could pull it together enough to read even the

lead paragraph of the article, Janet said, "There's more." Inside, on the front page of the Arts & Entertainment section, was a big ol' picture of Sappey, looking typically pretentious in a tight black turtleneck, his mouth curled in a sneer. The article seemed to be about his getting funding from an unnamed source—enough so that he could finally make "his film" without the interference of some studio machine.

Janet flipped the front page over so that my picture was next to Sappey's.

It didn't take a genius to make the connection.

"He sold me out," I said. "He sold my story to make his crappy movie. Right?"

Janet nodded. "I'm not sure, but it's the most logical explanation."

"Except how did he *know*?" I felt like I was going to puke.

"LaTanya could have told him," Janet said. "She's in your film class, right?"

I nodded, folding my arms across my stomach. "But she wouldn't have said anything. She signed an agreement." I filled her in on the details of Sam's payoff.

"Think, Morgan," Janet said. "What about your guardian?"

"She's never even met Sappey!" I exploded. "In fact, I don't know anyone who has contact with the man—no one, except maybe . . . *you*."

Her face went completely white. "No, Morgan. I never said a word to anyone."

I stared at her—hard. She blinked.

I was so pissed. All I could think was that Janet Moore was the worst liar I'd ever met.

"If it wasn't you, then why do you look so guilty?" I

could feel the bile rising in the back of my throat. "It *was* you," I said. "How else could he have found out?"

"No," Janet said, but with much less conviction. "You have to believe me. When I promised you confidentiality, I meant it. Nothing you've said to me has been repeated anywhere. Not your problems, not your identity—*nothing*. You have to trust me, Morgan."

I picked up the newsprinted picture of Sappey's smirking face and ripped it half, letting the pieces flutter onto her floor. "That's what I think of your trust," I said, storming out.

The next several minutes were a blur. I ducked into the girls' bathroom to pull my head together. Nothing added up. The story had broken, yet where were the reporters outside Trudy's house? Or the school? I was shakily dialing Trudy's work number on my cell when a man's voice echoed against the tile:

"Miss Miller—Carter—whoever you are," Principal Barke boomed. "I can hear you in there, so you might as well come out."

I did as he said.

"Come to my office, young lady," he commanded. "You've got some explaining to do."

Once again, I ended up staring at him across his wide mahogany desk. "How much of it is true?" he asked.

I swallowed hard. "I don't know," I said. "I haven't read it yet."

He handed me a copy of the paper and said, "Read it now." Then he picked up the phone and started punching numbers hard. "I haven't been able to reach your guardian," he explained, "and I feel it's her responsibility to be here."

I nodded. In less than forty minutes, the halls of Snider

High would be crawling with students. Students whose parents subscribed to the *Journal Gazette*.

Students who'd now know exactly who I was and who'd want to know *why*.

Hands shaking, I tried to at least get the gist of the article. I saw phrases like "recovering addict," "washed up at the age of sixteen," and "barely passing her classes." Then I *really* wanted to puke. At least I figured out why there hadn't been anyone at the house: "While it is certain that Carter has been attending Snider High, her residence has not yet been verified."

But it was the last line that got me: "None of our sources could confirm why Carter chose Fort Wayne as her hideout or what she hoped to gain from the experience. Perhaps, as one of Carter's classmates joked, 'we've all been punk'd.'"

Classmate? LaTanya?

No. LaTanya wouldn't say "punk'd." During our class discussion of *Dude, Where's My Car?*, she'd made it very clear that she had nothing but disdain for Ashton Kutcher and everything he stood for.

That left . . . *Debbie Ackerman*?

Barke was still trying to get ahold of Trudy when his secretary burst in. She was shaking too, but for a different reason. "Sir," she said, "the school is crawling with reporters. They're starting to interrogate the students as they arrive."

"What happened to the police?" Barke asked. "They were told to remove all trespassers immediately."

"I know, sir," she said. "But it looks as if they've been outnumbered."

Barke slammed the phone down and pulled up the shade on his window. There were media vans parked on the lawn of the school, and there were cameras *everywhere*. For every one officer there were at least four hacks.

"Damn it!" Barke shouted. "Make sure they're sending backup. I don't want a lawsuit on my hands. And find this girl's guardian!"

But the reason Barke couldn't get ahold of Trudy was because she'd seen the paper too, when she stopped at Starbucks for her morning coffee. She never even made it to work—just raced over to school to rescue me.

My head wouldn't stop spinning. Barke started yelling at Trudy the minute she walked in, saying she'd put his school in jeopardy by exposing it to this kind of media attention, falsified records this, lawsuit that, blah blah blah. I pulled my cell out of my backpack and quickly dialed Sam.

He answered on the first ring.

"Morgan, baby, are you okay?" he asked.

The minute I heard his voice, I started to cry. "I guess you know, huh?"

"Your mom's booking a flight as we speak," he said. "We'll be there as soon as we can."

"What should I do in the meantime?" I said, sniffing. "This place is like Paparazzi Central."

"Lay low, honey bun," he said. "Get Trudy to take you someplace safe. Go to a police station if you have to. Just . . . keep your phone on. We're coming to get you."

We hung up. "Excuse me," I said, quietly at first and then louder: *"Excuse me!"*

When I'd gotten their attention, I said, "I need to get out of here."

"Not until you've explained some things!" Barke shrilled.

"It'll have to wait," I told him. To Trudy, I said, "Sam wants you to take me someplace 'safe.'"

She nodded. "Let's go."

Despite Barke's attempts to thwart our departure and the dense crush of students creating barriers around the office and the front entrance to the school, little Trudy turned into a top-notch linebacker, pushing through the throngs with brute force. We'd gotten about halfway to the car when I recognized one of the people she was trying to push away: Eli.

I wish I could describe the look on his face. There was shock, but it was more than that. It was like shock tinted with sadness and disappointment. Instantly I knew why. It was because I wasn't who I'd said I was.

I'd been living a lie, and in some ways, so had he. He'd based all of his feelings on the story of someone who doesn't exist.

I reached out to grab Eli's hand, but he pulled away like I'd burned him. Then he just stood there, staring at us as Trudy whisked me away.

When they realized we were leaving campus, the hacks started piling back into their vans and cars so they could tail us to whichever destination we were headed to. Trudy kept saying, "It's going to be okay; we just need a quiet place to figure things out," but all I could do was cry.

That was four, five hours ago. I'm writing this from the finished basement in Trudy's boyfriend Dave's house. What an introduction! We drove to her office first, dumped the car in the parking garage, and took off in Dave's Volvo. Dave, I should note, has been really awesome and supportive, making us soup and grilled cheese sandwiches while I had something of a meltdown.

"I can't stand to see you like this, Morgan," Trudy said. "You're breaking my heart." That's when she started crying too.

Ryan got home from kindergarten around one. He said, "Daddy, what's with all the scary ladies crying in our kitchen?" Trudy and I both cracked up at that. It was the first time either of us had laughed all day.

Then Sam called from Detroit, where apparently you can pick up a direct flight to Fort Wayne International Airport. He said they should be here by dinnertime, which made it sound like all six of us were going to pile into Dave's Volvo and grab a meal at Munchies. He can't get here soon enough. Even though Trudy and Dave have been great, I feel so completely alone right now. We'd never bothered to create a contingency plan if something like this happened. I need Sam to tell me what to do next, how to make this better.

The one thing I have tried to do is get in touch with Eli. I've called the house like half a dozen times since school let out, but no one's answering. I even tried to call from Dave's phone, figuring that way they wouldn't recognize the number, but it just rang and rang and rang, no answering machine or anything. They must've unplugged it. Doesn't surprise me; everyone knew I was friends with the twins. They're probably being stalked too.

We're watching the local news programs to see what they've got to say about me, and the weather dude just said that starting at midnight, we're in for our first snowstorm of the year. Snow! In October!

What else could possibly go wrong?

I'm going to kill that bitch.

Debbie Ackerman told the Channel 15 news team that the "whole school" had suspected I was a liar from the start and that she felt it was her "duty" to get to the bottom of things. I *knew* it! I knew she'd been snooping in my room. Turns out she *had* found something on my phone—the pictures Marissa and I took of each other in that bar in Chicago. Then they did a split screen with the picture that appeared in *People* next to the ones Debbie e-mailed herself from my phone.

She told them that Eli was my boyfriend and that I'd lied to him too. One reporter tried to get Eli to talk, but he said, "No comment," and walked away, Emily by his side. Janet pulled the no-comment thing too. I feel like such a shit for not having believed her when she said she had nothing to do with it.

Barke was the only other person who stopped for the cameras, and all he did was say that the school was looking into the matter, but as far as they were concerned, everything was a rumor until otherwise confirmed. "That's a good man," Dave remarked. If only he knew.

MSNBC was the first national news station to run a piece on the "scandal." It was awful. They pulled up all this old footage of me from my partying days and a snippet from the press conference Sam set up for me right before I went into rehab, when I was a soggy, red-eyed mess.

But the worst part? Jeannette Walls, who's not even a reporter but a *gossip columnist*, interviewed Leah Rozen from *People* magazine, who starts talking about how they were the first to run this photo of me and Marissa dancing at the Hunt Club, which appeared in last week's story about

Chicago being the new celebrity hot spot. They cut to a screen shot of said photo, with a digital red circle "drawn" around my shadowy frame. Then back to Leah, who goes, "We had a pretty strong suspicion that Morgan was the one accompanying Marissa on the town, but we couldn't confirm her identity before going to press."

The segment wrapped with Jeannette telling Ashleigh Banfield that "a lot of folks in Hollywood are concerned about Morgan. Several sources close to the actress tell me they're worried she's not taking her sobriety very seriously. Let's hope for her sake, she is."

Dave's got every TV in the house on and tuned to a different news channel, and he keeps running back and forth between them all to see who's saying what (he's such a sweet guy). Trudy's on the Internet, running Google News searches every five minutes, printing out every new version of the story she can find. As for me, I've been locked in the bathroom since the MSNBC piece aired, because I think if I have to watch another second of this, my meltdown will go Vesuvius.

Trudy's yelling through the door that Sam just called; he and Mom are at the airport and as soon as they secure a rental they'll race over here. Meanwhile, Ryan, Dave's son, is slipping me Kraft cheese slices under the door, saying, "Eat these, okay? They'll make you feel better." What a cute kid. If I ever get out of this hell I'm living in, I'll be sure to give him a big bear hug.

10/8—Much later

Sam and Bianca still aren't here. Apparently, there were reporters staking out the airport and they IDed them almost instantly. So now they're on the phone with Dave, trying to figure out where they can ditch the rental and have him pick them up. It's an unbelievable nightmare.

"Why are you trying to be all secret agent man?" I asked Sam, the last time I spoke with him.

"Because, my dear, no one knows where you're holed up right now," he said. "That gives us the advantage. But if some two-bit hack trails me to this Dave person's house, then there goes your safe place. You got it?"

I knew what he meant, but I still didn't understand the point. The press will find me eventually. It's not like I've been hiding out in Hong Kong.

It's so depressing. Just when I was starting to feel like a part of something—feeling like I really was more of a Claudia Miller than a Morgan Carter—

It's over before it really even began.

10/9—*Very early*

It's 2 a.m. and I haven't slept a wink. I'm still at Dave's house, only I moved from the bathroom to the basement and back up to the living room, where I'm now camped out on Dave's plaid, L.L. Bean–style couch. Sam and Bianca didn't even get in until almost midnight, thanks to the whole cloak-and-dagger routine. Sam's first words to me were, "Morgan, sweetheart—are you all right?" Bianca's? "Marissa was right—you *have* put on a lot of weight!" Sam shot her the evil eye, prompting an immediate apology from Mama Bianca, who then demanded that someone bring her a scotch neat ASAP. Dave looked at me, like, "Is this okay?" and I nodded my assent. I almost made a joke about him bringing me a double, but I didn't think it would play well with this crowd.

After some hugs and kisses and several minutes of Bianca flashing her twelve-carat engagement ring and matching pink-diamond-encrusted wedding band (how J.Lo!), we all sat down around the dining room table to figure out what came next.

SAM: The best-possible thing is for you to lay low for another day or two. Then we'll call a press conference—maybe at the high school—and you'll deliver an impassioned speech about how, after your near-death experience, you simply wanted to experience life as a normal teenager.

BIANCA (nodding): Perfect.

SAM: Oprah's people already called—they want an exclusive—but I think we should give it to Katie Couric. I've got a call in to Mira—remember her? The publicist we hired for you when *Girls on Top* came out? I'm thinking we'll put her on retainer again.

BIANCA: Is that the one with the green hair? She had very poor manners.

SAM (ignoring her): Lorne Michaels owes me a huge favor, so let's see if we can't get you on *Saturday Night Live*, maybe during November sweeps. And the next *Charlie's Angels* installment starts shooting in December, so we'll make sure you get a cameo, maybe with Marissa.

TRUDY: So that's just it? You're going to whisk her away from everything's she's been working on?

SAM: Well, *yes*. The whole reason she's here is to save her career. When the calls come, you answer.

TRUDY (turning to Mom): Bianca, this is crazy! You can't just yank her out of the school year. She's been doing so well!

BIANCA: She's an actor, Tru. Her life is in Hollywood—not here.

TRUDY: "She" has a name, you know. It's Morgan. She's your daughter, remember?

BIANCA: What are you implying?

TRUDY: Just for once, will you consider what's in her best interest instead of yours?

SAM: But Trudy—that's exactly what we're doing. How can you possibly compare a year in high school to a lifelong career?

TRUDY: That's my point! Morgan's spent her *entire childhood* working. Here she has the opportunity to be a normal kid—even if it *is* only for a year.

SAM: Look, I know you mean well, but you don't know the business. If she misses the window . . . well, that could be the end of things.

TRUDY: So what? Is that the worst-possible scenario? Maybe the girl could have college in her future. Maybe she'll find out she doesn't want to be an actress after all.

ME: Um, is anyone going to bother to ask me what I think? What *I* want?

DAVE: What do *you* want?

ME:

BIANCA: Well, Morgan? We're listening.

ME:

SAM: Morgan?

ME (quietly): I don't know.

At this point, Sam declared me exhausted and moved his strategy session to the basement. I turned off all the TVs, pulled a fleece blanket off the back of the couch, and curled up fetal style underneath it. But I can't fall asleep. I'd give anything to be unconscious right now, just for a little while, anyway, but apparently my body and my brain have other ideas.

Even through the floor I can hear cell phones ringing constantly. Why don't they just turn them off? I almost microwaved my own phone, just for the hell of it, but I'm still holding out the faintest hope that Eli might call. Turning off the ringer didn't help with the waiting part, so I chucked the whole unit into Dave's freezer. I'm still checking it every ten to fifteen minutes, though, so I'm not sure what the point is anymore.

I have got to get out of here.

10/9—*Much later*

Added to the long list of my offenses: grand theft auto.

Dave left the keys to his Volvo on the kitchen table. They were just sitting there, calling to me. Forget the fact that I don't technically have a license, or that I was venturing out at 2:30 a.m. completely unaccompanied when there was a small media circus in town searching for me, or that the weather dude was actually right for a change and the storm he predicted was coming on with a vengeance.

Nope, the only thing I could think was, *I have to see the twins.*

It took me a while to get there, not just because of the snow, but also because I'm usually in the passenger seat and therefore don't pay much attention to directions. But Dave's Volvo is a top-of-the-line model, with a way cool GPS system in it. So once I figured out how to use it, it led me to the Whitmarshes' lickety-split.

I'd expected the house itself to be dark, with some reporters camped on the front lawn. Instead, the light in the kitchen was on, and there was one lone security guard parked out front, snoozing, his windshield buried under an inch of powder. Even so, I circled the block again and parked a few houses away, trying to stick to the shadows until I got to the house. Except with that much snow on the ground, the neighborhood looked all lit up, even though it was the dead of night.

I was cold, I was wet, and I was feeling like a total criminal, peeking through the kitchen window. I probably would've been treated like one too if Eli's parents had been in the room instead of him.

He unlatched the back door and ushered me in. "What

are you doing here?" he asked, keeping his voice low. "And why aren't you wearing a coat?"

"I stole a car," I said. "Well, that's not exactly true. I borrowed a car. Only Dave doesn't know I borrowed it yet. And please don't ask me who Dave is because it's a really long story and we have way more important things to talk about."

Eli sat me down at the table and ducked into the guest bathroom for a couple of hand towels so I could dry off. Then he said, "You want some coffee?"

I nodded. "Where's Em?"

"Sleeping," he replied. "It *is* almost three in the morning."

"So why are you awake?"

"Take a guess."

Fair enough. The next several minutes were beyond awkward, but eventually Eli brought two steaming mugs to the table and sat down.

"Hi," he said.

"Hi," I said back.

He sighed. "So why are you here?"

"Here like Fort Wayne?" I asked. "Or here like your house?"

"Both."

I told him all about the Witless Protection Program and what it was supposed to accomplish. He didn't interrupt, not even once, so I had no way of gauging his reaction. Then I said, "I came here—to your house—because they're saying these really horrible things about me on TV, and I didn't want you thinking they were true."

"Oh?" he said. "You mean you're *not* really hiding out from your abusive, dog-murdering bastard of a father?"

I shook my head, guilt flooding every inch of my body.

254

"Just tell me one thing," Eli said. "How much of it was a lie?"

"Well," I began, "my name's not really Claudia Miller."

ELI: Besides that.

ME: I don't have a boyfriend named Evan Walsh, famous or otherwise. And you've probably already figured out who "Daisy" is.

ELI: Okay.

ME: Obviously the dad story was a bit of a fabrication.

ELI: Nice touch there, by the way. Stealing the plot from a TV movie. IMDb is so helpful when you find out the girl you're into is actually a world-renowned celebrity. Anyway, go on.

ME: Other than that and the fact that I was—*am*—an actress . . . it was all true. I mean, even Emily knew about the rehab thing.

ELI: So she said.

ME: Does she hate me?

ELI: I don't think so.

ME: Do you?

ELI: No. I just . . .

ME: What?

ELI: Why didn't you tell us?

ME: I wasn't supposed to tell anybody! LaTanya only found out because she wrote her film paper about this movie I did when I was thirteen. And Debbie knew because she snuck into my room and went through my cell phone.

ELI: I know. She was bragging about it all day long. That's why she missed all those days this week. She and her parents were running around, trying to broker the best deal.

ME: Deal?

ELI: She's doing all the talk shows.

ME: That little—

ELI: I know. I know.

ME: I am going to kill her!

ELI: Shhh—you'll wake my parents.

ME (whispering): I mean it—I'm going to tear her apart! This is all because of you, you know.

ELI: What are you talking about?

ME: It's because she's in love with you, and she knew that you were in love with . . . someone else.

ELI (staring straight at me): I don't know about *love*. I liked her a lot, though.

ME: She liked you too. *Likes* you. A lot.

ELI: Why is that?

ME: Because you're really smart and weird and funny. But mostly it's because you actually listen to what I have to say. You're more concerned with what I'm thinking and feeling than how I could boost your press coverage or how good I'd look on your arm. I don't even think you *care* about how I look on your arm—just that I'm there.

ELI: So that wasn't part of the act?

ME: No. Absolutely not.

ELI: That's good to know.

I told him about the "rules" of sobriety and how it's highly frowned upon to enter a romantic relationship during the first year. "They say relationships make you vulnerable," I explained.

"Tell me about it," he said, with a small smile.

It was the smile that did me in.

ME: They want me to go back.

ELI: Who? Back where?

ME: Sam—that's my manager, and actually he's sort of my stepfather now, but that's another story entirely—anyway, he's been getting all these calls since the story broke. Like from Oprah? He wants me to go back to L.A. and, I don't know, be me again.

ELI: That's good, right? I mean, isn't that what you wanted?

ME: I thought it was what I wanted. But when they started talking about taking me back, the first thing I thought was, "I can't leave yet. Halloween Village opens in two weeks."

ELI (laughing): You're kidding.

ME: No, I'm not. That's the strangest part. I was starting to like this place, you know? Going to school, doing homework—well, okay, not the homework part. But you know, hanging out with you and Em. Scooby Snacks at Munchies. Mean-girl slumber parties. All of it.

ELI: So don't go.

ME: It's not that easy.

ELI: Why not?

ME: Because part of what I liked about being here was that I was anonymous. I was mousy Claudia Miller, hiding behind fake glasses and a bad dye job. Now I'll be the Snider High freak show. Everyone will be staring at me, asking me questions, making me feel like . . . I don't know. *Different.*

ELI (shrugging): They'll get used to it. Look at me! I'm already used to it.

ME: Really?

ELI: No. But I will be.

We talked until four in the morning. Or mostly I talked and he listened. At one point I said my hands were cold and Eli took them into his own to warm them up. It was the sort of gesture that in a movie would have led to a kiss.

But this wasn't a movie. This was our lives.

"Can I stay here?" I asked him. "Tonight, I mean. The snow's coming down pretty hard."

"Sure," he said. "But I should warn you—my parents might freak out."

"That's okay," I assured him. "Mine probably already are."

He snuck me up to his bedroom and gave me a sweat-shirt and a pair of boxers to change into, then left the room so I could have some privacy. When he returned, he had a sleeping bag under one arm.

"Is that for me?" I asked.

"No," he said. "You take the bed."

He had a full-size mattress—one that would easily accommodate the two of us. "We could both take the bed," I said. "If you wanted to."

Eli shook his head no. "You've already forgotten the part about my parents freaking out, haven't you?"

I asked him to at least put his sleeping bag close so I wouldn't feel so alone, and he obliged. "Thanks," I whispered to him once the lights were out. "I mean it."

His response? "Sweet dreams, you."

So there it is. How I made my decision. And no, it wasn't because of—as Bianca put it when I told her—"some boy." I mean, I like Eli. I like him a lot. But I wouldn't change my entire life for a possible boyfriend.

It was more like what Eli said: they'll get used it. The kids, my teachers, the lovely citizens of Fort Wayne. Sam and Bianca. Sure, it will be weird at first, but the media will get bored real quick, especially when they find out I'm still clean and sober. Maybe I could do *Oprah* and clear what's left of my good name. But that will have to wait until after we open the Haunted Village—maybe until after I pass my midterms, even.

And of course, I still have to figure out how I'm going to get back at Debbie Ackerman. This will be no quick retaliation. Oh, no. This will be *war*.

Anyway, here's the rundown of how everyone took the news that I'd decided to stay and finish out the year:

SAM: Shocked, semi-crushed

BIANCA: Also shocked, but not quite as crushed

TRUDY: Clearly pleased

DAVE: Just really relieved I didn't crash his Volvo

RYAN: Indifferent (of course)

ELI: Pretty far from indifferent—happy, even

EMILY: Also happy, surprisingly enough

MR. & MRS. WHITMARSH: Pretended to be happy but really are quite horrified that their son is in love—er, *like*—with a former Hollywood starlet (i.e., me)

DEBBIE ACKERMAN: Doesn't know yet but will probably freak when she finds out. According to Em, she thought that "outing" me would turn everyone against me—that they'd hate me because I'd duped them all. But celebrity worship is alive and well at Snider High, and Emily says that yesterday was like one big game of "six degrees of Morgan Carter." ("Me and E. won," she joked.)

My mom and Sam are flying back to Cali tomorrow. They were going to stay on a few extra days, but Marissa's lawyer has been calling Sam's cell nonstop. Apparently Marissa is afraid that *we* think she's the one who exposed my secret and that Bianca's gearing up to sue her for everything she's worth. I would've told her the truth myself, but her lawyer told Sam he's advised Marissa not to accept my calls until this matter has been settled.

In other words, it's business as usual.

So now I have a little over a day to prepare for my all-new role. I mean, it's one thing to pretend to be Claudia Miller going to high school in Fort Wayne, Indiana. It's entirely another to play the same part *as myself*. I'm pretty terrified, actually. Walking through the doors of Snider Monday morning . . . well, let's just say I have more than a little stage fright.

But I'm also sort of excited. No more secrets, no more lies. Just me, Morgan, finally allowed to be myself—maybe for the first time ever.

That's why I've decided to retire this diary. Not that I'm going to stop journaling—I mean, God, it's been my saving grace! I just keep thinking that I'm about to start a new chapter in my life, as clichéd as that sounds. And even though my birthday was last week, tomorrow is like . . . like my *re*birthday.

Besides, I like the idea of a new book. I love the idea of a blank page.

It's been real, but it's about to get even realer.

Morgan

The confessions continue when the world

learns that Morgan Carter ditched

Hollywood for high school.

Turn the page

for a sneak peek at

MORE CONFESSIONS

OF A HOLLYWOOD STARLET.

Week
THIRTEEN

11/9

Just got back from Chicago, a two-day quickie trip to make my first TV appearance since I was "outed" exactly one month ago today. Sam is still tweaked that I insisted on *Oprah* even after *60 Minutes* begged for an exclusive, but there's something about that Katie Couric that totally freaks me out. I mean, she *seems* nice enough, but her eternal perkiness is more cloying than Mama Bianca's $250 bottle of Shalimar perfume.

Frankly, if anyone should be tweaked, it's *me*. Sam failed to warn me that Bianca would be at the taping. And yes, I understand that he's Bianca's husband now, but he's still my manager, and after all these years, you'd think he'd show at least a *little* loyalty to his favorite client–turned–stepdaughter.

But that's another entry entirely.

Can I tell you how much I love Oprah? Not only did she leave this gorgeous, buttery, red leather journal and an assortment of her favorite Philosophy bath and beauty products in my dressing room, she also made sure to come down pre-taping to say hello. That, and to tell me that she appreciates me sharing my story with her audience. "Truly inspiring," quoth O.—and she wasn't all fake about it either, like a certain large-chinned late-night talk show host I can't stand who's *still* cracking farm girl jokes at my expense. No, she actually *meant* what she said.

Oh, but the best part? Oprah surprised me during the interview with all these lovely videotaped messages of encouragement from people like Drew Barrymore, Corey Feldman, and this old-school actress Tatum O'Neal—fellow former child stars who, like me, triumphed over their drug and alcohol addictions. It was almost as nice as the thousands of cards, letters, and care packages I received when news broke that I'd been hiding out at Fort Wayne, Indiana's, own Snider High.

I have to admit, though, that I hope my eventual comeback is more like Drew's than Corey's. I mean, hello! *Duplex* wasn't great art, but it's a hell of a lot better than becoming a cast member on *The Surreal Life*.

Speaking of, that dude who co-created *The Real World* left like a dozen messages on the machine while we were away. Apparently, Mr. Jonathan Murray has this idea that I could be the next big reality TV star. "Just like Paris and Nicole!" he kept saying, as if that was some sort of incentive. He's not the only one who's come sniffing around either. But hi—doesn't *anyone* get it? These days I'm trying to get *away* from the spotlight, not run farther into it.

Back to *Oprah*: Trudy came to Chicago with me as my chaperone, and everyone kept mistaking her for my mother. It made us giggle and Mama Bianca frown, but what does she expect? Trudy's been more of a mom to me these past several months than Bianca has been these past several *years*. Although I have to give Mama B. credit for trying: she's still begging me to meet her and Sam at some tropical location for Christmas. I told her I'd think about it if she and Sam would come to Indiana for Thanksgiving. Her perfectly collagen-plumped lips frowned; I knew she was counting on doing Turkey Day California style (read: nab invite to cushy catered dinner at celebrity couple's mansion *or* throw similar cushy catered dinner at one's own abode).

We'll just see about that, won't we?

I'd wanted to bring the twins to Chi-town for my *Oprah* appearance, too. After all, they were the best friends I'd made since I moved to the Fort. And they'd been awesome to me even when they didn't know I was really Morgan Carter. But Emily has some big project going at church, and there's no way Mrs. Whitmarsh was going to let Eli come with me without his sister's protection. She's been rather wary of me as of late, especially when it comes to her son. I guess I can't blame her entirely; after all, she *did* catch me sleeping in Eli's bed the morning after the news about my true identity broke.

It didn't quite matter that Eli had been a total gentleman and slept on the floor. I think it was the shock of finding *any* girl in her little boy's bed, especially since Eli was still using these ghastly kiddie sheets from one of the newer Star Wars movies.

Actually, if Mrs. Whitmarsh stopped to think about it, she would realize those sheets were, like, an anti-aphrodisiac. I mean, who wants to hook up on top of a cartoonified version of Natalie Portman's pseudo-geisha face?

Anyway, where was I? Oh, right—*Oprah*.

Except I just looked at the clock and realized that I'd better power down for the night. Oprah or no Oprah, if I don't show up for first-period geometry tomorrow, Mrs. Chappelle's going to kick my hypotenuse but good.

Can't sleep. Too wired from *Oprah*, or maybe it's that grande Sumatra that I picked up at O'Hare while Tru and I were waiting for our flight to board. According to *Teen Vogue*, caffeine addiction is the new high school epidemic.

I'm sorry, but after kicking booze, pills, pot, and all manner of snortable substances, a coffee jones is the *least* of my worries.

These past few weeks have been such a blur. At first it was fun, you know, getting to ditch Claudia's chunky glasses, sensible shoes, and lackluster style—not to mention her blander-than-bland brown hair. (Bianca insisted I color it immediately, and for once, I was in total agreement.) The deep red I now sport is a far cry from my former trademark blond, but even Mama B. admits that it suits the new me. It says serious. It says *survivor*.

Too bad she's keeping the bulk of my California wardrobe hostage—"It makes for better press if you keep wearing Old Navy," she explained, "like you really *are* just an average teenager"—as I have several Anna Sui pieces in varying shades of blue that would look smashing against my crushed-cherry-colored waves. Oh, well.

The truth is, I'm almost nostalgic for the days of attending Snider as Claudia Miller, average American high school student. "Claudia" could roll out of bed fifteen minutes before first bell and not worry about sleep hair or a lack of makeup. *She* could float from class to class in a fairly anonymous fashion. *She* had the luxury of privacy, something I'd otherwise never known.

And honestly? I wish I'd been more prepared to be Morgan Carter again. I mean, I'd spent six full paparazzi-free months in rehab at Crapplewood before being whisked into Indiana obscurity.

After the outing . . . well, let's just say it's been tantamount to a night of clubbing in Hollywood with Lindsay Lohan *and* Nicole Richie. I'm out of practice—you know, in terms of evading the stalkerazzi—and I've seen so many flashbulbs in the past thirty days that I'm surprised I haven't gone permanently blind.

I'd hoped that school might become a haven of sorts since Principal Barke was so adamant that no hacks be allowed on campus. But my classmates have been even *worse*.

At first, most of them gawked at me like I was a rare albino liger on exhibit at the Fort Wayne Children's Zoo. Then came the questions: did I know Brad Pitt/Ashton Kutcher/Ben Affleck/insert name of male hottie here? Was it true that I'd had a lesbian fling with my best friend (and current "it girl"), Marissa Dahl? When I OD'd outside the Viper Room, did the ghost of River Phoenix appear to me, telling me to run into the light?

Then there were those intrepid souls who snapped surreptitious shots of me with their camera phones and e-mailed the images to each other or, even better, to their blogs.

A scant few actually dared to exhibit groupie-like behavior, including Delia Lambert (aka Morgan Carter's biggest fan). It was flattering at first, but one quickly tires of being fawned over 24/7, especially by an over-exuberant cheerleader who has made it her mission in life to copy every single thing you do.

Finally, there were the haters, led by my very own nemesis, Debbie Ackerman.

Debbie. *Ackerman*. I can't even write her name without

feeling my claws come out. She will pay for what she did to me—for spilling my secret to the entire world. I haven't figured out how exactly, but she. Will. *Pay*.

I'll have to bide my time, though. There's too much attention on me right now, and I'd get so totally busted exacting my revenge. Then wouldn't it look like sour grapes? Me, Morgan Carter, attacking a pudgy, pathetic nobody like Debbie Ackerman? It's . . . I don't know. Unseemly? I'm going to have to be very, very careful with this one—make sure I don't leave any tracks when the moment is finally right.

God, do I sound insane or what? Who cares about stupid Debbie Ackerman? Instead of cooking up half-brained revenge schemes, I *should* be trying to get to sleep. It's now going on 1 a.m. and I was hoping to get to school early tomorrow. I only have three more days to talk Ms. Janet Moore out of resigning from her job as school guidance counselor, and tomorrow's mission is going to require some serious physical stamina. Let's hope it works!

11/10

Operation "Save Ms. Janet Moore" has been aborted.

Why? Well, for one thing, it's become increasingly clear that Ms. Janet Moore doesn't want to be saved. All this time, I thought that she was leaving because of me—because I wigged out on her after my secret identity had been revealed.

I had assumed *she'd* been the one doing the revealing. And I was wrong—so wrong.

But it turns out that while Ms. Janet Moore *was* hurt

that I hadn't trusted her—or believed her when she said she'd kept my secrets in the strictest of confidence—her wanting to leave has absolutely nothing to do with me.

It does, however, have everything to do with a cushy new position as career counselor at a posh, all-girl boarding school in western Massachusetts.

"What if I promise to bring you M&M's every single school day from now until I graduate?" I asked, preying on her biggest weakness.

She shook her head and chuckled. "Sorry, Morgan, but candy doesn't make a very convincing counteroffer."

Turns out this boarding school offers free housing to its staff *and* a stipend for groceries and other expenses. This on top of a salary that Janet says is almost double what she's making at Snider. Plus, she'll be close enough to Amherst that she can take part-time classes if she wants.

"What kind of classes?" I demanded.

But she didn't answer. She just said, "I don't understand why you're so upset."

I couldn't figure out if she was genuinely clueless or if she was fishing for compliments—making me pay for my earlier transgressions.

Before Debbie Ackerman sold me out to the press, Janet and I were meeting in her office three mornings a week. She was the first person I'd ever confided in about what that sleazeball Harlan Darly did to me. And she was the first Fort Wayner outside of Trudy to know about my struggles with sobriety. Hell, she'd even been the one to tell me it was okay to make out with Eli Whitmarsh, regardless of what my Narcotics Anonymous sponsor thought about romantic relationships during the first year of recovery.

But before I could put any of that into actual words, Ms. Janet Moore leaned forward and patted my knee reassuringly. "I'll miss you too, you know. But you're going to be just fine, and you don't need me to tell you that."

"I suppose not," I agreed reluctantly.

She ripped a piece of paper off a mini yellow legal pad and scribbled down her new address and phone number. When she handed it to me, she said, "Promise me you'll keep in touch?"

So there you have it. No more Ms. Janet Moore. No more before-sunrise psych appointments, no more endless supplies of peanut M&M's.

Sigh.

Another sixty minutes until lunch—the highlight of my day. I don't mean that sarcastically, either. I mean that lately lunch is the only guaranteed time of the day when I get to see Eli.

When I was working on the Halloween Village fundraiser last month, Eli, Em, and I were practically together 24/7. But we were almost never alone. Now it's been a week since the village shut down, and I was sure this would mean Eli and I would have some actual quality time together. But between me fielding press requests and trying to stay on top of my studies and Eli's yearbook duties and his new obsession with a specialty camera he found at the Goodwill on Maplecrest a couple of weeks ago (a Helga or Holga or something he uses to do early-morning shoots, rendering him unable to give me rides to school), we haven't even had one hour together—let alone the time to go on an actual date. Yet.

Is it possible that Tater Tots have some hidden aphrodisiac quality that's yet to be discovered?

Yeah, didn't think so.

11/10—*Later*

So guess what? Turns out that Ms. Bowman, the woman they hired to replace Mr. Sappey, isn't just the new film studies teacher—she's also in charge of the drama program. How do I know this? Because Ms. Bowman cornered me after class today to ask if I had any intention of trying out for the spring musical. When I said no, she launched into this big speech about how great it would be for me to get involved.

"Just imagine," she said, a dreamy look in her eye, "how much you could teach the others!"

I told her I'd think about it, but my mind is made up. The answer is *no*. First of all, I can't commit to yet another activity. Thanks to Em, I'm still a Very Involved Panther, which means VIP meetings every other Wednesday afternoon (plus supplemental meetings when we're working on a big project like the Haunted Halloween Village fundraiser).

I still have my NarcAnon meetings every Thursday night to make sure I stay sober. Also, Trudy and I made a solemn pact to actually visit the gym three times a week—and yes, I'd like to leave a little bit of the time that's left open for a certain amateur photographer I know, whom I've grown quite fond of.

But besides all of that? I know the girls who'll be trying out for the play. Half of them are in my film class. And these are not girls who'd be okay with me, a onetime Oscar nominee, stealing the lead right out from under them.

Plus, LaTanya told me that Debbie Ackerman is a decent soprano and has landed fairly juicy parts in the last three musicals that Snider's put on. So, no. I don't see myself voluntarily joining a cast like that anytime soon.

Speaking of Debbie Ackerman . . . the bitch has gotten bold. It was bad enough when her pathetic social status was actually *elevated* by her role in my outing. But now it seems her confidence has been bolstered by a brand-new band of bimbo supporters.

Just a minute ago, in the lunch line, she actually approached me directly. *Directly*. I kid you not.

She walked right up to me and said, sweet as pie, "Have I told you that I like your new hair color, Morgan? It really thins out your face."

As if *she's* one to talk about chubby cheeks—I mean, the girl is shaped like a lawn troll!

But what really pissed me off—the thing that totally sent me over the edge—is the car. *Debbie's* car. The sporty, brand-new, silver Jetta GLS she purchased with some of the blood money she received for selling me out. (I say "some" because I know a good chunk of change went toward her two-hundred-dollar highlights, new wardrobe, and half the makeup from the Clinique counter at Marshall Fields.)

Where is *my* car? I want to know. Hell, I don't even have my license, and I'm seventeen!

Plus, last week I went to meet Eli in the yearbook room, and Debbie was actually draped over him like some kind of human pashmina. It's like, "Back off, slut! You can take my dignity, but you are *not* taking my man!"

Hmmm. Maybe I've been watching too much *Laguna Beach*.

My *Oprah* episode is set to air tomorrow, and to cele-brate, Delia Lambert is throwing an *Oprah*-viewing party. At first I thought it was sort of sweet, but then I found out her mother is having it *catered*. While the Lamberts are far from poor, they aren't exactly the catered-party type either. At least, this is what Emily tells me. She also tells me that Delia's mom rented a large-screen projection TV that is so big, the delivery guys had to remove the bay window just to get it into the family room.

LaTanya got this photocopied invite that she said Meadow Forrester was passing out to their entire Spanish class, which is weird—I know for a fact that Delia can't stand Meadow Forrester, because Delia has told me six times now about how boobalicious Meadow hooked up with Delia's homecoming date under the bleachers last year before the dance was even *over*.

So now I'm stuck being the guest of honor at this overblown event I never asked for, when really I'd much rather be in my own living room with Trudy, Eli, and Emily.

Well, there's one consolation. Debbie Ackerman and her crew will *not* be in attendance, as Delia and the rest of the cheerleading squad have made it their mission in life to help me take Debbie down.

Sometimes it's good to have friends with pom-poms.

11/10—*Much later*

Eli surprised me as we were leaving the caf and asked me if I was free for dinner. I told him yes, even though Trudy and I were supposed to hit the Y to try out that new hot yoga class where the room temp hovers around eighty-five degrees. I figured Trudy would understand, seeing as I've been dying for me and E. to go on a real date, but then Eli said the invitation actually came from his *mother*.

"I don't get it," I said. "Why the formal request for my presence?"

Eli shrugged. "I think she just wants to get to know you better."

Sounded innocuous enough, right? Still, I felt suspicious. See, when I was Claudia, Mr. and Mrs. Whitmarsh were, like, totally in love with me. But then, after the outing, something changed. A big thing, actually.

First, Mr. Whitmarsh turned into this frat-guy dad, visibly pleased that it was *his* son who had snagged the starlet's heart. And then Mrs. Whitmarsh, who'd always seemed so genuine, started talking to me with a tight, practiced smile on her face—the kind people give you when they don't actually like you but are too mannered to say so.

"But your mother hates me," I practically whined.

"No, she doesn't," Eli said, for what must've been the hundredth time. "Besides, you have to come over. I want to show you the new prints I've been working on."

I called Trudy to postpone our gym date. She actually sounded relieved—like there was some other way *she* wanted to spend her evening too. (Most likely with Dave, her hot-'n'-heavy honey.)

My feelings might've been hurt—if I hadn't reminded myself I was the one to ditch her for a dude first.

Then it turned out that Emily had to stay after school—some student council meeting about a lack of fundage for the upcoming Winter Wonderdance—so Eli and I were actually alone for the first time in I don't know how long.

In the car, I asked, "Is your mom expecting us right away?"

Eli shook his head. "Why? Want to make a Munchies run?"

"Actually," I said slyly, "I *am* craving a little something—but not food."

"What? Starbucks?" Eli offered.

I batted my eyelashes a bit and said, "What do you think?" in my most suggestive tone.

I was rewarded with a blank stare.

I ran the tip of my tongue over my top lip, hoping that would help Eli get the message. It was something a director had me do once. According to Marissa, it made half the men in the crew pant.

Not so young Eli. All he said was, "You need some Chapstick?" and offered me a cherry-flavored tube.

"Oh, for Christ's sake!" I said, swatting the lip balm away. "Playing coy with you is like . . . like trying to teach Hilary Duff how to use eyeliner!"

"Relax," E. said with a grin. "I was thinking we could go somewhere private too. But I had to give you a hard time. Don't want you to think I'm easy."

I laughed, and Eli turned down a leafy little lane somewhere between the seminary school and the golf course.

He turned off the ignition and pulled me to him, kissing me softly at first and then, gradually, with a little more urgency. It was so nice I almost didn't notice the parking brake digging into my side.

But then the inevitable happened—

Flashbulbs popping on all four sides of the car. There must've been a dozen or so photographers swarming all around us. One guy was so gutsy, he'd shimmied up the front of the Camry, pressing his lens against the windshield while sprawling across the hood.

My cheeks grew hot; this was the first time the paparazzi had caught me and Eli in a "compromising position."

"Sam's going to kill me," I murmured, pulling a pair of oversized shades from my purse and slipping them over my eyes.

Eli, visibly shaken, rolled down his window. "Step away from the car, gentlemen, or I swear to God, I'll run you over."

This was not much of a deterrent, and I knew why. Sam had called me a couple of weeks ago to tell me the tabloids were offering between ten and twenty thousand for a clear shot of me snogging Eli (or, as the press had dubbed him, my "Midwestern Boy Toy"). He thought it was fabulous—Sam, I mean—and made me promise to hold off getting photographed with E. until he'd given the go-ahead. As much as I loved Sam, his pure glee at the possibility of capitalizing on my relationship with Eli made me feel a little uneasy.

Eli's face reddened as the hacks continued to shoot and call out things like, "Kiss her again!" and, "Come on, give us a little tongue!" The redder his face got, the more I knew his sweet-tempered nature was being stretched thin.

"Just start the car," I advised. "If you give it a little gas, they'll lay off."

Sure enough, when Eli revved the engine, the hacks backed away—all except Belly Boy, that is, who was still lying flat on the hood of the car.

Now *I* was getting pissed. It was bad enough that these jerks harassed me, but now they were messing with my man?

I rolled down my window. "Excuse me," I said, "I think

you got what you needed. Now please get off the car before we call the cops."

Belly Boy didn't move. In fact, I heard him say, "Oh, that's good. Keep it coming, honey—you look hot when you're angry."

I rolled up the window and turned to Eli. "Throw the car in reverse. He'll skid right off."

"Won't that hurt him?" Eli asked.

"Do you even care?"

But of course Eli cared, because he was still new to this whole "invasion of privacy" game.

So I tried to think of what Marissa would do in a situation like this. The idea came to me instantly and made me grin. I told Eli to close his eyes and keep them that way until I said it was okay. Then I rolled my window down again and leaned my torso out.

"Hey, slimeball. Over here."

I pulled my sweater up far enough to give Belly Boy a generous view of my black lace demi-cup bra. It had the desired effect; to get a proper shot, Belly Boy had to swing the lower half of his body to the right. In his excitement, he overshot his mark and slid right off the car onto the tar of the parking lot.

"Hit it!" I called to Eli, pulling my sweater back down and buckling myself into the passenger seat. "Open your eyes now and drive!"

Belly Boy was struggling to his feet just as E. peeled away.

"What did you do?" Eli asked when we were headed down the road.

"Ummm . . . nothing?" I said.

"Morgan." Eli's voice sounded stern. "What did you *do*?"

I sighed. "I flashed him, okay? But don't worry. He was too stunned to get the shot."

Eli's jaw tightened; I could see he wasn't pleased with my performance.

"Don't worry about it," I assured him. "Marissa and I used to do stuff like that all of the time. It's a . . . a defense technique."

He nodded silently.

"Come on, Eli," I said. "Don't let this ruin our afternoon, okay?"

After a pause, Eli's jaw relaxed. "Yeah, okay," he said. "Let's pretend the whole thing never happened."

It was a good plan. The problem was, after we turned onto the main road, we found ourselves followed by at least three more hacks. We tried to lose them, but to no avail. Eventually, we just gave up and headed over to the Whitmarshes'.